PROJECTION

RISA GREEN

Copyright © 2013 by Soho Press, Inc. and Risa Green

Published in the United States in 2013 by Soho Teen
an imprint of
Soho Press, Inc.
853 Broadway
New York, NY 10003

Library of Congress Cataloging-in-Publication Data

Green, Risa.
Projection / Risa Green.
p. cm
ISBN 978-1-61695-200-6 (alk. paper)
eISBN 978-1-61695-201-3
1. Secret societies—Fiction. 2. Astral projection—Fiction.
3. Murder—Fiction. 4. Mystery and detective stories. I. Title.
PZ7.G82618Pr 2013
[Fic]—dc23   2013008768

Interior design by Janine Agro, Soho Press, Inc.

Printed in the United States of America

10 9 8 7 6 5 4 3 2 1

CHAPTER ONE
ROME 249 A.D.

Amphiclea watched the awkward young slave girl. Her posture was perfect as she maneuvered through the garden, her expression blank, her arms loaded with a ceramic plate full of figs, olives, cheese, and flatbread. *She could be beautiful if she weren't unclean,* Amphiclea thought. *She looks like me.* The girl placed the plate gently on the table in front of Gemina. In an instant almost too quick to catch, the slave's eyes flickered to the warm loaves, and Gemina—who never missed a thing—caught the hungry glance. She ripped off a piece of the bread, wrapping a hunk of cheese and some olives inside of it.

"Here," Gemina said. She held it toward the slave.

A test. Everything was a test with Gemina.

The girl masked her fear with a polite, "No." She'd only recently been acquired by Gemina's husband, the influential Senator Castricius. Amphiclea knew that the girl's last owner would have beaten her just for looking at the bread.

Gemina nodded at the girl's hesitation. "Take it," she

insisted, picking up the girl's hand and placing the food into it. "I won't tolerate hungry slaves in this household."

Without a word, the girl curtsied, clutching the bread against her chest like it was a precious child. She ran back toward the house.

Amphiclea shuddered. "You shouldn't touch the slaves. They're . . ."

"Unclean?" Gemina finished impatiently, mocking her. "I know. Have you not been listening to Plotinus? To me? We are all the same. All of us—slaves, senators, philosophers, the entire universe—we are all one. We all come from The One." Gemina flung open her slender arms to illustrate her point. Her expression quickly turned to disgust as the gold bracelets adorning her wrists clanged against each other. "Plotinus says that nothing material matters. Not this house, not this food, not this jewelry. Even our bodies are irrelevant. They are merely prisons for our souls."

Amphiclea glanced around the garden to make sure no one had heard or approached. She lowered her voice. "Has he been successful?"

Gemina smiled conspiratorially, her high cheekbones revealing themselves like smooth rocks beneath her skin. "Twice now he has done it. He has projected his soul through the Oculus. He has passed through the highest part of the Pantheon, leaving his body behind while his soul floated among the stars!" She gripped Amphiclea's arm, her bracelets jangling again. "And soon he will teach me to do the same."

Amphiclea shook Gemina's hands free. "Stop it. Don't talk this way. You're not permitted to eat in the same room as your husband, let alone study with a philosopher—"

"Enough," Gemina interrupted. "It doesn't matter. Plotinus has shown me the truth. All of creation emanates from

The One. Men, women, slaves, animals, even these figs!" She leaned closer and whispered. "But you are right to be cautious. Castricius is no student of philosophy. He only tolerates Plotinus because he believes it raises his stature in the Senate to be viewed as a patron of a philosopher. The beneficent Castricius," she said with mock grandiosity, "patron of a great philosophical mind." She sat back, straightened the food on her plate.

"Of course, he'd never let it be known what he really thinks of Plotinus."

Amphiclea leaned closer, unable to keep from taking the bait. "Why? What does he think of him?"

"He thinks he's absolutely mad, Amphiclea!"

"Yes, of course he does." She should have known, given how often she'd listened to Gemina complain about Castricius in the two years since their marriage. The senator was not an open-minded man, and though he was hailed for being a shrewd and ruthless politician, such qualities left much to be desired in a husband. To be fair, he had seemed fond of Gemina during their courtship and in the early days. But when she'd borne him a daughter—little Gaia—he'd been furious. More than a year later, he still hadn't forgiven her for the transgression.

Gemina straightened herself in her chair. Both were seventeen, but today Amphiclea felt much younger than her friend.

"What my dear husband doesn't know about Plotinus," Gemina continued, "is that on Sunday last, he witnessed Castricius leaving the bedroom of the same woman who accused my poor father of forging Senate documents."

"Lucretia Iusta?" Amphiclea exclaimed with a start. "She nearly had your family banished from Rome!" Amphiclea held a hand up to her mouth. "Is this . . . ?" She couldn't finish the thought, because it could only lead to one place—a place where Gemina would be taken from her forever to pay for the sins of her father.

The accusations against Gemina's father had been *the* scandal last winter. All of Rome had gossiped about the charges—ultimately proved baseless—but Gemina's family name nearly had been ruined. And the taint remained. Amphiclea knew that some still believed the claim to be valid, though most thought only that Lucretia Iusta was a wicked, vengeful woman. It was hardly a secret that Lucretia had wanted Castricius for herself and that she'd been furious when Gemina's father had arranged for Gemina to be his bride instead.

"How could he?" Amphiclea whispered.

Gemina grimaced. "Oh, don't be so naïve. What man could resist a woman who is so desperate to have him?" She waved away Castricius's infidelity as if it were a bug. "I care not what he does in her bedroom. He only married me because of my father's fortune." She lowered her voice, her dark eyes flashing with anger. "But he appears to be taking money—money meant for *me*, and for Gaia, from the dowry given to him by *my* father—and giving it to that lying wench of a woman."

Amphiclea swallowed. "You truly believe that he's stealing from you?"

"I *know* it."

"But can you prove it?"

"Not yet. The proof I need is in the Curia, where the Senate meets and where Castricius keeps his ledgers. It would be impossible for a woman to be seen sneaking around there. Of course, if I were a man, I could find what I needed without arousing suspicion . . ."

Amphiclea blinked, fighting back the fear and sadness.

"And if I were a cat, I could lie around all day and do nothing but drink milk."

To her surprise, Gemina laughed. "Yes," she conceded. "But you can't become a cat, and I *can* become a man."

Amphiclea searched her friend's eyes for the hint of a prank, as was Gemina's way. All she saw was icy resolve. "And how do you propose to do that, exactly?" she asked in a teasing tone, ignoring the shudder down her spine.

Gemina stared back. "I told you that Plotinus is going to teach me how to project my soul, but not through the Oculus. He's going to teach me to project my soul into his body. My mind, my consciousness, will inhabit him like a crab in a shell, and his will inhabit me. We're going to trade our souls, Amphiclea. But we can't do it without your help."

Amphiclea went pale. "Gemina, you are like a sister to me. I would help you with anything. But this . . . this sounds impossible. Not to mention dangerous if anyone were to find out."

"It's not impossible," Gemina insisted. "It can be done if you believe in the idea of The One."

Amphiclea held herself steady. Gemina's face had tensed. A blue vein appeared by her temple. *Gemina believes what she is saying. This is no prank.*

"How could I help?"

"We need a witness. A *mártyras*. Plotinus says that without one, we can't ensure that we'll be able to return to our own bodies. Will you do it, Amphiclea?"

Amphiclea's thoughts raced for reasons, excuses. Had Gemina ever refused *her*? She'd consoled Amphiclea when her mother had died; she'd helped prepare her for her wedding night; she'd taught her how to run a household. This was the first time Gemina had ever asked her for anything in return. Amphiclea couldn't possibly say no, even though what Gemina was proposing was both risky and insane. She lowered her eyes.

"Of course. Anything for you, Gemina."

Gemina smiled, seemingly more to herself than to Amphiclea. The strained look vanished from her face. The blue vein receded.

"I knew you wouldn't disappoint me." She placed her hand on top of Amphiclea's. With her other hand, she reached beneath the table and emerged with a small, leather pouch. She opened it, revealing a delicate gold strand adorned with a disc of nearly translucent amber.

Amphiclea gasped. "Gemina, it's so beautiful."

"It's a gift to you. For your loyalty, trust and friendship." She reached out for Amphiclea's tiny wrist, frowning as she wrapped the chain around it. "Oh, it's much too big. Amphiclea, you must eat more!"

In spite of herself, Amphiclea laughed. "I shall wear it on a thicker limb instead." She lifted up the hem of her purple stola and fastened the chain around her right ankle. It fit perfectly. She held out her bare leg, and for a blissful fleeting moment, the two girls admired her new accessory, as if it were nothing more than another fancy gift bestowed upon a lady of the Roman Empire.

Gemina's face darkened. "I know you doubt me, Amphiclea, but you will see that what I say is the truth. I *will* become Plotinus, and as him I will find the proof against my husband that I require." She paused for a moment, lost in thought, and then squeezed Amphiclea's fingers. "And when I do, Castricius will get the justice he deserves."

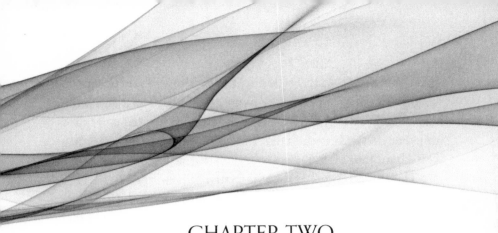

CHAPTER TWO
DELPHI, CALIFORNIA
TWO YEARS AGO

Gretchen reached up with her right hand and carefully adjusted one of the bobby pins holding her graduation cap in place. She'd had her hair blown out that morning, and her long, shiny, dark layers fell perfectly around her face in a way that she could never achieve on her own, no matter how hard she tried or how many times she'd studied her hairdresser's technique in the mirror.

"That's the fiftieth time you've fixed that bobby pin," whispered Jessica.

"It's messing up my blow-out," Gretchen complained. She snapped her compact shut and frowned at her best friend. It was bad enough having to sit in the sun in folding chairs, or for that matter, having to endure this ceremony in the first place. "I don't even understand why we have to wear these stupid hats anyway. We're only graduating from eighth grade. It's not like we're going out to save the world."

The school chorus finally finished singing its medley of seriously patriotic songs, followed by a round of applause.

Mr. Tobin, their soon-to-be former headmaster, approached the podium. Eleven o'clock in the morning, and Mr. Tobin was already sweaty. Gretchen couldn't help but feel sorry for him. He dabbed at the edge of his receding hairline with a white handkerchief.

"Thank you, boys and girls, that was beautiful."

"That was lame," said a too-loud voice behind Gretchen, setting off a round of snickering. Gretchen and Jessica rolled their eyes at each other. The voice belonged to Ariel Miller (of course), the girl who, despite everyone's best efforts, still hadn't figured out that "it's best to shut up and let everyone think you're an outsider than to open your mouth and remove all doubt." The funny part? Ariel had actually said those words herself. After which she'd said that she was "paraphrasing Mark Twain." Whatever the hell that meant.

Which, in a way, was the point: Ariel could have been friends with Gretchen and Jessica if she weren't so freaking weird. When she'd first moved to Delphi in the fourth grade, Gretchen and Jessica had reached out. It should have been a no-brainer. Ariel was pretty and very smart (smarter than Gretchen, probably) and since they wore school uniforms, nobody knew if she had the right clothes or not. Gretchen wanted her to be popular; they all did. But there was just something *off* about her. Mostly, she had zero respect for the social hierarchy that had formed long before her arrival. And when everyone found out that her mom was a lunch lady . . . well, after that it was full-blown banishment.

Not that Gretchen had anything against lunch ladies. Or Ariel's mom. But Ariel should have copped to her true identity the second she'd set foot in school. Gretchen would have in *her* shoes.

"And now," continued Mr. Tobin, his voice stronger in

an attempt both to quash and ignore the laughter, "I'll ask you to welcome Mrs. Octavia Harris, Former President of the Oculus Society and its chief Ambassador. She is here to present the Plotinus Award to the female student who best embodies the ideals of a classical Greek scholar . . ."

"If my mom waves at me, I'll kill her," Gretchen whispered to Jessica

Ariel snorted loudly. "God forbid the Oinkulus Society shouldn't be the center of attention at a public event."

Gretchen bit her tongue. She resisted the urge to spin around in her chair and tell Ariel to shut up. The girl was just jealous, obviously. That was where her weirdness and anger came from. It had nothing to do with her fired-lunch-lady mom. It had to do with the fact Ariel would never be part of the Oculus Society. And Gretchen knew that she was lucky; *her* mom was a two-time President. Their family could trace their lineage back to one of the founding members. But Gretchen's mom was something special, too. She'd given the Oculus Society (a formerly stodgy Junior-League-type organization as far as Gretchen could tell) a glamorous makeover. With her flair for entertaining, Octavia Harris was responsible for some of Delphi's most talked about parties. Gretchen clapped extra hard—as much in appreciation as to banish Ariel from her thoughts—as her mother rose from one of the white folding chairs on the stage and strode to the podium.

Octavia Harris smiled at her but didn't wave.

Someday I'll look like she does, Gretchen thought, smiling back.

Octavia Harris was raven-haired, petite, and beautiful. She wore a white linen suit, well-chosen both for the weather and to stand out against her olive complexion. Beige patent leather Jimmy Choo pumps complemented the ensemble. And the mysterious finishing touch: a thin gold anklet set around a yellowish-orange stone that always reminded Gretchen of honey in a jar. It seemed to glow as it caught the sunlight. Mom only wore it for special occasions. It was puzzling, though; it just didn't seem to match her style, admittedly more nouveau-riche sparkle than bohemian glow. Gretchen had asked her once if it had sentimental value, but her response had been nonchalant. *Oh, it's nothing. Just something I found at a vintage shop on vacation with your father before you were born. I thought it looked pretty.*

It did look pretty. Gretchen made a mental note that in addition to the Jimmy Choo heels, she would borrow it when she was older.

"Hello, graduates!" Mom's voice boomed over the lawn. "Congratulations to you all. The Oculus Society was founded in nineteen oh-seven by six women of Greek origin whose husbands had made their fortunes in the silver mines of the American West. Appalled by the curricula of most public schools at the time—notably the failure to teach the works of great Greek philosophers such as Socrates, Plato, and Aristotle—these women set out to improve education in the United States in the classical Greek tradition. Named after the eye-like, circular window built into the dome of the Roman Pantheon, the Oculus Society continues its mission today, not only to improve education, but also to raise money for various charitable causes."

"Yeah, right!" Ariel blurted from behind Gretchen's chair. "Because getting wasted on ouzo at a black-tie dinner counts as charity."

Gretchen's hands balled up into fists. Jessica gently laid a hand on her shoulder as if to say, *not now*, but enough was enough. Gretchen turned around in her seat, careful not to move her head so much that her cap fell off. Ariel's dirty blonde hair had been blown out into a flip that grazed the tops of her shoulders. Her emerald eyes were rimmed in dark brown eyeliner. Gretchen hated to admit that the girl was beautiful.

"Will you just shut up?" she hissed. "You're ruining my graduation."

Ariel smirked. "*Your* graduation?"

"Give it up, Ariel," Jessica chimed in, simultaneously trying to steer Gretchen back to face forward. "Nobody's interested."

"Really?" Ariel's voice rose. "Then why are we having this conversation?"

Onstage, Gretchen's mom fumbled with an envelope. "On behalf of the Oculus Society, I'm pleased to announce that the winner of this year's Plotinus Award, which includes a five hundred dollar savings bond to be put toward college, is . . ." She held the paper at arm's length so she could see it. It was something she'd been doing a lot lately. Reading glasses were out of the question, however. She was only forty-five. Her mother was not a big believer in succumbing to the aging process. As her eyes registered what was on the paper, she placed a hand over her mouth and then laughed. "Oh, my goodness. I swear, I had nothing to do with this, it's the faculty and administration who make the decision . . . Gretchen Harris!"

Her mother's voice echoed from the loudspeakers.

Gretchen whirled to find her classmates and the rest of the crowd staring at her and applauding. The red mortarboard on her head started to slide. Despite the shock and confusion, she reached up and caught it, expertly adjusting the bobby pin once again.

"I knew you'd win!" Jessica whispered excitedly. She squeezed her arm. "You were a shoo-in!"

Mr. Tobin stepped in front of the microphone. "Congratulations, Gretchen! Would you please stand up?"

Gretchen mustered a gracious smile and stood. Her heart
thumped. She offered an embarrassed bow and wave to the
crowd. But even with all of the cheering and clapping, she
still could hear Ariel grumbling behind her.

"Well, now graduation's been ruined for me, too. So I
guess we're even."

Gretchen's face was starting to hurt from smiling. Every time
she thought she'd posed for her last picture, someone else ran
up to her. *I've gotta have a picture with the class president!*
they all explained, as if it were the same thing as having a picture taken with the President of the United States. As she faced
yet another camera, she felt a sudden wave of nostalgia. She'd
miss middle school. She'd worked hard, and it wasn't going
to be easy to start at the bottom again as a freshman at the
high school. On the other hand, how hard could it be? Some
of Delphi's wealthiest sent their kids to private schools, even
boarding schools down the California coast or in New England. But the true elite sent their kids to the only public school
in town because the Oculus Society's primary mission was to
improve public education. Gretchen's mom and Jessica's aunt
and all the rest of them poured their hearts and souls and fun-
draising efforts into making Delphi High a shining example.
Very noble and very convenient. *And worth every penny of the
real estate tax*, Mom always said, whatever that meant.

Finally, after the last of the obligatory pictures had been
taken and her classmates had gravitated back to their usual
cliques, she grabbed Jessica.

"Come here," she said. "You're the only person in this
entire school I haven't taken a picture with today."

"The only one? Really?" Jessica asked, arching an eyebrow. "Will I be seeing a picture of you and Ariel up on Facebook later, then?"

Gretchen made a mock-serious face. "Absolutely. And the caption's going to say: buy a sweater because hell *has* frozen over!"

Jessica smirked, then threw her arm around Gretchen's shoulder. Together they beamed into Gretchen's phone. *This one,* she thought, *goes up on the bulletin board in my room.*

"Wait, what are you wearing tonight again?" Jessica asked.

"I *told* you already, remember? The green dress and the gold shoes."

She'd been through all of this with Jessica over texts: Mom had made a two-hour drive into Beverly Hills last weekend (which was why Gretchen couldn't hang out). They'd gone in search of a perfect dress for her to wear to the graduation party that Mom and Dad were throwing for the whole eighth grade class. They'd settled on a long, pale green Haute Hippie—elegant but casual. They'd also found a pair of gold Prada wedge sandals that she knew she'd wear all summer long. Normally, Mom didn't make such an outrageous fuss on clothes and shoes for Gretchen, but she kept insisting it was such a special occasion and important for the future . . .

"Oh, right," Jessica said.

Only then did it hit her. Mom had known all along that she was going to win that Oculus Society Award. Mom had been lying at the podium.

"I'm just asking because I don't know what *I* should wear," Jessica added.

Gretchen blinked. Her annoyance melted away. She felt a twinge of guilt. Jessica had no parents to take *her* shopping for a dress in Beverly Hills. Gretchen had been so busy thinking about herself that she hadn't even considered how hard this was for her best friend: no family present at one of the most important days of her life.

"Is your aunt here?" Gretchen asked, searching the swarm of families.

"I *told* you already, remember?" Jessica muttered, mimicking Gretchen. "She had to work this morning. Rob's here, though. He went like this when I got my diploma." She held up the thumb and pinkie of her left hand, then shrugged. "Michelle said she was going to try to make it."

Michelle should rot in hell, Gretchen thought, not for the first time. Without thinking, she looped her arm under Jessica's and leaned in close. Since Jessica's parents had died seven years ago in a car accident, she'd been living with her aunt Michelle. There was only one problem: Michelle didn't comprehend that she was supposed to act—if not like Jessica's mother exactly—then at least like someone who gave a shit. Worse, she made no secret that she resented being burdened with her sister's kid before she had any kids of her own. (Once, Jessica had confided that Michelle had slapped her after she'd gotten caught snooping around in Michelle's lingerie drawer.) The only upside was Michelle's husband, Rob. He was a really nice guy— though more in a cool, older brother way than in a stepdad way. So while he could talk *Girls* (which Jessica wasn't supposed to watch) and Adele (which he didn't consider "real music"), he didn't offer much in the way of parental guidance. And his problem was that he never intervened when Michelle got out of hand.

If it had been up to Gretchen, she would have called Child Protective Services and invited Jessica come live with her family. But Octavia Harris refused to get involved. Michelle was a member of the Oculus Society, as was Jessica, as was Jessica's deceased mother. And members of the Oculus Society didn't cause problems in each other's lives. Period.

"I just remembered that I have a white dress that would look *amazing* on you," Gretchen heard herself say. "You should come over and try it on."

Jessica didn't hesitate. "Well, I was going to wear that black dress that I wore to the Valentine's Dance, but if you think this would look better, I mean, I guess I could try it."

"Definitely," Gretchen said. And then she flipped her hand up in front of Jessica's face, knocking her cap right off of her head.

"Hey!" Jessica laughed. She flipped her hand up to Gretchen's cap and did it right back to her. Bobby pins went flying in all directions.

"Oh, thank God," Gretchen said, smoothing down her dark hair. "I am seriously considering flunking out of high school just so I never have to wear one of those again."

CHAPTER THREE

From her bedroom window, Gretchen surveyed the backyard. It was transformed to the point that she didn't recognize it, and she'd lived here her entire life. An enormous white tent covered most of the lawn; inside, hot pink and orange floor pillows lay strewn Moroccan-style around low tables covered with rich purple linens. Giant gold lanterns festooned the ceiling; potted plants lined the walls. Even the pool had been filled with floating candles and covered with a translucent dance floor. Gretchen knew exactly what Mom was going for: the illusion that you could dance above a cloud of fireflies.

It didn't look *real*. Gretchen tried to stop smiling but couldn't. Tearing herself from the window, she slipped her dress over her head and smoothed her hair one final time, then ran down the staircase and out the sliding glass doors to get a closer look.

Mom was inside the tent supervising the last-minute adjustments, having changed from her white linen suit into

black tank dress with a high slit up one side—all the better to show off all the hard work she'd been doing with her
private trainer, a tattoo-covered guy named Rick who came
to the house three mornings a week. She'd switched out her
diamond studs for gold hoop earrings. One wrist was stacked
with thick gold bangles. The anklet rested just above the strap
of her black, high-heeled Louboutin sandals.

"This is unbelievable!" Gretchen whispered.

Mom squeezed her hand without looking at her. "I'm so
glad you like it!" Her forehead creased with concern. "Do
you think your friends will get it?"

Gretchen positioned herself in front of her mom's distracted gaze. "Mom, *I* don't get it. I can't believe you did all
of this. I mean, it's just an eighth grade graduation party. I
don't know how you can possibly top this when I graduate
from high school."

Her mother offered a brittle smile. "It's not *just* an eighth
grade graduation party. Of course, that's what the invitation
says, but it's not why I did this." She placed her hands on
Gretchen's shoulders. "This is a very special time, Stretchy."
Mom hadn't called her by her family nickname in a while,
maybe a month. Her black eyes bored into Gretchen's own.
"Good. I have your attention. You're not a little girl anymore. You're going into high school, becoming a teenager.
Things are going to start happening to you. Things you can't
even imagine."

Gretchen's cheeks flushed. "Uh, Mom, maybe you forgot,
but I got my period, like, almost a year ago. So if you're about
to give me the 'you're becoming a woman' speech, you're a
little late."

Her mom laughed and gave her a quick kiss on the forehead. "That's not where I was going with that, but thanks

for the reminder." She dropped her hands from Gretchen's shoulders and straightened her dress, as if the conversation were over. Her eyes wandered back across the tent.

"Then what did you mean?" Gretchen insisted. "What's going to happen to me?"

"Not to worry. Tonight is just the beginning. Now, if you'll excuse me, darling, I need to go inside to start greeting our guests. Have fun and make the most of it!"

By seven o'clock the tent was overflowing with people. It seemed like the entire eighth grade and their parents had shown up, even though Gretchen was pretty sure her mom hadn't invited all of them. But it didn't matter. The only crasher she cared about was Ariel Miller. Unfortunately Ariel had a habit of showing up in places where she wasn't wanted—or invited. Like last year, for example, when Molly Carson had thrown a party at the bowling alley, and Ariel had conveniently shown up to go bowling at the very same time, as if it were all some big coincidence.

If she crashes this party, I am personally going to be the one to kick her out.

But Ariel aside, Gretchen felt like she was floating with happiness, and she knew Jessica was happy, too. She was stunning in Gretchen's white dress, with her long blonde hair and her tan skin. The picture of summer. The two of them had attracted a crowd of boys on the pillows around their table. Best of all, they'd attracted Nick Ford. A lot of the boys in their grade hadn't grown very much in the last three years. The majority came up to Gretchen's shoulders, or maybe her neck. But Nick was already taller than she was, taller than Jessica. Plus, he was the star center on the Delphi Middle School lacrosse team. They'd won the regional championship . . . or something; Dad always kept track of school sports better than she did.

The only minor annoyance was that Nick's blue eyes kept wandering to Jessica, not to her.

"Hey, did I ever tell you about the time my dad got seasick in Hawaii?" Gretchen asked in a loud voice. Both Nick and Jessica turned.

"So he leaned over the side of the boat and puked into the ocean, and, like, twenty minutes later all of these guys who were snorkeling came up to the boat asking, 'Who's the guy who puked?' Everyone pointed at my dad, and he was all embarrassed, but then they started thanking him and giving him high fives. They said all these fish came out of their caves to eat the puke, and it was, like, the best snorkeling they'd had all week!"

"Ewww," Jessica cried, but the boys all laughed, including Nick. Gretchen caught Nick's eye. He flashed a crooked smile that made her insides flutter. *That's more like it.* She glanced over at Jessica to see if she'd seen it, but Jessica had turned away, craning her neck as if she had spotted someone. A moment later she leaned over and whispered in Gretchen's ear.

"My uncle just walked in. Do you want a drink? He'll totally get them for us."

"I don't know," Gretchen answered. "My mom would kill me if she found out I was drinking."

Jessica rolled her eyes. "It's just one drink. And I'll tell him to get you something sweet, like an apple martini." She glanced at Nick. "We can get one for him, too."

Gretchen thought about this for a second. It *would* be cool to have a drink with Nick Ford. She tapped him on the leg. "Do you want a drink?" she asked in a low voice, so the other guys wouldn't hear. "Jess's uncle will get them for us."

He nodded at her. "Sure. I'll take a whiskey sour."

Gretchen raised an eyebrow. "Whiskey *what*?"

Nick shrugged. "I had, like, six of them at Jon Goldman's bar mitzvah last year."

He stood first and reached down so Gretchen could grab his hand. She allowed him to pull her up from the cushion on the floor and expected him to drop it as soon as they were side by side, but his fingers intertwined with hers. Gretchen saw Jessica take in the whole thing. Was she jealous? Did it matter? Nick dragged Gretchen behind him, following Jessica to the back of the tent.

Uncle Rob stood by himself near a speaker, holding a drink and moving his head to the beat of the music. With his free hand, he moved his fingers up and down the frets of an imaginary guitar. Gretchen knew that he was a musician; he played in a local band. According to Jessica, "even though Rob knows they're totally old," (her words) they were on the verge of getting signed by an indie record label down in LA.

Once, at the Country Club, Gretchen had overheard her mom and some of her friends talking about him. A lost soul, one of them had said though Gretchen didn't really get what that was supposed to mean. But they all agreed he was good-looking. Gretchen studied him with a critical eye. He was wearing a grey suit with no tie, and his white shirt was unbuttoned at the collar. His dark, curly hair was slicked back with some kind of gel that made it look shiny and stiff, and a stretch of stubble grew out of his smooth, dark skin. She could see it . . . maybe? It was weird to think about your best friend's stepdad that way.

"Hey, Uncle Rob," Jessica said, leaning forward to give him a hug.

"Hey, Jess," he replied, hugging her back. "You look nice."

"Thanks. You know Gretchen, and this is our friend, Nick."

Nick dropped Gretchen's hand and reached out to shake Rob's. She hoped he'd take hers again, but he didn't.

"Nice to meet you," Rob said. "So, congratulations are due to you all, I guess. Eighth grade graduation!" He smirked at Gretchen. "You must be pretty special to warrant a party like this, huh? I think I got a pen for mine."

Gretchen blushed. "I think it was just an excuse for my mom to throw a big party. I'm not sure the graduation has all that much to do with it."

"But we *are* celebrating," Jessica added, giving Gretchen a look that said she would take it from here. "And we thought you might be able to help our celebration become a little more liquid." She emphasized the word *liquid* not so subtly, making sure he understood her point.

"Ah, I see," Rob answered. "And what kind of *liquids* did you have in mind?"

Jessica smiled. "Two apple martinis and a whiskey sour would be much appreciated."

Rob laughed. "If your aunt finds out, she'll kill me."

"Oh, come on." Jessica wriggled her eyebrows. "After you got your pen in the eighth grade, didn't you feel short-changed?"

"Do I have to answer?" Rob rolled his eyes. "Fine. But you better keep this amongst yourselves." He sauntered off in the direction of the bar.

Jessica gasped and grabbed Gretchen's arm. "Michelle's here! She saw us ask Rob for drinks!"

Gretchen's brow furrowed, and then her jaw dropped. Jessica wasn't lying. She watched as Michelle grabbed Rob from behind and spun him around. Like most of the women in the Oculus Society, Michelle was beautiful: tall and thin with long, wavy, auburn-colored hair and a nearly perfect nose—it sloped at just the right angle and turned up just the right amount at the tip. (Gretchen's mom privately theorized that Michelle's nose had clinched her longstanding job as the local TV weathergirl. She was the only person who looked better in profile than she did head-on.) Tonight she was wearing a short, one-shouldered black dress. Correction: she would have been beautiful if her face wasn't twisted in fury.

"I will not have my husband be responsible for getting thirteen-year-olds drunk," she barked.

A hush passed over the tent.

Rob shrugged and laughed. "No idea what you're talking about, dear."

Michelle glowered at Jessica, but then her face softened into a smile as she spotted something on the other side of the tent. Gretchen looked to see what had caught Michelle's attention; it was Tina Holt, the current President of the Oculus Society. Michelle was making a beeline straight toward her. It made sense: Tina was Mom's handpicked successor, the one woman every grown-up wanted to talk to these days.

Jessica buried her face in her hands. Gradually, the conversation in the tent picked back up. Gretchen's gaze turned from Michelle—now cozied up with Tina Holt—back to Rob. He kept right on toward the bar.

"She's gone," Gretchen whispered.

"She didn't even say hi to you," Nick observed.

Jessica dropped her hands and frowned, but before she could respond, a waiter appeared before them with a tray of drinks. "I was told to deliver these to the two beautiful ladies and their handsome friend," he said.

Gretchen spotted Rob standing in the corner, watching. He raised his glass at them discreetly before turning away.

"Dude, your uncle's cool," Nick whispered. "You're so lucky."

"Yeah," Jessica said, her sarcasm subtle enough for Nick to miss but not so subtle that Gretchen didn't notice. "I'm the luckiest girl in the world."

Gretchen sipped slowly, pacing herself. She didn't want to drink too much too fast and get caught being drunk at her own party. And besides, she was enjoying the warm feeling that spread through her more and more with each sip. The sweetness of the apple liqueur softened the bitter taste of the vodka but didn't mask it completely. The drink reminded her of air freshener that doesn't quite eliminate a bad odor. But it didn't matter. She wanted this night to last forever and ever. She tuned out Jessica and Nick, gazing over the tent and beyond, where the party had spilled out on to the lawn—

What the hell?

Out of the corner of her eye, she saw someone quietly open the gate to the side yard and tip-toe up to the kitchen door. She couldn't make out a face, but it was a girl, and her hair was flipped up at the edges, grazing the tops of her shoulder blades. *Ariel Miller.* Gretchen was sure of it.

"That little bitch," she muttered. She tossed back the rest of her apple martini in one gulp and handed the glass to Jessica. "Hold this for me. I'll be right back."

Gretchen stormed across the yard, ignoring Jessica's calls for her to wait. But Jessica caught up to her before she made it into the house. "Gretchen, what are you doing?"

"I just saw Ariel Miller sneak into my house, and I'm going

in there to find her and kick her out." Gretchen crossed her arms defiantly in front of her chest.

"That's it? That's why you left Nick Ford half drunk and standing by himself in the darkest part of your backyard? Because you thought you saw Ariel Miller? Jeez, Gretch. I was just about to excuse myself and leave the two of you alone. Talk about a wasted opportunity."

Gretchen found herself grinning. "You were?"

Jessica grinned back. "Forget it. We might as well find Ariel now. We'll get you some alone time with Nick later on."

Leave it to Ariel Miller to ruin everything, she thought, shaking her head. "I saw her going in through the kitchen door, but she could be anywhere in the house by now."

She strode across the patio, Jessica on her heels, through the sliding glass doors and into the crowded den with its high ceilings and dark wood floors set off against the white, paneled walls. Small groups of people huddled together, talking and laughing, while waiters wove through them carrying silver trays of champagne and hors d'oeuvres.

A blood-curdling scream from upstairs shattered the conversation.

Everyone froze. A woman dropped her glass. The pieces shattered at Gretchen's feet. "Call nine-one-one!" a man's voice shrieked.

The spell broke instantly. The guests in the den began scurrying in different directions. Gretchen pushed her way through them, trying to make her way toward the stairs. Her heart pounded. Someone must have fallen in the bathroom, slipped on something; there must be a lot of blood, and people were drunk and over-dramatic, and that's why there were screams . . . of course, it had to be something like that.

But when she finally made it to the stairwell, the faces of the adults told a different story.

She scrambled up the steps. Sirens blared in the distance, growing louder. In the hallway outside the master bedroom, she found her father slumped against Tina Holt. His body was shaking, his face in his hands as Tina patted his shoulder, murmuring to him in a low voice.

It was Tina who saw Gretchen first. She said Gretchen's name out loud, more as a warning than as a greeting. Dad's head jolted up. His eyes were red, and there were long, uneven streaks running down his face.

"What's going on?" she demanded. "Dad?"

He reached out to her with both hands. "Gretchen," he said. He opened his mouth again to speak, but all that came out was a choked sob. Gretchen glanced at the open door to her parents' bedroom. Tina quickly stepped forward to block her.

"You don't want to do that, sweetie," she said in a low voice. But she was too slow. Gretchen darted around her and into the room. Her eyes instantly fell on the king-sized bed, with its extra-wide headboard in tufted suede that her mother had custom-built two summers ago. Mom was sprawled on the left side—face down, her arms splayed out beside her, her hands balled up into fists, her legs hanging indecorously off the edge so that her ankles twisted to the side, exposing the red soles of her shoes.

Gretchen blinked. This wasn't possible. She couldn't reconcile the lifeless body on the bed with the woman she had talked to just a few hours ago. She could see the warm smile, the legs peeking out from her black dress when she walked, the honey-colored anklet shifting as she moved. Gretchen's wide eyes flashed again at her mother's twisted ankles. They were bare.

A gentle hand fell on her shoulder.

It was Tina, pulling her away from the door. From behind her she could hear urgent voices, the crackle of a radio, heavy steps on the stairs. Men in uniforms were pushing past her, carrying bags and equipment. Their voices sounded muddled and far away, as if under water.

Forty-five-year-old female.

"Come on, Gretchen," Tina said softly, leading her away.

Dead on arrival.

"Let's go downstairs and make you some tea."

Neck wounds consistent with strangulation.

"Your dad wants to talk to you."

Homicide detectives on their way.

CHAPTER FOUR

The day of the funeral was bright and sunny, the type of perfect California day that Octavia Harris had always loved. Gretchen could just picture her mom throwing open the curtains and insisting that they all go do something outside because a day like this was too good to waste. As she sat in the backseat of the hearse with her father, Gretchen stared out the window and wondered if sunny days would make her sad now for the rest of her life.

The detective assigned to her mother's case had no suspects and no leads. He had interviewed everyone who'd been at the party, but it was impossible to pinpoint exactly where each guest had been at the crucial moment. Nobody remembered seeing her mom arguing with anyone that night, either. In fact, nobody even really remembered seeing her mom at all, aside from when she greeted them at the front door. A few different people reported seeing a shadowy figure running out of the side yard shortly after they heard the scream, but their descriptions were too vague to be of any value.

Gretchen, however, was not about to let things drop so quickly. There was a nagging voice in the back of her head, and it kept telling her that the detectives had missed something. Rather *someone*: Ariel Miller. Gretchen was positive she'd seen Ariel sneaking in through the kitchen door that night.

Of course, at Gretchen's insistence, the detectives had questioned Ariel, but they had come back with nothing. Her story was solid, they explained. She went out to an early dinner with her mother, then the two of them went home and watched a movie together. They'd questioned both Ariel and her mother separately, and both had provided the exact same story. Besides, the detectives reasoned, there were dozens of people in the kitchen the whole night. If Ariel had snuck in, someone would have noticed her. Not a single person at the party could recall seeing her there.

What they said made sense, but still, Gretchen wasn't convinced.

She held her father's hand as they walked through the cemetery toward the fresh mound of earth that had been removed from the ground to make space for her mother's casket. Her father broke into heavy sobs as they approached the grave site, but Gretchen just stared straight ahead. It had been four days since her mother was murdered, and still, she hadn't cried.

My mother is dead. My mother is dead. My mother is dead.

She'd been repeating this to herself every night as she lay in bed staring at the ceiling. While her brain knew it to be true, the rest of her just didn't—couldn't—believe it. She had no emotions, just questions. Who would want to do this? Why? And most of all, what had her mother meant when she said that things were going to happen to her? *Things you can't even imagine.* The words fluttered in Gretchen's mind like a sheet on a clothesline, twisting and turning in the wind.

The funeral was packed; everyone from the Oculus Society was there—along with Gretchen's friends and teachers from school, business associates of her father, and random friends her mom had picked up along the course of her life. Gretchen appreciated them all coming to show their respect. But the only person she wanted to see was her best friend. Jessica's parents had both died in a horrible car accident when she was six. She was the only other person Gretchen knew who had lost her mother. She was the only person in the world who could possibly understand what Gretchen was feeling. She'd already proven it: Jessica had been by the house every night, sitting with Gretchen for hours at a stretch, talking about nothing in particular, just trying to keep her mind from drifting back to what she'd seen in her parents' bedroom.

Gretchen spotted her in the crowd of people, standing almost directly across from the white folding chairs that had been set up graveside for the family. The chairs reminded her of graduation, and her chest tightened. How was it possible that it was just four days ago when it felt like four years ago? She remembered her mother standing on stage in her white suit with her beige pumps and the amber in her anklet glowing in the sunlight.

That was another nagging question: what had happened to her mother's anklet? After the police had left that first night, and after her father had taken a sleeping pill and passed out in the guest room, Gretchen had gone to her mother's closet and opened the drawer where she kept all of her jewelry. But the anklet wasn't there. The next morning, as soon as there was enough sunlight to see the ground, she'd scoured the floor of the tent and the grass around the pool. She'd even dug up an old metal detector from the garage. When she was younger she'd gone through a period of wanting to be an archeologist (to impress her ancient-Greece-obsessed mother, she could now admit), and Tina had given her the metal detector as a birthday present. It was old and kind of crappy, but it still worked. Maybe the anklet had come unclasped and fallen off at some point during the night. But Gretchen never found it. It bothered her that it was missing, almost as much as it bothered her that nobody else had seen Ariel Miller at the party.

The women from the Oculus Society stood together in a semicircle next to the grave, all in black suits and dresses. To Gretchen, they looked like a coven of beautiful witches. Not evil. *Special,* powerful, removed from the rest of the crowd, and bound to her mother by a secret bond. She tried to keep her eyes focused on them and away from the mound of dirt and the casket that held her mother's body. As the priest began to speak, Gretchen noticed that some of them—Michelle, Tina Holt, her mother's friend Joan—were whispering fiercely to one another. She fought to decipher the conversation but was jolted back to the ceremony by the priest, who, in keeping with Greek Orthodox tradition, had begun to loudly sing the Trisagion.

"*Agios o Theos, Agios ischyros, Agios athanatos, eleison imas.*"

He sprinkled dirt on the coffin in the shape of a cross, then invited everyone to place a flower on the casket. Gretchen watched as the guests formed a line. It seemed endless. There were her cousins and her aunts and uncles. There were some of her friends from school. There was Jessica's uncle Rob, and there was Nick Ford, who made a somber face at her as he passed by her chair. Then came the members of the Oculus Society. Tina went first, then Joan. Gretchen expected some of the older, more senior members to be next. To her surprise, Tina ushered Jessica to the front.

That's strange, Gretchen thought.

And then it was all over, and she and her father were being led away to a car, leaving her mother behind in a dark wood casket where a mound of earth used to be.

CHAPTER FIVE

The summer wore on slowly and painfully. In the first days after her mother's murder, Gretchen cancelled her plans to spend four weeks at sleepaway camp. She wasn't up for all of the laughing and lightheartedness; she wasn't ready yet to pretend that she was fine. She knew that was coming, of course. Once school started, she'd have to act breezy and strong. But with nothing to do all day except sit home and be sad, she grew bored and anxious.

Worse, Jessica was beginning to distance herself. She'd been calling and texting less and less; she hadn't come by in almost two weeks. Not that Gretchen could really blame her for it. No doubt Jessica was gearing up for high school. Ninth grade at Delphi High comprises two eighth grade classes; one from Delphi Middle School, where they had gone, and another from Outer Delphi, the other middle school in their township. That meant there would be another two hundred kids to navigate and another "cool crowd" vying for popularity. No doubt Jessica was also anticipating the gossip that would be swirling around Gretchen; she would be "the girl whose mom had been murdered in her own house." She got it. If she were Jessica, she wouldn't want to be associated too closely with her, either. But still, they were best friends, and if you couldn't count on your best friend at a time like this . . .

As if thinking about her loneliness had somehow conjured some company, there was a knock at her door.

"Hey, Gretch?"

It was just her dad: the same zombie she passed in the silent halls of their home, day in and day out. She tried to muster a smile from bed as he pushed open the door. He'd lost weight since the funeral. He'd also stopped caring about his appearance. His hair was uncombed, his pale jowls unshaven. His face looked sunken and hollow.

"What's up?" Gretchen asked.

He shifted his weight from one foot to the other. "Do you remember that anklet that Mom used to wear? The one with the orange-y stone in it? I can't find it anywhere. Have you seen it by any chance?"

Gretchen's heart skipped a beat. "Actually, I've been looking for it, too. She was wearing it the night of the . . . party."

His eyes sharpened. "She was? Are you sure?"

"I'm positive. We were talking in the tent right before everyone came, and I remember noticing it. But when she, um, when she was, you know, in the bedroom . . . it wasn't on her. I looked in her jewelry drawer, and I checked in the tent and in the backyard. I thought maybe it had fallen off. But I never found it."

Her father's brow creased. He shifted on his feet again. "Why were you looking for it?"

"I don't know. It was pretty, and she was wearing it that night, and it reminded me of her. I just wanted to have it."

Gretchen paused and sat up in bed, tossing the covers aside. "Why are *you* looking for it?"

"Same reason," he said with a shrug. He started to turn, then hesitated. "Did you mention to the police that it was missing?"

"No. Why? What's so important about it?" Suddenly, it dawned on her what he was thinking. "You don't think . . . Dad? Do you think whoever killed her stole the anklet? It wasn't valuable, was it? She told me it was something she found at a vintage store."

He shook his head. "No. That's not what I'm thinking. It was an old piece of junk, like you said. Nobody would want it." He coughed twice—two staccato, *huh-huh*s into his hand. Gretchen crossed her arms in front of her chest. Her dad always did that when he was holding something back. Her mom used to joke that he would have made a pathetic poker player because he had such an obvious tell.

"What are you not telling me?" Gretchen demanded.

"Nothing." He forced a strained smile. "I mean it, Gretch. I just wanted it for the same reason you did. It reminds me of her, that's all." His eyes were welling up. He saw her looking at him, and he dropped his head for a few moments to collect himself before he could speak again. "I've got some work to do, okay? I'll see you in the morning."

He closed the door. Gretchen didn't bother mentioning that he'd probably see her at dinner, too. It was only 4:30 in the afternoon.

Gretchen texted Jessica twice the next day—hey, miss u, what's going on? Did u get my text b4?—and once the day after that—r u ok? Haven't heard from u in a while.

No response.

It was just plain rude at this point. On the morning of the third day, Gretchen's heart pounded as she reached for her phone.

WTF Jess?? The radio silence is NOT COOL.

Her finger hovered over the send button, but she hit delete instead. She curled back up on her bed. Maybe she should never leave. (It wasn't as if she left her bed much anymore, anyway.) Was she really going to be an outcast at Delphi High? How would she ever get through the year? How would she even get through the first day? She could just picture everyone whispering about her and the fake sympathy smiles she would get in the hallways. Worse, she kept imagining herself having to see Ariel Miller.

Gretchen picked up her phone without moving from the fetal position.

I know u were at my house that night. Just admit it already.

This time she had no trouble hitting the send button. Then again, this was the sixth time this summer that she'd sent the exact same text.

Maybe I could transfer to a private school, she thought. One of them might still have a spot left for the fall. *Or maybe boarding school, even.* She could get the hell out of Delphi and away from all of the reminders . . . But, no, she could never leave her dad. Besides, she couldn't even imagine how she would introduce an idea like that to him.

Her phone vibrated.

U r sick. Text me again, and I WILL call the police.

Gretchen texted her back immediately.

Go ahead. Maybe they'll question u again and find out the truth.

The doorbell rang just as she hit send, startling her. *Shit.* She threw the phone on her bed. It was probably just a real estate agent. Ever since her mom had died, a new one had been popping by every week or so. *Just canvassing the neighborhood, checking to see if anyone is thinking about selling and might need some help.* As if they hadn't heard the gossip about the woman who'd been killed in her bedroom. Most people, Gretchen imagined, probably would want to sell after something like that. But despite the fact that her father hadn't set foot in the master bedroom since the murder, he hadn't even mentioned the possibility of moving. Instead, he just slammed the door in the agents' faces, yelling that they were worse than ambulance chasers.

Gretchen thought about ignoring this latest one at the door, but she walked downstairs anyway. It had been over a week since she'd talked to anyone but her dad. At this point, even a real estate agent would be a welcome distraction.

"Who is it?" she called through the door.

"It's Jess. Can I come in?"

Gretchen's pulse quickened. She unlocked the door and found her friend standing on the welcome mat, dressed in cut-off jean shorts and a White Stripes T-shirt that Gretchen had never seen before.

"Hey," Jessica mumbled, looking down at the ground. "I'm really sorry that I've been MIA. Things have been crazy busy for me." Gretchen wanted so badly to be the kind of person who could just forgive and forget. The kind of person who wouldn't ask where she'd been or be mad at her for having disappeared. But she wasn't.

"Oh, yeah, I've been really busy, too," she said, sarcastically. "It takes up a lot of time to sit by yourself all day, wondering who killed your mom and why your best friend doesn't respond to your texts anymore."

Jessica bit the already red, chewed-up skin around her fingernails. It was a gross habit she had, one that Gretchen knew got worse when she was stressed out. "I know, and I'm sorry. I've been a shitty friend."

"Yeah, you have." She was trying to sound angry, but her voice broke, giving away the raw hurt underneath.

The two of them stared at each other in awkward silence.

"Would you forgive me if I did Mr. Pants?" Jessica finally asked.

Gretchen did her best not to smile. Mr. Pants was Jessica's favorite stuffed animal from when she was little: a worn, brown bear that for some reason wore a pair of bright yellow pants. They used to put on plays with him when they were younger, and Jessica had this crazy Mr. Pants voice that Gretchen could never get her to do anymore, no matter how much she begged.

Gretchen raised her eyebrows. *She must feel really bad if she's willing to do Mr. Pants.* "Maybe."

Jessica smiled. She tucked her chin down into her neck and raised her shoulders up by her ears. "Hello, Gretchen," she said in a deep, raspy, vaguely Southern smoker's voice. "Mr. Pants sure wishes that you wouldn't be mad at his pal Jessica anymore. Hey, do you know why I wear these yellow pants, anyway?"

Gretchen kept a straight face and shook her head.

"Well now, it's simple. If I didn't wear pants, everyone would be able to see my junk."

In spite of her best efforts, Gretchen smiled. She rolled her eyes. "Come on," she said, resignedly, as she waved Jessica into the foyer. "You had me at hello."

Jessica's eyes refused to stay put while Gretchen talked; they kept darting around the bedroom. "I was thinking before that I wish I could just leave here and go to boarding school,"

Gretchen admitted. "But I don't think my dad could handle it. Do you?"

"Uh-huh," Jessica replied, nodding.

Gretchen gave her a confused look. "You *do* think he could handle it?"

Finally, Jessica's eyes focused on Gretchen. "Wait, what?" she asked.

Gretchen crossed her arms in front of her chest. "Is something wrong? Because you're acting really weird."

Jessica bit her lip and stared at the floor, and then looked Gretchen in the eye. "I need to talk to you."

"I'm right here," Gretchen said, exasperated. "Talk."

"Okay, well, I really don't know how to say this, like, at *all*. And the thing is it sounds crazy . . . it sounds like *I'm* crazy, but I'm not, and so you have to believe me that what I'm about to tell you really is true."

"Just say it," Gretchen demanded.

Jessica inhaled, then let it out in one long, deep breath. "The Oculus Society is not just about promoting classical Greek education and doing philanthropy. That's what they tell everyone, and it's what most of the members think. But its real purpose is to protect a secret that's been passed down from generation to generation since, well, since the early days of the Roman Empire." She paused.

Gretchen's eyes narrowed. This was definitely *not* what she'd been expecting from Jessica. "What's the secret?"

"Okay so, this is where it gets weird." She dug into her bag and pulled out around a dozen pages of printouts. "I did some research."

Gretchen frowned. "Can't you summarize? I really don't feel like reading all of that right now."

Jessica sat down on the edge of the bed. Her eyes flitted

around the room again, as if she were searching for some-thing that might help her to explain.

"Okay," she finally said. "Here's the deal: there was this guy named Plotinus, who was a Greek philosopher who lived in Rome. He believed that everything in the universe was all part of something he called The One. But that part's not really important—the important thing is that he believed people could project their souls out of their bodies. In the beginning, he projected his soul through the Oculus in the Pantheon. He described himself floating with the stars, and he said he could see the Earth below him, including his own body, which looked asleep. Are you following me so far?"

Gretchen nodded. She was following, but she couldn't imagine where Jessica was going.

Jessica continued. "Well, later on, he realized that he could do more than that. Instead of just projecting his soul into space or wherever, he figured out that he could actually project into another person, and they could project into him. They could trade souls."

"Like in *Freaky Friday*?" Gretchen asked, skeptically.

Jessica smiled. "Exactly like in *Freaky Friday*."

Gretchen grinned again, in spite of herself. *This is so Jes-sica,* she thought. *Leave it to her to make up a crazy story to take my mind off of my problems.* She had to admit it, though; it was working. She couldn't remember the last time she'd actually smiled.

She rubbed her palms back and forth against each other, getting into the game. "Okay, so let me guess how they did it. Let's see . . . they both wished they could become the other at exactly the moment a bolt of lightning struck. No, wait. That's too cliché. Okay, I know. They both threw a penny into a foun-tain and made the same wish at the same exact time."

"No," Jessica said. "It's nothing like that." She hesitated for a moment. "They had to kiss."

Gretchen blinked. "Oh. That's good." She gave Jessica a look that said *you are so bad* and continued to play along. "And of course, people in the Oculus Society do this. They kiss each other and trade souls."

"Not people," Jessica corrected. "Only one person. Well, obviously you need two people, but only one person is chosen by the Oculus Society to do it," she explained. "She's called the *Odeetees*. It's Greek for leader."

"And who's that?" Gretchen asked with a smile. "Who has this magical power to trade souls with whoever they want?"

Jessica sighed. "It was your mom, Gretch."

Gretchen stopped smiling. Stopped breathing, actually. "My mom?" She shook her head. "That's not funny, Jessica."

"I'm not trying to be funny, Gretchen."

Gretchen looked Jessica in the eye. "You're saying this is all true? And that my mom could trade souls with people?"

"Not with people," Jessica corrected, again. "With one member of the Oculus Society. A member of her choosing. The *Etaíros*."

"Who?"

"Tina Holt."

Gretchen's lips twisted in a grimace. "You think my mom made out with Tina Holt? I don't believe you. This is ridiculous." She felt her eyes welling up with tears; if she hadn't been able to cry in the days following her mother's death, she was sure making up for it now. It felt like all she did anymore was cry. She crossed her arms and turned around so Jessica wouldn't see her tears.

"They didn't *make out*," Jessica explained. "It's more like breathing into someone else's mouth than kissing." She paused. "I'm sorry, Gretch. I know this is a lot to take in. I just . . . I had to tell you. There's so much going on right now, and it's all really confusing, and I couldn't keep it from you any longer."

Gretchen wiped the tears out of her eyes. Her hand was shaking. If this was a joke, it had gone way too far.

"There's something else," Jessica said, slowly.

Great, Gretchen thought. She didn't say anything, and she still wasn't willing to turn around; she just waited for Jessica to go on.

"I think my aunt might have had something to do with your mom's murder."

CHAPTER SIX

A mphiclea arrived at the Pantheon just before midnight, exactly as Gemina had instructed. The moon was full, perfectly aligned with the great round window in the ceiling, casting a soft light across the marble floor.

A few white-plumed pigeons strutted by her, pecking at the ground. She watched them so intently that she didn't notice Gemina and Plotinus entering behind her. Gemina placed a hand on her shoulder, and Amphiclea jumped. She wasn't doing anything illegal, but nonetheless, her heart pounded at the unfamiliar feeling of being out so late at night without her husband.

Amphiclea and Gemina kissed each other on each of their cheeks, and Plotinus reached out and took Amphiclea's hand. He was a small man, hardly taller than Gemina, and though he was only in his forties, his hair had already turned white. With his somber disposition, he appeared much older than he was. He spoke in a quiet, low voice, and Amphiclea had to lean in to hear him.

"Dear Amphiclea, we are indebted to you for agreeing to join us here tonight."

"It is my honor," Amphiclea replied.

Plotinus smiled slightly. "I trust Gemina has explained to you your role here?"

Amphiclea nodded. "I am to be a witness, but beyond that, I'm afraid I am not exactly clear on what it is I am to do."

Gemina looked sheepishly at Plotinus. There was just enough moonlight for Amphiclea to see that her cheeks had turned red. "I'm embarrassed to admit that I didn't quite understand it myself, Plotinus, so I did not know how to explain it to another."

"Ah, yes, I see," Plotinus said. "The concept of projection can be quite confusing to the uninitiated. But it's really quite simple. As the witness, you will watch me and Gemina simultaneously project, or trade, our souls. Only you will know that we are not really who we appear to be. Should something happen to either of us where we must reveal the truth, it is your responsibility to step forward and corroborate our story. But most importantly, you must ensure that we return to our proper bodies."

"But how?"

Plotinus's expression turned grave. "What Gemina and I are doing is very dangerous. If she or I were to be caught and imprisoned, it is imperative that we be able to see each other so that we can project ourselves back. It is your duty, Amphiclea, to make sure that happens. No matter what, you must find a way for us to be together, even if only for a few minutes."

Amphiclea felt like she might faint. This was more than she had bargained for. Sensing her distress, Gemina put her arm around Amphiclea's shoulder.

"It won't happen," she assured her. "Plotinus and I will be careful, and we'll return to ourselves as quickly as possible."

Amphiclea nodded, trying to be brave. "I understand," she said.

"One more thing," Plotinus added. "You must wear the anklet Gemina gave you at all times. I made reference to it in my writings: 'she who wears the anklet shall know the truth.' If you must come forward, show my diary, and the anklet will serve as further proof that what you say is true."

"I'm wearing it," Amphiclea said. She lifted her robe to reveal the amber disc on the gold chain; it glowed as it caught the moonlight.

"Then we're ready to proceed," Plotinus whispered. He took Gemina by the hand and led her forward, directly under the oculus. The two of them sat down on the ground facing each other, and Gemina placed her hands on top of Plotinus's own. Amphiclea stood back, watching them in silence.

"Close your eyes," Plotinus instructed Gemina in a low voice. "Now breathe slowly, and picture the universe. Picture the people and the animals and the plants and the trees. Picture everything that's living. And now picture them free of their mortal bodies, floating together as one great energy. Feel that energy in you, Gemina. Feel it in your toes, in your legs, in your stomach. Feel it in your fingers and your hands, in your breast, in your throat. Feel it in your heart. Feel it in your mind." He lowered his voice and spoke quietly in Greek, the phrase that he'd been perfecting for nearly a year. The phrase that would release their souls. "*Écho exorísei aíma egó dió xei ostó n, proválloun ti n psychí mou se állo spíti.*" He leaned in toward Gemina, placing his lips on hers. "Now, breathe deeply and exhale," he whispered.

Amphiclea closed her eyes. It felt wrong for them to be so

intimate with each other, and more wrong still for her to be watching them. She heard them both loudly exhale, and then she heard the soft tinkle of Gemina's laugh, like the bells rung in town after a baby has been born.

She opened her eyes. They were still sitting there, except instead of holding hands, Plotinus was touching Gemina's face as if he'd never seen it before.

"This is miraculous," he said, running his fingers over Gemina's lips. "I feel so . . ." he looked down at himself, turning his hands over and then touching his chest, his stomach, his hips. "I feel so strong!" he exclaimed.

Gemina laughed again. "And I feel so soft. It's quite remarkable."

Suddenly, Plotinus jumped up and ran toward Amphiclea, hugging her excitedly. "Did you see it happen? Was there any sign of it?"

Amphiclea backed away from Plotinus uncomfortably. "A sign of what?"

Plotinus laughed, his eyes sparkling in a way that Amphiclea had never seen before. "Amphiclea, it's me! Gemina! It worked!" Amphiclea stared at Plotinus, disbelieving. "Ask me something," Plotinus said. "Something only I—I mean, Gemina—would know."

Amphiclea thought for a moment. "What did you say to me about my father the night before I was married?"

Plotinus let out a deep, hearty chuckle. "I said that your father surely must love your sister more, because the husband he chose for her is rich and handsome, while the one he chose for you is just rich."

Amphiclea's mouth fell open. "Can it really be?" she whispered. She looked back at Gemina, who was still standing under the oculus. Her eyes shone in the moonlight, but they looked duller somehow, as if something had been extinguished inside of her. Gemina took a step closer to her.

"She speaks the truth. It is I, Plotinus, in this woman's body. You are witness to something extraordinary, Amphiclea. Do not forget what we discussed earlier. You alone know the truth."

Amphiclea felt dizzy, and her heart began to beat in triple time. She looked again at Plotinus. *Is he really Gemina? But how?* The words spun in her head. And suddenly, everything went black.

CHAPTER SEVEN

Gretchen tried to read the Wikipedia pages that Jessica had laid out on her desk, but she couldn't focus on the words. The names were all so confusing, and the philosophical explanations were so dense that she was having a hard time wrapping her brain around it all. She took a deep breath and tried again, reading from the beginning.

*"**Plotinus** (Greek: Πλωτῖνος) (ca. CE 204/5–270) was a philosopher of the ancient world. His most important theory taught that there is a supreme, transcendent One beyond all categorization of being and not being. His metaphysical writings have influenced centuries of pagan, Christian, Jewish, Islamic, and Gnostic metaphysicians and mystics."*

Gretchen looked up, bewildered and just the slightest bit angry. "Jessica, I can't read this right now. I'm sorry. You can't tell me that my mother had some mystical power and was trading souls with Tina Holt, then say that you think your aunt had something to do with my mother's murder, and then hand me a stack of boring pages to read. I need you to tell me what you're talking about. I need you to tell me *now*."

Jessica seemed to waver, then gave in with a sigh. "Okay, okay." She sat down on the edge of Gretchen's bed. "After your mom died, things got really crazy. There was an emergency meeting of the Oculus Society to discuss, like, what kinds of flowers we were going to send to the funeral home and who was going to make meals for you and your dad the first few weeks. Then, about two weeks ago, we had the regular, monthly meeting. I thought maybe you would come—"

"I'm not ready," Gretchen interrupted. "I just can't handle seeing all of those moms and daughters together right now. I don't know if I'll ever be able to handle it."

"I know," Jessica said, patting her on the arm. "I know it's so hard, Gretch, but I swear to you, it does get easier. It never gets easy, but it will become easier than it is right now."

"I wish I believed you," she said. Gretchen gulped down the lump in her throat. "Anyway, go on. What happened at the meeting?"

"Well, nothing really. I mean, everything seemed normal, but then when it was over, Michelle came to me and said that I was needed for something. She took me to this back room that I didn't even know existed. Tina Holt and a few of the other, older members were sitting behind a long table, and they were wearing white robes, and it was all really, really creepy. And they tell me about this secret—they call it the Plotinus Ability—and how they're members of a secret board that is charged with protecting it. And then they tell me that you were next in line to get it."

"Me!" Gretchen exclaimed. "Why me?"

"Okay, stay with me for a minute. Your mom, I guess, was finished with being the *Odeetees*. I don't know why; they didn't get into it. But for the last few months she had changed her role in the whole thing. Instead of being the one who projects, she became the *mártyras*—the witness. The one who watches the other two project and makes sure that everything goes smoothly."

"And who were the other two?" Gretchen asked.

"Well, it was still Tina Holt and then also Joan Hedley."

"Joan Hedley!" Gretchen shouted. Joan Hedley was the quietest, meekest woman she'd ever met. Joan Hedly blushed every time she opened her mouth to speak; how could she kiss another woman? Gretchen just couldn't believe what Jessica was telling her right now. But it was obvious that Jessica did. A chill went down Gretchen's spine. *What did they do to her in that ceremony?* she wondered. *What did they say to make her believe this craziness?*

"Anyway," Jessica went on, "it was only supposed to be a temporary arrangement, until the board decided who was going to be chosen next. Your mom, I guess, had lobbied really hard that it should be you. She felt it was time to bring in some new blood, to get the next generation involved. And your mom felt that you were the best candidate. You know, winner of the Plotinus Award at graduation and all that. They were going to tell you this summer."

Gretchen's eyes got watery again. *Things are going to happen to you,* she heard her mother's voice say. *Things you can't even imagine.*

"So why haven't they told me?" Gretchen wanted to know.

Jessica lowered her eyes. "Well, I guess some of the board members weren't sure if you were ready. They didn't know if you would be able to handle the responsibility right now since you're, you know, emotionally distraught or whatever."

Gretchen sniffed. "Who's on this board, exactly?"

"Well, that's the thing. It's Tina Holt, obviously, and your mom was on it, and Joan Hedley, of course. And then there's also Kristen Renwick, and . . ." Jessica paused.

"Your aunt," Gretchen guessed.

"Yes," Jessica said. "But there's one other person, too."

"And who's that?"

Jessica closed her eyes for a moment, then opened them to meet Gretchen's searching gaze. "Me."

"You! I don't understand. How come you never told me about this? How could you keep something like that from me?"

Jessica shook her head. "I didn't keep it from you. It just happened that night. I just told you: they called me into the room out of the blue, and they told me that I had been chosen to be on the board. They made me take an oath of secrecy and everything. That's why I haven't called you or answered any of your texts. I didn't know what to do. I felt like I should tell you, but they made me swear not to say anything to anyone. And I didn't know how you'd react. I mean, don't you think I know how crazy all of this sounds? But you're my best friend, Gretchen. If it were me, I'd want you to tell me the truth."

Gretchen had to sit down. This was all too much . . . too much. "So let me get this straight," she said slowly. "The board chose you to fill the seat that was left behind by my mother, and then you all discussed whether or not I was emotionally capable of inheriting the Plotinus Ability? And where did you come out on that?"

"I said you were fine!" Jessica insisted. "I said that if it was what your mother wanted, then we should respect her wishes! I was on your side!" Jessica took a deep breath. Her face was red, and her hands were shaking. "At first everyone agreed with me. Joan, Kristen, Tina, all of them. But then Michelle got up and started arguing that you couldn't possibly be stable enough to handle it. They asked me what my impressions were, and I told them that you were a strong person and that you would be fine. But Michelle wouldn't let it go. She kept insisting that it wasn't in your best interest right now, and she managed to convince Tina and Kristen. It was three against two."

"And that's why you think Michelle had something to do with the murder?"

Jessica nodded. "But it's not just that. After it was settled that it wasn't going to be you, we had to decide who it would be. And guess who didn't hesitate to volunteer?"

Gretchen shrugged. "Okay, so she wanted to be the one to get this . . . this power or whatever. So what? That doesn't mean she killed my mom."

"I can't explain it, Gretch. She was so forceful about the whole thing. It was like she had planned it all out: your mom dying, getting you ousted as her successor, and then volunteering to take your place. I just have a bad feeling about it."

Gretchen picked up a strand of hair and twirled it around her finger. She couldn't help thinking that everyone in the Oculus Society—or at least the people on this "secret board"—had gone completely insane. *They have so much real power in this town. They've somehow convinced themselves that they've got magical powers now, too.*

"Okay. Let's say you're right. Let's say that Michelle really believes this magical power exists, and she wanted it so badly that she was willing to kill my mother for it. What are we supposed to do? Go to the police? They'd never believe us, and you'd get kicked out of the Oculus Society for telling them."

"No, we obviously couldn't tell the police. We'd have to find evidence first and then go to them with that. But at least I have a lead."

Gretchen shook her head stubbornly. "I have a lead, too. And her name is Ariel Miller."

Jessica rolled her eyes. "You're still on that? Gretch, nobody saw her that night. She wasn't there."

"*I* saw her. I know she had something to do with it, Jessica. I can't prove it yet, but God help me, I will." She crossed her arms. "You have your bad feelings, I have mine. What's harder to believe, anyway? That a girl who hates me killed my mom, or that my mom was killed over some make-believe secret power?"

Jessica tapped her index finger on the desk, bouncing it up and down over and over and over again in quick, even bursts. Then she stopped. "Maybe there's a way for both of us to confirm our suspicions."

"Yeah? What's that?"

"I didn't finish telling you about the Plotinus Ability."

"Does it really matter? You said they gave it to Michelle."

Jessica shook her head. "No. I said that Michelle volunteered."

Gretchen arched an eyebrow. "But they didn't give it to her?"

"Nope. They gave it to me."

Gretchen paced back and forth in her room, tears stinging her eyes as she replayed the fight in her head. She'd kicked Jessica out, told her she couldn't handle this right now—couldn't handle *her* right now. And of course Jessica had cried. *Gretchen, you don't understand. I just want to help you.*

Well, boo-freaking-hoo, Gretchen thought, continuing the argument in her mind. *You ignore me for weeks and then come in here with this crazy story about trading souls and my mother kissing Tina Holt, and now suddenly you're the one who's next in line?* On the other hand, she could see why Jessica would want to believe all this BS. She'd be the most powerful person in the whole Oculus Society now. She was drunk with her own power. So drunk she actually believed she could become someone else.

Gretchen snatched up the papers that Jessica had left on her desk.

Please, just read them, she'd begged after Gretchen had told her to get out.

Oh, I'll read them, all right. I'll read them and tell everyone how crazy you all are for buying into this crap.

Suddenly, Gretchen didn't care if she never set foot in the Oculus Society ever again. It was as if she were seeing the whole thing for the very first time—an exclusionary, petty, power-hungry group of multi-generational social climbers—who had been completely deluded into thinking they're not only better than everyone else, but super human to boot. No wonder Ariel Miller hated them all so much.

Gretchen angrily flipped the pages, skimming through the paragraphs.

According to Plotinus's diary, he and his partner, Gemina, chose Gemina's closest friend, Amphiclea, to witness them trade souls. Plotinus was adamant about the existence of a witness. In his opinion, the witness was the most crucial part of the exchange, because only the witness knew that the partners had projected into each other's bodies. If something were to happen to

either of the partners, then it was the witness's respon-
sibility to come forward . . .

They want you to be the witness, Jessica had pleaded.
You'd still be a part of it.

Yeah, Gretchen had responded. *I'm sure you'd love that,*
too; having me on the sidelines while you get to be the big
star. She went back to the paper.

Further, Plotinus referenced an amber amulet that was
worn by Amphiclea in her role as witness. It is unknown
whether the amulet had powers that facilitated the
exchange, or whether it was merely a ritualistic symbol,
but his diary states, "She who wears the anklet shall
know the truth."

Gretchen felt like she'd been punched in the stomach. The
papers fell from her hands, floating in and out and landing
softly at her feet, like gentle waves lapping against a dock.
The anger she'd been feeling toward Jessica evaporated.

She picked up her phone and frantically dialed Jessica's
number.

"Hi," Jessica answered. Her voice sounded guarded and hurt.

"She wore an anklet," Gretchen blurted out. "My mother
was wearing an anklet the night she was murdered. It had an
amber stone on it."

"I know," Jessica said. "I saw it at graduation. That's why
I wanted you to read the papers."

"No, you don't understand. When she was in the bedroom . . . afterwards . . . the anklet was gone."

Jessica didn't say anything.

"Jess? Are you there?"

"Oh, my God," Jessica finally whispered. "Do you think someone killed her to get the anklet?"

Gretchen gripped the phone. "I think they might have. I mean, I thought it was just lost, but then my dad came around the other night asking me if I'd seen it."

"Your dad! Do you think he knew about the Plotinus Ability?"

"No," Gretchen said firmly. "My mom took the Oculus Society too seriously. If what you're saying is true, if she wasn't supposed to tell anyone, then she wouldn't have. Not even him." She paused as tears sprang to her eyes. "Not even me, either."

"Then why was he asking about the anklet?"

"I don't know," Gretchen admitted. "But if it's true that the anklet had some sort of power or special significance, then somebody might have wanted it badly enough to kill her for it."

"Yeah, somebody named Michelle."

Neither of them said anything as they thought through the implications of all of this.

"Do you believe me now?" Jessica asked.

Gretchen sighed. She could almost see the shimmering amber around her mother's ankle, could almost hear her mother's voice. *Things are going to start happening. Things you can't even imagine.* Her mother wasn't crazy; that much Gretchen knew for sure.

"I'm sorry," Gretchen answered, purposely avoiding the question. "I shouldn't have said those things to you."

"It's okay. I'm sorry for springing it all on you like that."

"You said you had an idea," Gretchen reminded her. "Something about how we could both confirm our suspicions."

"Yeah. I was thinking, the board told me that I don't have

to make any decisions yet. They said there was something
they needed to take care of before I could officially begin.
Something they needed in order for the ritual to be complete.
I'll bet you they're looking for the anklet. I'll bet you they
called your dad to ask him if he had it."

"That would make sense. Especially if it's the key to trading souls. If the anklet has the power, then you wouldn't be
able to do it without it."

"But what if it doesn't?" Jessica said. "What if it's like the
articles say—just a ritualistic symbol?"

"What does it matter? Either way, you need the anklet to
trade souls."

"No, that's the thing," Jessica said. "If it's just a symbol,
then you don't need it. You can do it without it."

"What are you saying, Jess?"

"I'm saying: We need to gather as much information as
possible. Gretchen, you know things that I don't know about
your mother, things maybe even only you and the killer know.
Michelle would never mention those things to *you*. But if she
thought you were me . . . I'm saying we trade souls without a
witness. And that way, I can find out things about Ariel that
she'd never say to *you*. If it turns out Michelle wasn't involved,
no harm no foul. Same for Ariel."

Gretchen frowned. She was a rule follower, and the quality
she most hated and also most admired in Jessica was the ease
with which she ignored rules.

"Jess, the papers say that Plotinus thought the witness was
the most crucial part of the exchange, and now you're saying
we should just skip the whole witness thing. Do you think
that's a good idea?"

"I think that in ancient Rome it probably was crucial to
have a witness, because if a woman got caught snooping

around where she wasn't supposed to be, she could get her head cut off or something. But seriously, what could happen to us? So we snoop around a little and pretend to be each other. Who cares?"

"I don't know," Gretchen hedged. "And anyway, do you even know how to do it? It can't be as simple as just kissing. People kiss all the time, and they don't open their eyes and find that they're in the other person's body. Even if it's not the anklet, there has to be something that makes it happen."

"Let me worry about that," Jessica answered. "I just need to know if you're on board."

Gretchen paused to think it over. All she wanted was to solve her mother's murder and to have Jessica on her side to help her do it. If that meant she had to kiss Jessica in some weird, Oculus Society ritual, then so be it. "All right." She sighed. "I'm in. What do we need to do?"

"I'll need a couple of days to get everything together," Jessica said. "And we can't do it at either of our houses. It's got to be somewhere totally private. Remember, we have to kiss. If anyone saw us . . ."

"So where, then?"

Jessica didn't answer right away. "I know," she said finally. "There's a park I used to go to when I was little. It has a sandbox and a giant pirate ship. Did you ever go there?"

"Yeah, of course. But that's totally out in the open."

"I know, but there's that play structure there. It's like a teepee, and you can go inside of it. I used to play in there and pretend I was Pocahontas."

"I know what you're talking about. But is it enclosed?"

"Mostly. There's an opening on one side where you enter, but the rest of it is solid. If we go there at night, when it's dark, nobody will ever find us. It's the perfect spot."

"Okay then," Gretchen agreed. "Should we say Friday night? Is that enough time?"

"Yeah, that should be good. It gets dark a little before nine, so let's plan to meet there at nine fifteen. And Gretch, you should really read all of the papers I left you," she suggested. "I think it will help you understand things a little bit better."

"I will," Gretchen promised. She let out a quick laugh. "It's ironic, though, that you're telling me to read something."

"I know," Jessica laughed. "I don't think I've read that much since the time I found Michelle's diary."

"So I guess I'll see you on Friday, then."

"It's a date. I mean . . . you know what I mean."

Gretchen laughed. She couldn't help herself. It felt good.

"Oh, and Gretch, do me a favor? Don't eat any raw onions that day."

CHAPTER EIGHT

Gretchen awoke on Friday morning with an anxious pit in her stomach. She and Jessica hadn't even spoken since their phone call the other day, and Gretchen was feeling more confused than ever. Of course, she knew it couldn't be real. Just because the people in the Oculus Society thought it was real didn't *make* it real. She just couldn't imagine how her mom would have bought into this nonsense, even going so far as to wear the anklet. Was she just humoring Tina Holt, the way Gretchen was humoring Jessica? Or did she really believe it? Certainly her mom was no fool. She would have needed proof. She would have needed to have seen it for herself . . . Gretchen couldn't help opening that door the tiniest bit and letting just the slightest crack of light shine on the idea that it might—somehow, impossibly—be true.

She took out the folded Wikipedia printout that Jessica had left with her and read it again for the hundredth time.

Plotinus wrote in his diary that he was going to attempt to trade souls with his disciple, Gemina. However, his writings ended abruptly just a few days after that mention of her. Some of Plotinus's more fervent believers have theorized that this is because the two were successful and that Plotinus stopped detailing his activities out of caution. However, most respected scholars believe that Plotinus simply lost interest in philosophy because he and Gemina failed to achieve their goal of dual-projection. More recently, upon further examination of Plotinus's early life, many have also concluded that Plotinus may have been exhibiting signs of schizophrenia.

Gretchen stopped reading. No. It was ridiculous. This nonsense about The One and being able to project your soul were obviously just the ravings of a lunatic. She was tempted to call Jessica to tell her to forget the whole thing. And she would have, if it weren't for that stupid anklet. Because no matter how many different ways she tried to spin it, the anklet proved one thing that she couldn't deny: that her mother obviously believed in this stuff, or pretended to, anyway. Gretchen couldn't help feeling that she'd be disloyal to her mom if she didn't at least give it a chance.

Besides, Jessica was right. If people really believed that the anklet was the key, then, for the first time, they would have a real motive for why someone might have wanted to kill her mom. But unlike Jessica, Gretchen wasn't convinced that Michelle was the culprit.

In the days since Jessica had filled her in on the true nature of the Oculus Society, Gretchen's suspicions about Ariel Miller had only grown. What if, Gretchen wondered, Ariel somehow knew about the Oculus Society's secret? What if Ariel was secretly trying to destroy the Oculus Society? What if she knew about the anklet and wanted it to start a society of her own? Gretchen realized that a murderous plot of this magnitude would be a lot for a thirteen-year-old girl to carry out. Then again, thirteen-year-olds were capable of all sorts of terrible things. What about the thirteen-year-old who was caught trying to blow up a school bus filled with the kids who bullied him on a daily basis? Ariel was miserable about her social status at Delphi. As ridiculous as it might seem for Ariel to have committed a murder, Gretchen wouldn't put it past her.

She took out her phone and composed another text to Ariel. Despite the threat that Ariel had made in her last text, Gretchen didn't believe for one second that she would really call the police on her.

I know u h8 the Oculus Society. But enough to commit murder?

She hit the send button. Almost immediately, a text came back to her.

That's it. U r going to be sorry that u ever started with me. Consider yourself warned.

Gretchen's hands trembled just the slightest bit as she tossed the phone onto her desk.

The teepee was smaller than Gretchen had remembered. In her mind, it was big enough for them to stand in, but in reality, it was barely even tall enough for her to sit inside of it without having to hunch over. Gretchen looked up; there was a small opening at the top of the teepee where the plastic folded over itself, just like how there's a space at the bottom of a piece of paper when you roll it into a cone. Through the circle she could see a sliver of a constellation in the clear, night sky.

Jessica was late. It was already well past nine o'clock,

and the last vestiges of daylight had been replaced with a deep, lush blackness that enveloped Gretchen like one of her mother's cashmere sweaters. If it hadn't been for the full moon, she wouldn't have been able to see a thing.

Finally, she heard footsteps crunching in the wood chips beneath the play area. Jessica ducked inside the teepee, frowning.

"I remembered this being bigger," she said, glancing around as she took a seat on the ground next to Gretchen.

"It's definitely cozy in here," Gretchen agreed. "But you're right, I don't think anyone will find us." She sat on her hands so that Jessica wouldn't see them shaking. She still couldn't believe that her first kiss was going to be with Jessica and not with Nick Ford. If only she had seized upon the opportunity when it had presented itself that night at her party, instead of going inside to look for Ariel. She didn't know why that would have changed anything, but somehow, she felt that if she'd only stayed outside, if things had been just the slightest bit different, her mother would still be alive.

"Are you ready for this?" Jessica asked. Her tone had become serious.

"I think so. Do you even know what we're supposed to do?"

Jessica grinned. "Yup. Tina told me *everything*."

Gretchen raised her eyebrows. "How? How did you get her to talk?"

"I just told her the truth," Jessica said with a shrug. "I mean, the job was meant for you. I was plan B. So I was like, hey, I want to know what I'm getting into here if I'm taking on a responsibility that was supposed to be someone else's. And I want to know exactly what I'm supposed to do, or I'm not doing it."

"And she bought that?"

"Hell, yeah, she bought it. I made it sound like I was doing them a favor by agreeing to take your place. I think she really thought that I might turn them down. But do you want to hear something crazy?"

"What?"

"Tina's never even done it. None of them have. Not your mom or anyone."

Gretchen wasn't exactly surprised to hear this, but still, she felt relief roll over her, like an extra layer of clothes on a cold day. She couldn't believe that she even thought for a second that this might actually be real. Of course none of them had done it. And now she knew for sure that her mom didn't really believe it could work. She was just pretending so that she wouldn't upset everyone else. They probably all thought it was a big crock—her mom, Tina, Joan—but none of them wanted to admit it. The whole thing reminded Gretchen of when she and her friends used to play with a Ouija board at sleepovers. They all pushed it with their fingers, and they knew that everyone else did, too. But still, they pretended to believe that it was moving all by itself. It was just more fun that way.

Jessica continued. "Apparently, projection is only meant to be used when doing so will help right a wrong that's been done to another woman. Something about a tool for keeping justice in the balance. I don't know. Tina said they've only been guarding the secret, they've never actually had to use it."

"Well, it seems like now would be a pretty good time for them to start," Gretchen said indignantly. "I mean, I think my mom qualifies as a woman who's been wronged, don't you?"

Jessica flashed a sad smile. "Yes. And that's exactly why I want to do this. We can't wait for them to find the anklet. We need to get started *now*."

Gretchen shivered in the night air. She wrapped her arms around herself as Jessica went on to explain what Tina had told her. That the Plotinus Ability was really just a form of intense meditation. That you had to clear your mind of everything until you had no thoughts, no feelings, no sensations in your body. The goal was to feel that you'd become one with everything around you, and once you achieved that, all you had to do was breathe yourself into where you wanted to go.

"And," Jessica added, "you have to say something."

"What, like a spell?"

"I guess it's like a spell. Tina said that Plotinus thought of it more as 'words that help to release the soul.' But either way, it's in Greek, and it's a bitch to say. It took me forever to get it right."

"And what about the anklet?" Gretchen asked.

"She seems to think it's a necessary part of the equation," Jessica admitted. "She said something about how the anklet has a calming, grounding effect on the body, and when combined with the words, it allows the soul to become free." She shrugged. "I think it's just a placebo effect. But I guess we'll find out."

It's not going to work. It's not going to work. Gretchen repeated this to herself half a dozen times. But still, her heart was pounding, and she could feel herself starting to sweat despite the desert chill that always set in after the sun went down.

Jessica seemed so sure it was all for real; Gretchen wondered if she really believed it or if Jessica, too, was just bluffing.

"So what's the plan?" Gretchen asked.

"I think the plan is just to observe and to gather as much information as possible. It'll be like looking at our worlds with a whole new set of eyes. Things that seem normal to me might seem totally weird to you, and things that you would never think twice about might seem really suspicious to me. But I think we should both try to lay low. Try not to go out a lot, don't talk too much to anyone if you can help it. Remember, everyone is going to think that you're me and I'm you, so if we act different than normal, we're going to draw attention to ourselves. And the last thing we want is for people to be saying that either of us has been acting strange."

Gretchen nodded that she understood. "Assuming that this really works"—*it's not going to work*—"I think we should only do it for twenty-four hours."

"Agreed. We meet back here tomorrow night at ten P.M."

"Okay," Gretchen said with a long, nervous sigh. "Let's do this."

At first, Gretchen couldn't clear her head of anything. Her mind was racing in a million different directions—kissing Jessica, the anklet, Nick Ford, her mom, her dad, Ariel Miller, Michelle. She thought about starting high school, about the night of the party, about drinking the apple martini, and about how she left that part out when the police questioned her. She thought about how Jessica had appeared in the hallway and then quietly taken her aside, asking her not to say anything about Rob getting them drinks, or about Rob at all, actually. He didn't want Michelle to find out, and even in the state of shock Gretchen had been in, she'd understood. Michelle *was* terrifying.

"Clear your mind," Jessica said in a soft, low voice. "Clear your mind. Picture the anklet shining in the sun, and imagine that you are the warm amber. Nothing but warm. Nothing at all."

Gretchen could see the anklet on her mother's ankle, the sunlight glinting off of it. She relaxed into the image of it, letting all of her thoughts fall away as Jessica's voice trailed off. She was the amber. She was warm. *It's not going to work. It's not going to work. It's not going to work.* Her breathing slowed, her mind repeating the mantra with each exhale. *It's not going to work. It's not going to work.* She felt like nothing, like she was asleep and awake all at the same time.

She heard Jessica whispering in Greek. "*Écho exorísei aíma egó dió xei ostó n, proválloun ti n psychí mou se állo spíti.*" And then she felt Jessica's mouth on hers, and as she inhaled, a warmth like nothing she'd ever experienced was filling her up. It felt as if she'd swallowed the sun itself. And then she opened her eyes, and she felt cold again.

"Holy shit," Jessica said. Except it wasn't Jessica's mouth that formed the words, and it wasn't Jessica's voice that spoke them. It was hers. But yet, it wasn't hers, exactly. Her voice sounded different, coming out of Jessica's throat. It sounded just like the way it did whenever she heard herself on video.

I can't believe it worked! But before she could verbalize the thought, before she could examine her own face staring at her, before she could even pinch herself to make sure this was all real, she noticed a bright light coming from the door of the teepee. On instinct she turned toward it.

"Smile," said Ariel Miller's voice from behind the light. "You're on candid camera!" She let out a gleefully wicked laugh, and then the light disappeared, leaving nothing but the black cashmere darkness and the fast crunching of wood chips as she ran away.

"Oh, no," Gretchen said slowly. The realization of what had just happened sank in. Her own face, suddenly drained of color, stared back at her, eyes blinking. It felt different to speak with Jessica's mouth. She pushed her tongue against the unfamiliar front teeth, noting that they were further away than her own.

"We are so screwed," she said, trying it out again. "Do you understand what just happened? Ariel Miller just saw us trade souls!" She watched, fascinated, as Jessica shook Gretchen's own head from side to side. She realized that she, like everyone, had only ever seen herself reflected in a mirror. *What a cool thing,* she thought, *to be able to see myself the way everyone else does.*

"No," said her mouth, which, she'd never noticed before, was slightly lopsided. "She didn't see us trade souls. She has no idea about all of that. All she saw was us kissing for a split second. Big deal."

"But what if she does?" Gretchen asked, trying not to focus on the fact that she was actually Jessica. That she was *inhabiting* Jessica. "What if she knows about the Plotinus Ability?"

"Don't be ridiculous. How could she know? Nobody even talks to her, let alone shares secrets with her."

Gretchen revealed her theory about Ariel murdering her mom in order to steal the anklet and start a society of her own. Jessica just stared back at her with Gretchen's big, blue eyes, the long, dark lashes framing them like tiny spider legs.

"That doesn't even make sense, Gretchen. How could she possibly know about it? Who would ever have told her? She's not friends with anyone in the Oculus Society. Come on, think about it. There's no way she knows."

Gretchen crumbled a stray, brittle leaf between her fingers. She supposed that Jessica was right. There really was no way that Ariel could know about the Plotinus Ability—or the anklet, for that matter. She realized that maybe she'd indulged in a little wishful thinking of her own.

"All right, I see your point." She lifted her chin. "I still think she did it, though. I texted her tonight before we came here. I asked her if she hated the Oculus Society enough to commit murder."

"No, you did not. Please tell me you didn't do that," Jessica pleaded. But Gretchen just looked at her hands. At Jessica's hands. Ew. The skin around her fingers was red and raw, and the nails were jagged, gibbous moons in their nail beds. Jessica let out a long sigh at Gretchen's failure to respond.

"What did she say?" she finally asked.

Gretchen looked up. It startled her all over again to see her own face looking back at her. "She said that I would be sorry that I ever started with her. She said that I should consider myself warned."

Jessica shook her head. "Well, congratulations, then. You just unleashed the wrath of Ariel Miller." She sighed again. "When we switch back, you'd better go and apologize to her."

"Why?" Gretchen demanded.

"Because she may not know that we projected, but if she shows that video to anyone, our high school social lives will be over before they even start." She shook her head. "And if we end up like Ariel—us, the future leaders of the Oculus Society and the entire town of Delphi—we'll bring the whole Oculus Society down with us. Nobody will ever take them seriously again."

CHAPTER NINE

Jessica's room was a mess. Piles of clothes, damp towels, out-of-date magazines, and empty shopping bags covered the carpet like moss on a forest floor. As she dangled her foot in the air, looking for an empty spot to place it in, Gretchen was reminded of when she used to walk across tide pools at the beach, searching out rocks sturdy enough to step on.

It was strange enough being Jessica, but it wasn't until she walked into Jessica's room that she began to consider she might be in over her head. For starters, she had never been in Jessica's room alone. She felt like an intruder. As she caught sight of a dirty bra lying on the floor, she thought of how Jessica was alone in her room right now. She cursed herself for not taking a few minutes to tidy up and to make sure that nothing embarrassing was lying around. Not that she had anything to be embarrassed about. Compared to Jessica's, her room was spotless enough to be in a catalog.

At the foot of the bed, she caught sight of Mr. Pants. She

almost smiled. For the past few years, Jessica always made
sure to put the worn little bear away when Gretchen came
over. So clearly she wasn't worried about any secrets Gretchen
might discover.

She picked up a few of the wet towels and hung them up
in the bathroom, then searched through Jessica's drawers for
something to sleep in. The thought of having to wear Jessica's
underwear creeped her out a little, but she reminded herself
that it was Jessica's body, not hers. All she wanted to do was
hide out in Jessica's room and have as little human contact as
possible.

Gretchen slipped into a pair of sweatpants and an old
looking T-shirt, feeling that same sense of creepiness again
when she reached for Jessica's toothbrush. *There is nothing
gross about this*, she told herself as she brushed Jessica's teeth.
When she was ready for bed, she perused Jessica's book shelf.
It was mostly filled with books that had been required reading for school over the last few year: *To Kill a Mockingbird*,
Flowers for Algernon, *Lord of the Flies*, *Animal Farm*. But
Gretchen managed to find a paperback with some relatively
attractive, undead looking teenagers on the cover, and finally
slipped into Jessica's bed.

She'd read about three chapters when her stomach—no,
Jessica's stomach—began to growl. Suddenly, she was starv-
ing. She had no idea when, or if, Jessica had eaten dinner that
night. Jessica's stomach gurgled again, loudly. She had to eat
something. There was no way she was going to chance going
to the kitchen for a snack, but she knew Jessica always kept
a stash of candy in her bottom desk drawer, so Gretchen got
out of bed and opened it up.

Ick. Just a bag full of fun-sized Butterfingers. They were
Jessica's favorite, but Gretchen hated them. She couldn't

stand the taste of peanut butter, and besides, she liked chocolate bars that were smooth and creamy, like Milky Way or
Three Musketeers. The crunchy, flaky consistency of Butterfingers was nauseating to her.

Another grumble came, as if Jessica's stomach sensed the
presence of food. *Oh, what the hell,* Gretchen thought. She
reached for a piece of candy and peeled off the wrapper. It
was better than going hungry all night. She popped it in her
mouth and began to chew quickly, hoping it would go down
fast so she could get it over with and satisfy Jessica's noisy,
complaining gut. But as the crunchy inside of the chocolate
bar hit her taste buds, she slowed down and began to savor it.

This is delicious, she thought. *Why do I never eat these?*
She opened up another one and took a cautious bite. Still
delicious. For a second, she was confused—why did she suddenly like this?—but then she realized that she didn't. They
weren't her taste buds reacting this way to the Butterfingers.
They were Jessica's.

This is so freaking weird.

By the sixth piece of candy, Gretchen was feeling full again,
if not slightly ill. She crawled back into bed and picked up the
vampire book again. Four chapters later, there was a knock at
the door. Gretchen's heart sped up, and she felt panicky. Jessica had told her that Michelle and Rob were out that night;
the house had been empty when she'd gotten there earlier.
Crap. She needed more time to get used to the idea of being
Jessica before she had to actually talk to anyone. But now she
had no choice.

"Come in," she said, trying to control the shakiness in her
voice. The door pushed open. It was Rob.

"Hey," he said. His eyes narrowed as he took her in.
"Are you *reading*?" He said the word with a mix of disdain

and disbelief, as if he'd asked if she was plunging toilets. Of course: Jessica didn't read books. She tossed the book aside.

"Oh, yeah, it's just some book Gretchen told me to read. It's *really* boring."

Rob approached the bed and picked up the book, studying the back cover. He began to read from it an amused voice.

"After a summer romance, Emma and Kyle fall madly in love. But Emma doesn't know the ugly truth about Kyle's past or his real identity. Can you have a relationship when one person is hiding the most important part of himself?"

"I *know*," Gretchen said, trying to sound like Jessica. "It's *so* stupid."

"Gretchen told you read this, huh? How is Gretchen?" Rob asked.

Gretchen tried not to stiffen. "She's, um, you know. She's as good as she can be, I guess, under the circumstances."

Rob shook his head. "It's really such a shame what happened. Do they have any leads yet?"

"No. Not that I know of. The detectives told . . ." she almost said *me*, but caught herself just in time. "They told Gretchen that it's a cold case. No leads, no suspects. They can't find anyone who might have had a grudge against her or a reason for wanting her dead. And you know, normally the husband would automatically be a suspect, but like, a dozen people saw—" *Her* dad. Not *my* dad. *Her* dad. "Saw her dad downstairs while it was happening."

Rob nodded thoughtfully. "And what about Gretchen? What does she think?"

Gretchen forced a smile. "Oh, well, Gretchen thinks that it was a girl in our class."

Rob looked up, surprised. "A girl in your class? Who?"

"Ariel Miller. You wouldn't know her. She's a huge loser."

"Why would she want to kill Gretchen's mom?" *Shoot*, Gretchen thought. *I shouldn't have said anything. I can't tell him about the anklet.* She tried to backpedal.

"Oh, I don't know. It's crazy. I don't think she really thinks that. It's just, um, I think she's just looking for someone to blame, you know?"

Rob shrugged. "I guess. Must be hard."

Gretchen didn't want to talk about this anymore. She just wanted Rob to leave. "So what did you want, anyway?"

Rob didn't answer. He seemed distracted, as if he didn't hear her. "Sorry. What?"

"I said, what did you want? You know, how come you knocked on the door?"

"Oh, right." He seemed snapped back to reality. "I wanted to see if you wanted to play some Halo." He moved his thumbs around, playing an invisible video game. "I can't get through the next level without you."

Gretchen swallowed. She'd never played Halo in her life, and Rob would totally know something was up if she tried. She faked a yawn.

"I don't think so," she said. "I'm super tired."

Rob gave her a funny look. "Are you feeling okay? First you're reading and now you're turning down Halo? And you're going to bed before midnight?" He put his hand on her forehead as if to feel for a fever. "Nope. You're not warm."

"I think it's just all catching up with me. A girl needs to sleep sometimes, you know."

"You seem to do plenty of it during the day, what with all

of your sleeping till noon. I swear, sometimes I think you're a vampire. Maybe there's a reason Gretchen told you to read that book."

Gretchen pretended to laugh. "Maybe." The conversation was getting more awkward by the minute. There was a silence, and she seized it. "Okay, so, good night."

"Good night," Rob said, giving her that same funny look as before. "See you tomorrow."

"Yeah. See you tomorrow." He walked out and shut the door behind him.

Gretchen exhaled. *Tomorrow,* she thought. *How am I going to do this all day tomorrow?* She glanced at the window. Jessica's room was on the first floor of the house. She could easily sneak out right now. She could go home and switch back to herself tonight, and they could just forget the whole thing. But even as panic raced through her, she knew she couldn't. Jessica had given her a chance to find out the truth. Besides, Jessica hadn't panicked yet. Gretchen wouldn't be the first to back down.

The sunlight streaming in under the curtains was unfamiliar, too bright. Gretchen blinked and opened her eyes. The bed felt wrong, the mattress too hard, the sheets too heavy. For a few seconds, she had no idea where she was. She bolted upright. But then she glanced at the floor, covered with Jessica's dirty clothes.

I'm Jessica until tonight.

With a shaky sigh, Gretchen turned to the clock: 8 A.M., the same time she woke up every day. She'd wondered about that last night—about what would prevail, Jessica's body or her own mind. After all, Jessica's body was used to sleeping until noon. Gretchen's mind was in control of some things, after all. She picked up the book from the nightsta.. pulled the covers over her head to read. Best to stay in bed as long as possible so as not to arouse suspicion from Michelle or Rob . . .

By 10 A.M. Gretchen was certain she would pee in her pants. She crept out of bed and tiptoed into the bathroom (thank God it was private), leaving the door open so that nobody would hear it creak as it closed. But the second she sat down on the toilet, the door to Jessica's room flung open.

"I thought I heard you," Michelle said.

Instinctively, Gretchen crossed her legs and leaned forward in an attempt to conceal herself.

Michelle let out a derisive laugh. "What, you're shy all of a sudden? You think I don't know what you've got down there? Trust me, they're all the same."

Gretchen's jaw dropped. Her own mother would never have spoken to her like that. Or walked in on her without knocking, for that matter.

"It's Saturday," Michelle said, not noticing Gretchen's shock. "You have to take the trash cans to the curb, you have to do your laundry, and it's your day to do the dishes." She snorted with disgust as she turned back into the room. "And you have got to do something about this mess." With two fingers, Michelle picked up a pair of jeans off the floor, inspected them, and then let them drop like garbage. She walked out, calling over her shoulder: "Clean it up this morning, or you're not coming to the Club."

Gretchen's heart stopped. The Club. *Oh, my God.*

Delphi Hills Golf and Country Club had been the epicenter of Delphi's social scene since its founding, long before even Gretchen's mom was born. Before she started going to sleep

away camp, Gretchen had spent nearly every single day of
every summer there, taking tennis lessons, swimming lessons . . . preparing for the kind of life her parents had lived.
But neither Gretchen nor her father had been to the Club
once this summer. She wasn't ready to socialize, wasn't ready
for the prospect of passing by her mom's favorite pool chair
and finding someone else lying there.

Of course it hadn't occurred to her that Jessica had been
going all summer long without her. Why hadn't Jess warned
her? She could just imagine her in a tiny bikini with her long
tan legs, poring over trashy magazines, flirting with the boys,
and cementing herself with the cool crowd before high school
had even begun.

True, it wasn't fair for her to feel betrayed by Jessica having a life without her, especially now that she knew the truth
about the Oculus Society. But still, she couldn't help herself.
How far behind had she fallen by holing up in her room all
summer long?

The instructions Jessica had given her last night in the teepee floated to the top of her memory: *Try to lay low. Try not
to go out a lot.*

Gretchen shook her head. She began picking up the clothes
off of Jessica's floor. By the time she made the bed and finished
with the chores that Michelle had given her, it was almost
lunch time. She rifled through Jessica's drawers and found a
modest, one-piece bathing suit and put it on. It was a bathing
suit meant for swimming laps, and she turned around in front
of the mirror, examining Jessica's body in it from all angles.
Nothing sexy or revealing: it was perfect.

Rob knocked just as Gretchen was throwing on a cover up
and stuffing a towel into a beach bag.

"You ready?" he asked, peeking his head in from behind

the door. He scanned the floor. "Wow. I don't think I've seen this carpet in three years."

Gretchen shrugged. "Michelle told me I had to clean it up."

Rob raised his eyebrows. "She tells you that every weekend. It never motivated you before." He paused to study her. "Are you sure you're feeling okay? You just don't seem like yourself."

Gretchen gathered Jessica's hair and put it into a ponytail. She turned toward the mirror so she wouldn't have to look Rob in the eye. "I'm fine. I'm just, you know, I'm starting high school in a few weeks. It's time for me to grow up."

Rob smirked. "Wow. Look at you, all Miss Maturity. Next you're going to be telling me you want to start spending more time with Michelle."

"I wouldn't go that far," Gretchen muttered before she could catch herself. She turned from the mirror, but Rob was smiling.

"Good." He lowered his voice. "And by the way, Mommy Dearest is in a mood today in case you haven't already noticed. So steer clear."

"Will do. Thanks for the heads up."

Gretchen picked up the bag with Jessica's stuff in it and walked past Rob in the doorway. "Hey," he said, reaching out and grabbing her by the arm. His face was close. He looked her right in the eye. "I need you on my side, kid."

On your side for what? Gretchen wondered. She suddenly felt uncomfortable. It occurred to Gretchen that even though she and Jessica were best friends, even though they thought they knew everything about each other, they couldn't possibly scratch some very important surfaces. Knowing that a person's favorite candy is Butterfingers isn't the same as knowing how they act with a person they see every day. Particularly a parent figure. There was so much Jessica didn't know about Gretchen and her dad: that they only talked about safe topics, like the weather, or that they both pretended to be just fine even though neither of them were. Gretchen felt panic rise up in her, as if it were taking an elevator from her feet to the top of her head. Secrets were dangerous now; one slip and this whole thing could be blown.

"I know," Gretchen lied. Rob searched her face again, and Gretchen could tell that he still wasn't one hundred percent convinced by her acting.

"Okay," he finally said, dropping her arm. "Come on, then, let's go. We don't want keep the queen waiting."

Gretchen made a point of staying as far away as possible from the chair where her mother used to sit poolside. She stole a glance, remembering Octavia Harris stretched out under an umbrella—her dark, Mediterranean skin set off by her white bikini. Now the chair was occupied by a heavy-set woman Gretchen didn't recognize, with two young children snacking on Goldfish, spewing crumbs all over their towels.

Then she saw The Sirens.

It's how she always thought of Molly Carson, Katie Elliott, and Lily Ranger: three girls who weren't quite what she and Jessica were, but wanted to be. They were part of the Oculus Society through their moms, but of course more demi-goddess than goddess, with the same jealousies and temptations.

Molly spotted her and waved her over. Gretchen took a deep breath and started toward them, reminding herself to be as Jessica-like as possible. They sprawled out on lounge chairs in bikinis, their skin glistening with tanning oil.

"Hey, Jess," Molly said, pulling up her legs and patting the end of the chair. "You can share with me."

"Thanks," Gretchen replied. She spread a towel and sat down, Indian style. The girls snickered.

"What's with the Speedo?" Lily asked.

Gretchen rolled her eyes the way Jessica would. "It was all I could find this morning. My aunt is, like, on a cleaning binge, and she made me put everything that was on my floor in the wash. And of course all of my bikinis were on the floor."

"She's such a bitch," said Katie. "I don't know how you deal with her."

"Thank God for Rob," Molly added. "You'd be *so* screwed without him."

Lily leaned in toward her and lowered her voice. "My brother said he bought beer for a bunch of his friends last weekend."

Gretchen nodded. "Yeah, he's cool like that—"

"Psst," Katie interrupted. "Nick Ford, twelve o'clock."

By the time Gretchen had spun around in her chair, Nick was already approaching them. Her stomach dropped to her feet. He was tan, dripping from the pool, his long dark hair plastered to his head. He'd grown taller over the short and terrible summer. His body had filled out a bit, too. He looked amazing. Gretchen tried not to blush.

"Hey, Jess," he said, grinning at her. "I see you've changed your look."

Gretchen blinked. "You know, I like to mix things up every now and then. It keeps people on their toes."

Nick laughed. The Sirens giggled. "That's a racing suit, right?" he asked. You wanna race?"

Gretchen hesitated. She was a strong swimmer, but she hadn't been in a pool since last summer, and she had no idea what kind of a swimming shape Jessica was in.

The Sirens started chanting. "Race, race, race, race!"

Molly practically pushed Gretchen off the end of the chair. "What the hell?" Gretchen said, with her most Jessica-like nonchalance.

"I'll give you a ten-second head start," Nick yelled before diving into the deep end.

Gretchen jumped in behind him. The hairs on her arms stood up when they hit the cold water. *Am I having fun?* She wasn't even sure. But for a split-second, she forgot almost everything except the tingle she felt. It wasn't bad. She lined up next to Nick along the back wall, wiping the water from her eyes.

The Sirens appeared at the side of the pool. Molly stared at the second hand on her watch.

"And, go!" she called out.

Gretchen pushed off. She could feel Nick gaining on her, so she swam as hard and as fast as she could. She heard the girls calling her name above the water just as Nick came up beside her. When she touched the wall and opened her eyes, Nick was already there.

"You were so close!" Lily shouted. "He only beat you by half a second!"

"I'm impressed," Nick said to her. "Considering that's the first time you've gotten in the pool the whole summer."

Gretchen blinked at him, shivering and wet, her eyes stinging. She panicked. What did he mean? Did he know it was really her? How?

"What?" she asked, nervously.

"Oh, come on. You always just sit there and read magazines and talk. I haven't seen you get in the water once. Any of you, for that matter. You're all too worried about messing up your hair."

"Oh," Gretchen said. "Well, I'm in the water now."

He smiled. "There you go, Jess, mixing things up again."

Gretchen laughed, but then caught herself. *What am I doing? I don't want Nick flirting with Jessica. I want Nick flirting with me.* The ugly bathing suit idea had totally backfired. And besides, she didn't have time to waste with Nick. She only had a few more hours left as Jessica; she needed to get to work.

"I've got to go," she said, abruptly pushing herself out of the water. "I'll see you later."

Gretchen left him standing in the pool and hurried, soaked and hunched, to the cabana to get a towel. No way would she use the one she'd brought. That would mean socializing. A girl with shoulder-length hair in a club uniform was inside, folding towels with her back to the pool.

"Um, excuse me," Gretchen said politely. "Could I have a towel please?"

The girl turned. Gretchen's heart stopped. It was Ariel Miller.

"What are you doing here?" Gretchen asked.

Ariel glared at her, blue eyes frigid.

"Ha ha ha, you're so hilarious," she said, throwing a towel at her. "Like you and your loser friends haven't been pretending not to see me all summer. I'm shocked that you would even acknowledge that you know who I am."

Suddenly, Gretchen was self-conscious about her dripping hair and her ugly bathing suit. Jessica had never mentioned that Ariel was working at the Club this summer. But she quickly calculated the opportunity; if she made things right with Ariel now, while she was Jessica, she wouldn't have to apologize later. "Listen," she said, collecting herself. "About last night, at the park . . ."

Ariel smirked. "What? You don't want me to tell anyone about you and your girlfriend? Is that why you've been flirting with Nick Ford all summer? So nobody will suspect that you like girls?"

"I don't . . . it's not like that," Gretchen argued. Even in her anger, she couldn't help but note how Ariel said Jessica had been flirting with Nick *all summer*.

"Oh, I think it's just like that."

"I know you were involved in my—in Gretchen's mom's murder. So if you know what's good for you, you'll keep your mouth shut—"

"Oh, so now it's you, too?" Ariel interrupted. "I didn't know you and your best friend were both insane."

This was not going as planned. Gretchen heard Jessica's words echoing in her head: *If she shows that to anyone, our social lives will be over before they even start. And the Oculus Society will go down with us.* Gretchen took a deep breath and tried to start over. "I'm sorry, okay? That's not what I meant. I don't think you did it. It's just, if you know something about it, then you might be able to help, and then I could convince Gretchen that she's wrong about you."

Ariel scoffed at her. "Don't try to suck up to me now. Do you think I don't see right through you? And do you think I care what your stupid friend thinks?" She picked up a stack of towels and pushed the cabana door open with her hip. "I liked it better when you ignored me," she whispered, then walked away, leaving Gretchen standing there, alone.

Gretchen burst through the heavy, dark doors of the clubhouse and made a beeline for the ballroom. She had made a mess of everything, and she needed a quiet place to think, away from everyone. She'd been to countless events in the ballroom over the years, from Christmas parties to birthday parties to musicals put on by the Club's theater group, and she knew that at this time of day, it would be dark and empty. As she'd assumed, the room was dark. But it wasn't empty. There were sounds of people moving, then whispering. She flicked on the light switch.

In the back of the room near the stage, were Michelle and a man Gretchen had never seen before. Michelle was clutching her bikini top to her chest. The man was shirtless. Gretchen's eyes widened.

"Oh, my God," Michelle said when she saw who it was. She strode toward the front of the room. "What are you doing here, Jessica? Were you spying on me?"

"What? No! I was looking for somewhere quiet. I didn't know you were in here." She eyed the shirtless guy, who by now had turned the color of rare meat. He returned Gretchen's withering look with a feeble smile. Gretchen turned back to Michelle. "What are *you* doing?"

"Um, I've gotta run," the guy mumbled. He pushed open an emergency exit door in the back of the room and bolted through it. Michelle glared at her. "You are *not* to tell Rob about this," she hissed. "This is none of your business."

Gretchen thought fast. Jessica was going to have questions, and she wouldn't be able to bring this up with Michelle again. Now was her only chance. "Who is he?"

"I just told you this is none of your business."

"It's my business now, and if you don't answer my questions, I'm definitely going to tell Rob."

Michelle crossed her arms in front of her chest and frowned. "Fine," she spat. "You get two questions. That's it."

"So?"

"His name's Mike."

"And how long has this been going on?"

Michelle sighed and rolled her eyes. "Since June. I met him at Gretchen's graduation party."

"*What*?" Her voice rose. "When?"

"I just told you, I met him at the party. He knows Gretchen's dad." Gretchen's mind raced. She hadn't recognized Mike, but then again, her dad had dozens of colleagues and clients that she didn't know, and it was true that he'd invited most of them to the party. Michelle looked up at the ceiling. "We were, you know, *together*, when they found her mom." Michelle lowered her voice to a whisper as she adjusted her bathing suit. "Look, it doesn't mean anything. I'm just having a little fun, that's all. But you can't say anything, okay? I didn't want Rob to find out, so I lied to the police about where I was during the murder. I told them I was outside in the tent when I heard the screams, but—"

"But you weren't," Gretchen interrupted, feeling sick.

"No. I was in the laundry room with Mike."

CHAPTER TEN

Gretchen sat on the ground inside the teepee at the park. She was early. Jessica wasn't supposed to meet her for another ten minutes. She leaned back against the wall and took a few deep breaths. Her head felt jumbled, as if someone had gone inside of it and rearranged everything without her permission. All the neat ideas about who she was and where she stood in the world had been rifled through and left in disarray.

Jessica. They'd always been equals—well, in Gretchen's mind, she'd always had a slight edge over Jessica—but now, Gretchen felt like she was trailing behind, with no chance of ever catching up. She had been home all summer, wallowing in grief and obsessing over Ariel Miller. Meanwhile, Jessica had blossomed. Not only did she hang out with everyone at the Club and flirt with Nick Ford, but she'd been invited into the innermost sanctum of the Oculus Society and had been given power—real power—that had been meant for *her*. Jessica had literally replaced her.

Still . . . she'd lived Jessica's life for twenty-four hours, and yes, in many ways she was jealous. But she didn't want to *be* Jessica. There was a difference.

Gretchen checked the time on her phone, and her eye caught Jessica's raggedy, chewed fingernails. She took another deep breath. She could feel the panic elevator starting to rise. What if the Plotinus Ability didn't work this time? What if they couldn't switch back? Gretchen imagined herself being stuck as Jessica forever. Living in Jessica's house. Having Jessica's children. There was a very real chance she could be buried alive inside of Jessica's body.

Crunching footsteps on the wood chips outside the teepee shattered her claustrophobia; a few seconds later, Jessica ducked inside. *Finally.* Gretchen never imagined the relief she'd feel at seeing her own face and body again.

"Hey," Jessica said, breathlessly. "How'd it go?"

"You first," Gretchen said. "What did you do all day?"

"Okay. First of all, your life is super boring. I don't know how you've gotten through the whole summer without tearing your hair out. I basically sat in your house all day. Except for dinner. Your dad and I went to Vito's."

"You did?" Gretchen gasped. She and her dad hadn't been out to eat since the murder.

"Uh-huh. I suggested it, and he agreed. He said it was probably time to start going out in public again."

"He *did*? Did he notice that you—that I—seemed different at all?"

"Sort of. He said that I seemed happier than I'd been in a long time. I told him that I was starting to feel like I could maybe move on a little bit. So you're going to have to start acting a little cheerier when you get home, or he's going to think something's up."

Gretchen frowned. *Great,* she thought. *Leave it to Jessica to ruin the one place where I don't have to be fake.*

"Anyway," Jessica continued. "We talked a little bit."

"Oh, yeah?" Gretchen asked. "What did you talk about? Did he tell you he's worried that Spain might have to leave the EU because of their staggering debt crisis?"

"No. We talked about the anklet."

Oh, God, Gretchen thought. She and her dad never talked about anything having to do with her mom. This was exactly the kind of slip she'd been worried about.

"You heard me. I asked him what the deal was and why he had been looking for it."

Gretchen was too amazed to be panicked anymore. She wished she had half the nerve Jessica did. "What did he say?"

"He said that Tina Holt had called asking about it, just like we thought."

"Are you serious? Did she tell him why she wanted it?"

Jessica made a *pffffffft* sound. "Of course not. She made up some story about how the anklet is given to the outgoing President of the Oculus Society when her term is over, and that it's passed on to the next outgoing President in some kind of ceremony. So Tina said they needed it back for when her term is over and they elect someone new."

Gretchen couldn't believe what Jessica had done. "And did he believe her?"

Jessica shrugged. "Hard to say. Tina's called him three times to see if he's found it, so I think he's starting to get a little suspicious. He seems to think that maybe it was more valuable than your mom realized. It was all I could do not to tell him the truth. And that I think Michelle killed your mom for it."

Gretchen chewed on her bottom lip. "Yeah, about that. You're wrong."

Jessica cocked her head the way she always did when she was confused, and Gretchen was struck by the strangeness of seeing her friend's mannerisms in herself.

"What do you mean? How do you know that?"

"I was at the Club today," Gretchen said, pausing to let Jessica take in everything that statement meant and implied. Jessica looked down at the floor. "Anyway, I went into the ballroom for something, and I found Michelle in there. With another man."

Jessica's head snapped up. "*What*?"

"I know. I'm sorry."

"Sorry?" A smile broke on her face. "That's *awesome*. Maybe now she'll leave Rob."

"Why do you want her to leave Rob?"

Jessica rolled her eyes. "Because he's never going to leave her. He's too dependent on her. But if she leaves him, then I can live with him by myself, and I won't have to deal with her anymore. It would be the best thing ever."

"What's with you and Rob, anyway? He said something weird about how he needs you on his side. His side of what?"

"Gretch, in case you haven't noticed, Michelle is a total bitch. It's me and him against her, always." Jessica narrowed her eyes. "What did you do to make him say that?"

"Nothing. I just, I don't know, I guess I was acting more like me than like you. He thought it was weird that I was reading, and that I went to bed early, and that I didn't want to play Halo with him. Oh, and that I cleaned up your room." She allowed herself a little grin. "You're welcome, by the way."

"Oh, God. How am I going to explain all of that?"

"I told him that I'm starting high school in a few weeks and that it's time for me to grow up a little bit." Gretchen smiled.

"So you're going to have to start acting a little more mature when you get home, or he's going to think something's up."

"Touché," Jessica said, dryly. "But wait, you didn't finish telling me about Michelle. How do you know she wasn't involved with the murder?"

"Because when I caught her with that guy—his name's Mike, by the way, and apparently, he's a friend of my dad's—I asked her how long it had been going on. And guess where it all started?"

"Your party," Jessica said, flatly.

"Mmm-hmm. And she made me promise not to tell anyone, because she lied to the police about where she was when she heard the screams."

"She was with Mike," Jessica said in the same tone.

Gretchen nodded. "In the laundry room." Jessica chewed on Gretchen's thumbnail. "Can you not do that?" Gretchen asked, pointing to her hand. "It's disgusting. Maybe you don't mind your fingers looking like they've been through a meat grinder, but I do."

Jessica removed Gretchen's hand from her mouth and smiled sheepishly. "Sorry, I don't even realize when I'm doing it. But let me ask you something: do you believe her? About Mike?"

"Of course I believe her. I *saw* them."

"No," Jessica said, shaking Gretchen's head from side to side. "I mean, do you believe her that she was with Mike the night of the party? How do you know she's not just making that up?"

"Why would she make that up?"

"Why *wouldn't* she?" Jessica asked. Funny: her voice cracked in the same way Gretchen's did when Gretchen was upset. All of a sudden, Gretchen felt a palpable hunger to return to the body where she belonged. She'd go insane if she spent another second arguing with herself-as-Jessica or Jessica-as-herself. "You don't know her like I do. She lies all the time. She's a freaking news reporter; it's her *job*. Look, maybe she thinks I suspect her. Maybe she's trying to throw me off of her trail with this Mike story—"

"Listen, Jess," Gretchen interrupted. "I also talked to Ariel Miller. It didn't go well. And that sucks for both of us. And I'm sorry. I thought that if I talked to her while I was you, I'd be able to stay calm. But I was still me, and it was too hard for me to control my emotions. But can we please just . . . ?"

"Switch back?" Jessica nodded. Gretchen's own disapproving eyes stared back at her, filled with disappointment and anger and what? Agreement, at least. "We have to. Now. Look, I'll talk to Ariel tomorrow, and I'll apologize. For both of us," she added. "Let's just switch back."

Jessica closed her eyes first. This time it was easier for Gretchen to let go. She closed Jessica's eyes and breathed deeply. It was almost as if she could feel her body pulling her back, like they were magnets.

"*Écho exorísei aíma egó dió xei ostó n, proválloun ti n psychí mou se állo spíti,*" Jessica whispered. She leaned in and placed her mouth on top of Gretchen's, and Gretchen felt that thick warmth inside of her, as if her body were being filled up with sand that had been sitting in the hot sun.

When she opened her eyes, she looked down to find her own familiar hands resting on top of her own, familiar legs. She exhaled with relief.

"Oh-my-God-I'm-so-glad-that-worked," Jessica exhaled in a rush. Her eyes were moist. "Gretch, I had a moment there. I wondered if I'd have to live out the rest of my life as you."

Gretchen nodded. She'd never felt so relieved and ecstatic and confused. "Same," she managed in a hoarse whisper. *My own voice, in my own head!* She wiggled her own fingers and toes, swallowed with her own throat, blinked her own eyes. She felt calmer already. But she also knew something: she'd never look at herself the same way in a mirror again. Staring at her own body talking back at her was nothing like looking at a reflection. It was like looking at another person. A person she could judge and criticize and form opinions about. Videos and pictures were one thing . . .

Jessica reached into her pocket. "My phone's going crazy," she muttered.

Gretchen's phone started vibrating, as well. She typed in her pass code and clicked into her email. There were at least twenty messages in her inbox from school friends she hadn't spoken to all summer, and each one of them had the same forwarded message attached.

Delphi Teen Scandal, read the subject line. In the body of the message was a link to YouTube.

"Are you getting this?" Gretchen asked Jessica, as she waited for the video to buffer.

Jessica nodded, clearly horrified.

The video was only ten seconds: the kiss inside of the tee-pee. Gretchen read the caption. Popular Girls: Secret Lovers. The up and coming Oculus Society Elite. And we wonder why a murder took place? It had been posted by Anonymous.

Gretchen scanned the posting. It had been put up only ten minutes ago, and already there were over five hundred hits.

Jessica looked up. Her face was ashen, and her hands were shaking. "I think we're too late for apologies, Gretch."

CHAPTER ELEVEN

Gemina strode down the Roman street, Plotinus's short tunic exposing the lower part of her legs in a way that she was not accustomed to. It made her self-conscious, and she kept pulling at the robe in a futile attempt to make it longer. She had to remind herself to stop, lest people think that Plotinus had developed some sort of twitch.

So strange, being a man!

His feet were so much bigger than her own; she found it difficult not to trip over them, and she felt naked without her long hair to cover the back of her neck. The rough, itchy skin on his hands and forearms drove her crazy. A little sea mud would fix it. Men could afford not to take care of themselves. If only they knew! Gemina felt exhilarated by the freedom.

And the Roman Empire, she knew, was not as restrictive as Persia. Plotinus had told her that Persian women were treated almost as badly as the slaves: they were not permitted to show their faces in public, were not afforded any education; they were considered no better than kept animals.

So where did this fury come from? But she knew even
as she asked herself the question; she knew because there
were no women who walked as she walked in this part of
the city. She could not own property, even though her husband's house had been bought with her money. She could not
hold office or vote, even though the senators made laws that
directly affected her. She could not even meet with the money
lenders, let alone be given credit or a bank account of her
own, even though her husband was stealing from her. And
most infuriating of all, she could not enter the private rooms
within the Curia, where the senators surely hid the evidence
of their most incriminating secrets.

Gemina smiled to herself. *But I can now,* she thought,
resisting the urge to pull on her tunic again. The Curia,
however, was not the first stop on her itinerary. No, that dis-
tinction was reserved for Miss Lucretia Iusta.

The slave girl asked Gemina to wait while she fetched her
mistress, and a few moments later Lucretia emerged from a
long hallway. She was in her late twenties, her face creased
with the sharp angles of a woman who was no longer a child.
Her dark hair wound in long coils around the back of her
head. Though Gemina hated to admit it, Lucretia was quite
beautiful.

Lucretia curtsied before her. "Plotinus, to what do I owe
this honor?" She extended her right hand, and Gemina had
to remind herself that she was a man. Her skin crawled as she
took Lucretia's hand and gently placed her lips on it.

"Miss Iusta, the honor is mine, I can assure you. I was sent
here by my dear patron, Senator Castricius," Gemina lied.
"You do know him, do you not?"

Lucretia looked at the ground, and Gemina thought she

saw her cheeks turn pink. "I'm sure you have heard about my rather unfortunate history with his wife's family, sir, seeing as how she is such a devoted student of yours."

"Ah, yes, I believe I do recall there being something of a feud between the two of you. Now I see perhaps why the senator did not want to call upon you himself. At least not in the light of day," she added slyly.

This time Lucretia flushed a deep red. *You wicked woman,* Gemina thought. If only reddened cheeks could be held up as evidence in a court of justice.

"And what, kind sir, did the senator wish you to tell me?" Lucretia asked.

"Ah, yes, of course. I'm afraid it's a rather . . . delicate matter. You see, the senator has incurred some unexpected debts as a result of property investments that turned out to be less profitable than planned. The senator has asked me to inform you that, as a result, he'll be needing access to certain moneys that he *loaned* to you."

Gemina searched Lucretia's face for any sign of worry but saw none. "I'm sure I have no idea what you're talking about, sir. The senator has never loaned me any money. He must have me mistaken with someone else."

Gemina tried not to convey her surprise. She had fully expected Lucretia to react with outrage—or panic, perhaps, at the idea of having to return the money, *her* money—to Castricius. In a thousand years she would not have guessed that Lucretia would instead deny that money had been given to her at all.

Unless she suspects him, Gemina thought suddenly. *She knows that Plotinus is my friend. She might think he's acting on my behalf.* It crossed Gemina's mind that Castricius wasn't too fond of Plotinus and that if he had shared his opinions

with Lucretia, then she would never believe that Castricius
had sent him. *This was a terrible mistake,* Gemina realized.
A slow panic began to burn through her, making her feel as
if she were being suffocated from the inside out. *If she tells
Castricius of this meeting, I will be found out for sure.*

"I see," Gemina said, trying to match Lucretia's calmness.
"Perhaps you're correct, Miss Iusta. My mind gets so confused these days, I hardly know who I am anymore. You must
forgive me. And please, I beg you not to tell Castricius of my
error. I'm sure you can understand that a philosopher cannot
afford to upset his patrons, especially the ones who provide a
roof over his head."

Lucretia smiled forgivingly. "Of course, dear Plotinus. It
shall be our secret."

Gemina reached out to take Lucretia's hand, kissing it
once more, despite the foul taste. "You have my humblest
thanks," she said, backing out through the door and making
her way out of the courtyard as quickly as possible.

Plotinus was no more accustomed to wearing the long tunic
for women than Gemina was to wearing the short one for
men. He had to slow his natural gait considerably to accom-
modate the extra fabric at his feet. More than once he stepped
on the hem and almost tripped while walking to the Forum.
The heavy gold hoops Gemina wore on her ears made his head
feel as if it were being pulled down by stones. Plotinus had
always known that women were responsible for taking care of
a household, but he never fully understood the magnitude of
female responsibility until now.

Lugging baskets through the marketplace, he wondered
how Gemina—with her curious, intelligent mind—could bear
the day-in, day-out monotony of purchasing food, overseeing

slaves, educating Gaia, and hosting dinner guests. He never realized how much he took for granted the simple freedoms he enjoyed because he had been born a male. *It isn't right*, he thought for the hundredth time as he stepped around a group of women talking loudly in the street. *It isn't right at all. We all come from the same place. We are all but part of The One.*

He resolved then and there to write about the crime of gender inequality. He resolved to use his influence with Castricius and other senators to have the laws changed. As soon as he and Gemina switched back, he would show all of Rome the truth.

In the immediate moment, however, he was determined to help Gemina discover the truth about her husband. She had been such a loyal patron and friend; she introduced him to the best of Roman society, she convinced Castricius to host him in their home, and she had been the most eager and willing student he had yet known. Admittedly, he was concerned about what would happen to him if her allegations against Castricius proved to be true. But he flung those concerns aside. As a philosopher, he was committed to pursuing truth at all costs. If the truth about Castricius ruined his life, then so be it.

From the corner of his eye, Plotinus spotted Amphiclea filling a small basket with oranges. He approached her. The thought of not having to pretend to be Gemina for a few moments filled him with relief.

"Amphiclea!" he called out, still surprised to hear Gemina's voice emerging from his throat.

Amphiclea looked up and smiled at the familiar voice, but then eyed him warily, as if she'd just remembered that her friend was not who she appeared to be. He resisted the habitual urge to kiss her hand as he scurried up beside her. "Hello,

Gemina," she replied awkwardly, glancing at the woman sell-ing the oranges. "I wasn't expecting to see you at the market today."

"Well, I must carry on with my daily duties, must I not?"

Amphiclea frowned. "I suppose you must."

Plotinus took her by the arm and led her into a narrow alleyway, where they could talk without being overheard. "Have you heard from Gemina?" he whispered.

Amphiclea shook her head. "I have not, and I am wor-ried. Oh, Plotinus, what if she's caught? She has a daughter to think of. I'm afraid this might have been a terrible mistake."

"Gemina will be fine," Plotinus assured her. "She's the most intelligent woman I know. More so than many of the Roman men in power, I dare say. And with you as our witness, we are guaranteed to be successful in this endeavor. You still wear the anklet?" Amphiclea lifted her tunic to show him the gold chain encircling her ankle. Plotinus patted her paternally on the arm. "Then all shall be fine, my dear. I'm expecting her to be home this evening. If we have the opportunity to speak in private, I'll remind her to be careful."

Amphiclea thanked him and bid him farewell.

Lost in thought, Plotinus wandered back toward the Forum. He wasn't ready to return to the house quite yet, so he continued walking, wandering farther through the city, until he came upon more familiar territory. Here were the Coli-seum, the Pantheon, the Curia, the banks, and the library: places inhabited almost entirely by men, with the occasional female slave waiting by a chariot along the road. Here, in this part of the city, Plotinus began to feel like himself again. The woman's tunic he wore seemed to slip away, and he hardly felt the heavy gold earrings of which he'd been so conscious earlier. He looked upon the library with longing and found himself ascending the steep, marble stairs that led to the front door.

Inside, Plotinus hardly noticed the strange looks he received from the other patrons. The library was part of a complex that also housed a palestra for physical games, along with the baths; the room smelled faintly of the oils the men used to wash themselves. He purchased a reed pen and some parchment papers and began to give a written voice to the thoughts that had been germinating since he'd been enlightened.

If the perfect life is within human reach, the man attaining it attains happiness. Man, when he commands not merely the life of sensation but also of Reason and Truth, has realized the perfect life. But what of a woman? Can she not attain the same degree of Reason and Truth? Is this life something foreign to her nature? No: there exists no single human being who does not either potentially or effectively possess this thing which we hold to constitute happiness. But then if a woman can have a truly perfect life within, the same as a man, then why should she not be permitted the privileges of men without? Why should a woman not own property or take part in politics? If she has the same capabilities as man, why should a woman not become Emperor, even? Is it fear that leads men to keep the laws of women unequal? Fear that women might perhaps be better qualified to govern this Roman Empire?

Plotinus stopped writing and gazed off into the corner of the room. In the corridor across from the library, leading into the baths, he recognized a banker whom he'd met several times with Castricius. This man, he knew, would be familiar with Castricius's finances. Suddenly, Plotinus had an idea for how he might find out exactly what Castricius was doing with his money and bring swift justice; he quickly jotted down his ideas on the back of his paper in order to have them straight in his mind when he approached the man.

Senator Castricius has accounts with you. I'd like to open an account of my own.

Plotinus quickly gathered up his papers and followed the banker down the hallway and through the door, finally catching up with him just inside the baths.

"May I help you?" the banker asked, indignantly.

"Yes," Plotinus replied. But the voice that spoke was not his own.

Oh, no, he thought, delicate hands flying up to cover his mouth. *What have I done? How could I have forgotten that I was Gemina?*

"What do you want, woman?" the banker asked, angrily.

Plotinus said nothing as the other men in the room turned to stare at him. He began to back up.

"What is this?" the banker demanded, grabbing the paper out of Plotinus's hand. When he was finished reading it, he looked up, his face bright red. The banker let out what sounded like a roar.

"You follow me into the men's baths because you want to open a bank account? Guards! Guards! Arrest this woman!"

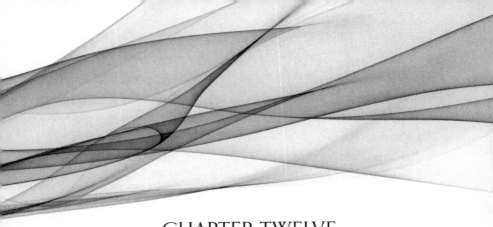

CHAPTER TWELVE
DELPHI, CALIFORNIA
PRESENT DAY

A group of fifteen or twenty soon-to-be juniors crammed around the oversized center island of Nick Ford's kitchen, surrounding Nick as he stood, shirtless, sloppily pouring shots of tequila into his mother's platinum-rimmed Wedgwood tea cups.

Ariel stood next to him. She was careful to strike the balance between possessive and nonchalant: keeping one arm resting on his smooth, hairless shoulder. The gold-plated bangle that she'd swiped from the counter of a local boutique yesterday glinted in the soft glow of the overhead light. With her other hand, Ariel discreetly pinched the top of her thigh, just under the hem of her white miniskirt. She pinched until her eyes smarted.

Yup, she thought. *This is definitely real.*

"*Ju-niors, ju-niors, ju-niors,*" the guys started to chant, banging their fists on the glossy marble.

It was the Saturday night before school started, and Nick's parents had conveniently decided to spend Labor

Day weekend in Martha's Vineyard. Ariel glanced around the kitchen at the familiar faces: classmates who had finally accepted her for what she knew she was always destined to be, the most popular girl in school. And Nick Ford—with his olive skin, bright blue eyes, and rippling muscles honed from two years of lacrosse practice—had fulfilled his destiny as her natural partner: the hottest guy at Delphi High.

It didn't matter anymore how she'd gotten here. She'd *gotten* here. That was all that counted. But still, a brief thought of her victims tried to push its way up to the surface. She told herself what she always did when the guilt surged: *I never meant for things to get so bad.* She'd never meant for them to leave Delphi altogether. Jessica, she knew, had quickly found a spot at a boarding school somewhere abroad. But Gretchen was a question mark. Ariel's hand trembled just the slightest bit on Nick's shoulder, and she quickly lowered it to her side.

I'm not going to think about that anymore, Ariel told herself. *It's a new year. A fresh start.* She could almost hear Mrs. Lackman, the school psychologist whom she secretly saw every week, repeating to her what she had said so many times before. *You can't change the past. All you can do is change how you behave in the future.*

Nick passed around the tea cups, gently handing the last one to Ariel. He raised his own, and Ariel caught a few of the girls around the table staring longingly at his outstretched bicep. She put her hand back on top of his shoulder.

"What should I toast to?" he whispered to her, his blue eyes glassy.

"To the future," Ariel said.

Everyone lifted up their cups. "To the future!" they all shouted back.

She threw her head back and tossed the tequila down her

throat, then placed her cup down on the counter without flinching. She could feel Nick watching her, and she fought the urge to make an ugly face as the alcohol burned her insides. He pulled her close to him, and she couldn't help noticing how much she liked the feel of her smooth arms against his bare chest.

"You look so hot tonight," he breathed in her ear. "I still can't believe it took us so long to hook up."

Ariel smiled. She'd gone to a lot of trouble to put this outfit together: a black, low-cut tank top that she'd put on in the dressing room under her T-shirt, and the white skirt (which she'd stuffed into her purse while the saleswoman wasn't looking). She tilted her head up to look at him—she was tall, five six and a half, five eight in her wedge heels—but Nick was easily six foot two. "You were worth waiting for," she said.

He leaned down and kissed her.

"Get a room!" yelled Connor Matthews, Nick's best friend and teammate.

Idiot, Ariel thought, her eyes still closed. Everyone knew that the only reason Connor hadn't been kicked out of school yet was because his father was a member of the City Council. He was always getting caught doing stupid shit—like the time he brought a live pig into the girl's locker room at school. But in keeping with the "boys will be boys" mentality of certain wealthy community leaders, he never got into any trouble. Ariel had never liked Connor—in fact, she resented the way he breezed through life without any consequences—but she would never say that to anyone. Especially not to Nick.

Everyone in the kitchen laughed. Finally, she pulled away from Nick, blushing. "I'm gonna go outside and get some fresh air," she murmured to him. "I'll find you later, okay?" He nodded, but before she'd even had a chance to kiss him on the cheek like she'd intended to do, Nick had already pounced on Connor and was now good-naturedly twisting his arm behind his back.

The fresh air felt good. Ariel could feel people staring at her as she walked by them. Three years ago, she would have snarled, but now she knew they were staring not because they hated her, but because they were envious. And she reveled in it. *This is going to be the best year ever.* She stumbled along through the backyard, trying to count how many shots she'd done. There was the one with Nick, and then a few more before that when she'd first gotten to the party. Four, at least. Her head was spinning, and she needed to just chill out somewhere for a little while. She was searching for a quiet spot where she could be alone when she spotted a hammock strung between two enormous maple trees at the far end of the yard. She was less than three feet away and already sinking into it in her mind when Brinley Porter stopped her in her tracks.

"Oh, Ariel, there you are! Have you heard?"

"Heard what?" Ariel asked, annoyed. Did she slur those words? It didn't matter. Ariel knew that Brinley couldn't stand her, and the feeling was mutual. They'd sort of been friends in middle school, but in ninth grade, when Ariel had begun to get popular, she'd dropped Brinley like a hot coal. To be honest, she reminded Ariel of the way she herself used to be. Whatever the news was, Ariel knew that it was going to be bad for her. If it wasn't, Brinley wouldn't have been trying so hard to find her.

"*Jessica Shaw* is here. She's back, and she's re-enrolling at Delphi. Can you believe that?"

Ariel narrowed her eyes. "*What* did you just say?"

For a moment, Brinley seemed surprised by Ariel's sudden intensity. Of course, she remembered just as well as Ariel did how Jessica used to ignore them both, or at best, sneer at them. "I *said*, Jessica Shaw is back. And she's here. At this party." Brinley could hardly contain her glee. "I take it you hadn't heard."

"Whatever," Ariel muttered, pushing past her and lumbering back toward the house. But her heart had started to pound. *Jessica Shaw is back*, she repeated to herself. *Jessica Shaw is back*. She hesitated for a moment and stayed hidden in the shadows. She wasn't sure if she even believed Brinley. Still . . . If Jessica was really here, Ariel wanted to see it for herself. She peered out from behind a large shrub and scanned the kitchen. There was Connor, acting stupid, as usual. There were some semi-popular, semi-attractive girls playing quarters with a few guys from the lacrosse team. And there was Nick, talking to— Ariel's heart stopped beating. He was talking to the prettiest girl she'd ever seen. Tall and thin with subtle curves, a full, pouty mouth, and long, beachy-blonde hair. She wasn't even moving, but you could see her self-confidence just in the way she stood, even from this distance.

Ariel felt herself deflating like an old pool raft at the end of the summer, her own confidence practically hissing as it leaked out of her. Nobody knew that Ariel was the one who released that video of Jessica and Gretchen kissing. She'd had to post it anonymously. If people had known the true source, they would have just chalked it up to Ariel being a jealous outcast instead of seeing it for the scandal that it really was. The only ones who knew the truth were Jessica and Gretchen themselves. And now here was Jessica, holding all of the cards yet again.

What if she tells everyone the truth about me? What if they all hate me again?

Her stomach sank as she watched Nick talking to her.

"You can't just hide from her like a scared little girl," came a voice from out of the darkness. Ariel turned around to find Brinley standing behind her.

"I'm not hiding," Ariel insisted.

Brinley crossed her arms as if to say *yeah, right*. "Look, Ariel, I know that you and I were never really friends, but I hate Jessica Shaw just as much as you do. You're in charge now, and you don't have to let her back in. Go in there and deal with her. Put your hand on Nick's ass, and let her know that she doesn't get to just waltz in here and take over like she never left. Let her know that you haven't forgotten about how she treated you."

Ariel took a deep breath. Brinley did have a point. After all, Ariel hadn't clawed her way up the social ladder just to have the rungs knocked out from under her. But then again, Brinley didn't know the truth, either. If she did, she'd think that Ariel was evil—and so would everyone else if they found out that she'd pulled a stunt like that on a girl whose mother had just been murdered.

What if Jessica tells? Ariel tried to put herself in Jessica's shoes: if she'd been scandalized for kissing another girl, then disappeared and suddenly re-emerged two years later, the last thing she'd want to do is bring up the scandal that sent her running off in the first place.

No, she thought. *She wouldn't dare bring it up again. The only reason she'd even come back is if she thought people had forgotten about it.*

"You're right," Ariel finally answered. "Thanks for the pep talk."

"You're welcome," Brinley said. "Now go put that girl in her place."

Ariel was already gone, striding through the French doors

with her head held high and her long, layered blonde hair bouncing at her shoulders. She was glad now that she'd done all of those shots earlier. She didn't think she'd have the nerve to do this sober. *Liquid courage*, she'd once heard her mom call it.

Ariel walked through the kitchen, making a beeline for Nick. Ignoring Jessica, she sidled up to him, sliding her hand across his back and then slowly making her way down until she reached the left back pocket of his jeans. She placed her hand inside and left it there.

"Nick," she cooed. "Where have you been? I've missed you."

"Hey, babe," he said, giving her a kiss on the mouth. Ariel made a big show of kissing him back, harder than she probably would have if Jessica weren't standing there watching them. But then Nick broke away from her, waving his hand toward Jessica. "Hey, Ariel, do you remember Jessica Shaw? She left right before ninth grade. And now she's back."

Ariel hesitated. She wasn't sure if she should pretend not to remember, or if she should give a terse acknowledgement. But Jessica beat her to it.

"Oh, my God! Ariel Miller? No way!" Jessica opened her arms and leaned in for a hug. Ariel awkwardly hugged her back, then braced herself for the punch line. But none came. There seemed to be no sign of the old Jessica. In fact, she seemed genuinely happy to see her again. "This is so crazy! You look amazing! Wow. I don't think I would have even recognized you! You're gorgeous!" She looked from Nick to Ariel and back again. "Are you two going out?"

"Umm, sort of," Nick answered. "We just started, you know, hanging out together the last week or two . . ."

"That's *so* amazing," Jessica said. She looked back to Ariel. "How have you been?"

Ariel tried to keep her jaw from hanging slack. Was it

possible that Jessica didn't realize that she was the one who
posted the video on YouTube? She didn't see how that could
be, given that she and Gretchen had seen her videoing their
kiss. So then, why was she being so gracious? Why didn't she
spit at her or yell at her, or accuse her of ruining her life? Of
ruining two lives? Ariel eyed her suspiciously. There had to be
a catch here somewhere.

"Um, I've been good," she managed. "Things are good."

Jessica smiled broadly. "That's great. I'm so glad to hear
that."

On the other side of the kitchen, there was a loud crash as
something ceramic fell to the floor.

"Party foul!" yelled Connor, slurring his words.

"Oh, shit," Nick muttered. "Let me go deal with this."

"I can help you," Ariel volunteered.

"No, it's okay. Connor gets hostile when he's drunk. It's
better if I do it myself. I'll find you later." He hurried off,
leaving Ariel alone with Jessica. *Now she'll show her true
colors,* Ariel thought.

She got right to the point. "So. How come you're back?"

Jessica smiled, but this time it was wistful. "My aunt got
tired of paying for boarding school. But you know, I'm glad
to be back. I missed Delphi."

Ariel thought about what Brinley had said: *You have to let
her know that she doesn't get to just waltz in here and take
over like she never left.* She inhaled deeply. "Listen, Jessica,
things have changed since you left. *I've* changed."

Jessica laughed. "I can see that. But I've changed, too. If
you're worried that I'm going to try to take over, you don't
need to. You're the It Girl now. I get it."

Ariel's forehead creased. "So you're not . . . you know,
upset about what happened anymore?"

"Honestly, Ariel, it was probably the best thing that ever happened to me. I got to get out of here and get a totally different perspective on things. I'm not upset about it all. I forgive you completely."

Ariel's heart raced again. She lowered her voice. "I appreciate that. But, you know, nobody knows that it was . . . that I had anything to do with it."

Jessica nodded sympathetically. "I'm not going to tell anyone, Ariel. I was too ashamed to accuse you before. Besides, nobody would have believed me, anyway. That video took on a life of its own." She sighed. "Your secret's safe with me. I just want to put the past behind us. I was hoping, actually, that you and I could be friends."

Ariel blinked a few times. Her eyes were moist. She was already feeling pretty good from the alcohol, but she suddenly felt amazing, as if all of the horrible guilt she'd carried these last few years had shattered like that vase Nick was trying to clean up. She could hardly even believe her luck. Could someone really change this much? Could someone really be this forgiving and forward thinking, the way that she herself so desperately wanted to be? Ariel thought of Brinley, still bitter and angry about the past. Girls like Brinley, she realized, were the problem. Girls who couldn't get beyond things that had happened years ago. But Jessica was an inspiration. If she could be gracious enough to forgive Ariel, then Ariel could certainly be gracious enough to forgive her back. There was just the one big question mark.

"What about Gretchen?" Ariel asked. She'd heard all kinds of things when Gretchen had first gone away; that she refused to speak to anyone, that she slept for fifteen, sometimes twenty, hours a day, that she was undergoing shock therapy treatments. It was these images that caused Ariel to stick her finger down her throat for nearly a year, these images that compelled her to shoplift, and these images that, ultimately, sent her running to Mrs. Lackman's office every week.

Jessica's face darkened. "I don't talk to Gretchen anymore," she said.

Ariel thought about the kiss between them that she'd filmed. *Had they been in a relationship? Had there been a bitter break up?* But she didn't dare ask.

And then, just like that, the light went back into Jessica's face. She stuck her hand out toward Ariel. "So, what do you say? Friends?"

Ariel hesitated for just a fraction of a second. She still couldn't quite believe that this was for real. But she reached out and shook Jessica's hand. "Okay. Friends."

Jessica smiled. She held up one finger, signaling for Ariel to wait for her, and she ran off toward the kitchen. A few moments later she was back, carrying two Wedgwood teacups filled with tequila. She handed one to Ariel.

"To new beginnings," Jessica said, clinking her cup gently against Ariel's.

"To new beginnings," Ariel agreed.

She tossed hers back.

As she lowered her cup, she caught sight of Brinley watching her from outside. She felt a flush creep up her neck and into her cheeks, but it wasn't from the tequila. Brinley shook her head and walked away. *Yes, I get the message,* Ariel thought. *Melodramatic enough?* She smiled at Jessica. It didn't matter what Brinley thought. Brinley was the pathetic one; if she couldn't move on from something that had happened in middle school, then that was her problem.

CHAPTER THIRTEEN

A horn honked in the driveway. Ariel lifted the curtain that hung from the lone window in her tiny bedroom and peeked out at the black Acura idling in the driveway. It belonged to Jessica's uncle Rob—Ariel recognized it from when she'd worked at the Club—but she caught a glimpse of Jessica's streaky-blonde hair in the driver's seat. Was this really happening? Was she really old enough now to have friends who could drive to school? Doubt quickly snaked its way into her mind like a curl of smoke. *Is Jessica Shaw really my friend?*

She'd nearly choked on the tortilla chip she'd been eating when she'd seen the text from Jessica last night: U need a ride to school tmrw? Ariel had secretly been hoping that Nick would drive her to school this year, but that ship had sailed once she'd learned that he had daily 6 A.M. practices. A ride from Jessica Shaw was something she had never even considered or even dreamed of.

Ariel tried once again to put herself in Jessica's shoes.

Tainted by scandal. Out of the loop for two years. Former
best friend institutionalized. Slowly, it dawned on her. Jessica
Shaw needed her. She thought back to what Jessica had said
at the party: *You're the It Girl now, I get it.* Ariel tried to
imagine what would happen if Jessica showed up for school
today alone, out of the blue. Everyone would whisper. *But if
she shows up with me . . .* Ariel had to admire Jessica's fore-
thought. She'd done her homework on who's who at Delphi
High these days. For a second, it crossed Ariel's mind that she
could still decline the ride. She could say she wasn't feeling
well and let Jessica fend for herself without the protection of
Ariel's popularity. But Ariel knew that that would be a mistake. After all, she needed Jessica, too. She needed her to keep
her mouth shut. The best way to ensure that she did would be
to keep her happy and to let her think that Ariel didn't have
her all figured out.

Oh, stop being so cynical, Ariel told herself. After all,
she was trying to move on. Maybe Jessica was just trying to
do so, too. She heard Mrs. Lackman's voice in her head: *A
grudge is not a life preserver. It's not a healthy thing to hold
onto.* Ariel wondered if maybe Jessica had been seeing her
own Mrs. Lackman these last two years.

She dropped the curtain and walked into the kitchen. Her
mom had left for work before Ariel had even woken up, but
she'd left a homemade blueberry muffin on the counter for
her. Next to it was a note.

*Love you, sweetie. Hope you have a great first day of
school. I'll be home by eight. Dinner's in the fridge.*
                                        Love, mom

Ever since her mom had lost her job as a nutritional

consultant for the Delphi School District, she'd been commuting to another town over an hour away. Some days they didn't even see each other at all. Ariel cringed as she remembered how her mother would show up in the school cafeteria to check in with the staff, her hair covered in a mesh hairnet. At first, she pretended not to know her. But how could she? Her mom was a single mom, her only parent, her best friend, her ally. And eventually they all found out, as they always did.

Your mom's a lunch lesbo, the kids would sneer. *Where's your hairnet, loser?*

She wondered if the other kids' moms had been home by five every night. Not to mention weekends. When the other girls were having sleepovers or going to events for the Oculus Society, she and her mom would go to the movies or bake cupcakes at home. Now their primary means of communication took the form of notes left on the kitchen counter.

But on the other hand, nobody asks me where my hairnet is anymore.

Ariel slung her backpack over her shoulder, grabbed the muffin, and ran out the front door to where Jessica was waiting.

She could sense the unease as soon as she and Jessica pulled up in the school parking lot. Everyone was staring at them.

Her heart raced. Maybe she'd made a mistake. Maybe *she* was the one who was going to end up stuck in Loserville if people didn't accept Jessica. She breathed in deeply. No. The other kids would be taking their cues from her. All she had to do was act like everything was normal, and everyone would follow suit. So she did. As she and Jessica walked toward the eleventh grade homeroom wing. Sure enough,

by the time they reached their lockers, everyone was smiling, welcoming Jessica with open arms. For the first time
since she could remember, Ariel felt like a good person. She
wanted to cling to that sense of benevolence—as strange as
it was intoxicating.

When the bell rang, releasing them from homeroom, Ariel was
feeling so light-hearted and magnanimous, she practically
floated out into the hallway. She resolved to stop shoplifting,
effective immediately. She studied her schedule, trying to figure out when would be the soonest time she could sneak into
Mrs. Lackman's office to report all of her good news.

But when she shut her locker door and found Jessica on
the other side of it, looking white as a sheet of paper, her hope
fizzled. Something was wrong. Ariel glanced around. Not too
many people, but there was a low buzz, a few urgent whis-
pers behind cupped hands.

"What's going on?"

Jessica seemed to look right through her. She didn't answer
for a moment, and Ariel sensed that she was having some
kind of inner dialogue with herself. Then, suddenly, the color
came back into her face. She straightened as if she'd made up
her mind about something.

"Gretchen's back," she answered.

Ariel's pulse quickened. Jessica, she could handle. Jessica,
she *had* handled. But Gretchen was the one who haunted her.
A million questions ran through her mind. How could she
be back? Wasn't she in an institution? How come nobody
knew she was re-enrolling? Finally Ariel's thoughts came
back around to herself. *What if she tells everyone what I did?*

Ariel wanted to frantically throw all of these questions at
Jessica at once, but something in her gut was telling her that

she should play it cool. "Wow. That's a coincidence, both of you coming back at the same time."

Suddenly, the buzz in the hallway stopped, giving way to dead silence. Ariel's head whipped around. There she was. Gretchen. She was taller, of course, and she'd shed the baby fat she had still been carrying back in middle school. She'd given up her long, smooth layers for a choppier, shoulder-length cut with side-swept bangs—but her dark blue eyes were still striking, her cheekbones still high and prominent.

The only real difference was in the way she carried herself. Before, Gretchen had been all confidence. Now she walked with her shoulders slumped, her head turned down, eyes focused on the floor in front of her. Impulsively, Ariel started to lift her hand in a wave. If she could save Jessica, shouldn't she do the same for Gretchen? As if reading Ariel's mind, Jessica slammed her locker shut, breaking the silence. The hallway instantly began to buzz again. Jessica turned on her heel and walked off in the other direction.

"Jess," Ariel called out to her. "Wait up!"

Jessica turned around, and when she saw that Ariel was alone, she waited. "What was that about?" Ariel wanted to know. "How come you didn't say hi to her?"

Jessica frowned. "Are you joking? Didn't you see her, shuffling her feet and looking at the floor? Seriously, Ariel. The girl is crazy. You don't want to be associated with someone like that. All she'll do is drag you down."

Ariel stared back at her. Jessica lowered her eyes. Ariel again thought back to the kiss in the teepee that night: maybe only one of them had wanted to be more than friends. Maybe Gretchen had kissed Jessica unexpectedly, and maybe Jessica hadn't known how to handle the advance. On the other hand, how could she? Her best friend had wanted to be something more?

Ariel sighed. Ignoring Gretchen didn't sit well with the
fresh start she'd made just half an hour ago. But Jessica was
probably right. Gretchen *did* seem pathetic, and the last thing
Ariel wanted was to be deemed pathetic by association. She
decided to trust Jessica on this one. After all, she did have
experience with this kind of thing. And besides, she had to
admit: she was dying to know what had happened between
the two of them. If she went along, she just might be able to
find out.

At lunch, Jessica regaled them with funny stories about boarding school.

"You wouldn't even believe this one girl. She had a whole
advance team come in and decorate her dorm room before
she arrived, like she was the Queen of England . . ."

Ariel glanced around their table: Nick's friends and the
Oculus Society princesses. Everyone was rapt. Amazing:
Jessica seamlessly fit back in; she made herself the center of
attention, but Ariel didn't feel at all displaced. It was as if the
rest of them were a giant puzzle, and all this time they'd had
no idea that they'd been missing the final piece.

But Ariel also couldn't help noticing how Gretchen sat by
herself in the corner, reading a book as she ate. The seats
around her were conspicuously empty. Unpopularity was
the most contagious disease. She knew that better than anyone. And yet she'd been cured. Ariel turned back to Jessica,
waiting for her to notice, too, but she never even glanced
in Gretchen's direction. The dynamic was starting to make
Ariel paranoid. She desperately wanted to speak to Gretchen,
to put what had happened between them behind her once
and for all. But she was afraid to approach her, and not just
because Jessica forbade it. After all, Gretchen might not be as

forgiving as Jessica was, and Ariel worried that bringing up the past with her might open a Pandora's box that she'd never be able to close.

But what if she tells? For the thousandth time, Ariel thought back to the aftermath of the "Secret Lovers" video: the explosion in hits, the scorn heaped upon Jessica and Gretchen, the questioning of all things Oculus Society, their abrupt disappearance . . . and now this. Two years ago it had been a delicious game with Ariel as sole victor. But the video had faded into oblivion, the way all YouTube videos do. And the Oculus Society had never lost any influence or power in Delphi. They had denounced the anonymous poster as cruel and tasteless and depraved. And soon even their denouncements were forgotten.

Ariel glanced over at Gretchen again. She wished she would look up so that she could catch her eye and maybe get a read on how Gretchen was feeling toward her. Everyone at the table suddenly burst out laughing.

Ariel noticed that Jessica looked only at Nick, and smiled at him as their eyes met. Connor was staring at Jessica in a way that was almost creepy. Instinctively, Ariel put her arm around Nick's waist. When Jessica wasn't looking, she whispered in his ear.

"I think Connor likes Jessica," she said. "He was listening to her story like it was the most interesting thing he'd ever heard. Wouldn't they be cute together?"

Nick looked at her, bewildered. "What? Does she like him?"

Ariel nodded. "Yeah," she lied. "She told me this morning that she thinks he's really hot. Did he say anything about her to you?"

Nick frowned. "No. We haven't talked about it. But I'll find out."

Ariel kissed him on the mouth, then pulled away seductively. "It would be fun if they went out. We could double date."

Jessica drove Ariel home in silence, steering with her left hand and chewing at the skin around the nails of her right hand. Ariel hadn't counted on the tension. She wished Nick could have driven her home.

"So how was your first day back?" Ariel finally asked. "It seemed like things went pretty well for you."

Jessica shrugged. "It was fine, I guess. Kind of feels like I never left."

Ariel nodded. Something was obviously bothering her. Maybe Jessica was having second thoughts about being friends with her now that she'd been back at school. Maybe someone had said something to her about the video. Maybe Jessica had realized that it bothered her more than she'd thought it would.

"Listen, Jessica, I just want to apologize to you again about, you know, everything that happened before," Ariel blurted out. "I'm sure it was weird for you to be back around everyone today, knowing that they all know about, um, what happened." She was still too ashamed to even say the words.

But Jessica seemed unfazed. "You really need to stop apologizing, Ariel. I told you: it's all in the past. And today wasn't weird for me at all. I swear, it's all good."

"Okay. I just felt like maybe something was wrong, and I thought maybe you were still mad at me."

"I'm not mad at *you*," Jessica answered.

"Is it Gretchen?" Ariel asked in a flood of relief. "What went on between the two of you, anyway?"

Jessica's face tightened. "Ariel, you can ask me pretty much anything you want, but what happened with me and Gretchen stays between me and Gretchen. Okay?"

Ariel slumped back into the passenger seat. Jessica's face relaxed again. "Hey, what's the deal with Connor?" she asked, changing the subject.

Ariel raised her eyebrows. She hadn't thought that Jessica had even noticed Connor. "I think he's into you. I even said so to Nick at lunch."

"Really?" Jessica seemed surprised to hear it. "I think he's hot. Do you think Nick would, like, set us up?"

Ariel tried not to cringe. She supposed that, objectively, Connor was good looking. But he was such a jerk, Ariel couldn't see how anyone could find him remotely attractive. But she didn't feel the need to point this out to Jessica. "Definitely," Ariel answered. "I'll make sure of it."

The next few weeks passed in a blur. There were her classes, and homework, and Nick. But mostly, she focused on Jessica. The two of them had become nearly inseparable. Jessica sought her out at every opportunity. In the same way Jessica and Gretchen had always been attached at the hip in middle school, Ariel and Jessica were now. She imagined that Jessica probably had a best friend like this at boarding school, too. Sometimes if she thought about it long enough, it made her feel disposable, like a drummer who gets replaced in a band and nobody even notices.

But mostly, Ariel liked it. She'd never really had a close friendship with a girl before. Yes, she was sort of friendly with some of the less popular girls, like Brinley. But the relationships were always tinged with sadness and depression and anger, and doomed to fail. Even last year, when her popularity suddenly sprouted like a weed, she mostly hung out with the guys. The reigning girls welcomed her, but they'd been a tight clique for years. Ariel always felt like an outsider around them.

Now Jessica was an outsider, too, and she and Ariel—impossibly, unimaginably—had quickly become best friends. Jessica complained about her aunt Michelle, gushed about her uncle Rob, and confided every last detail about her budding relationship with Connor Matthews. Ariel told Jessica things she'd never told anyone before: about how she missed her mom, about how she never even really knew her father, about what she had—and hadn't—done with Nick Ford.

There was only one thing the two of them never spoke about, and that was the video that Ariel had taken of Jessica and Gretchen kissing.

The last week of September was warmer than usual. After school let out that Friday, Ariel, Nick, Jessica, and Connor piled into Nick's car.

"It's so hot," Ariel complained. "It sucks so much to live in California and not be close to a beach."

"Dude," Connor said, addressing Nick. "Let's go swimming at your house."

Nick shook his head. "We can't. My parents are having a party tonight, and my mom's been setting up the backyard all day. Why can't we swim at your house?"

Connor frowned. "Dude, my mom." The four of them sat in silence. "Okay," Nick finally said. "Somebody tell me where to go, because I'm driving around in circles."

Silence again. Then Jessica made a suggestion from the backseat. "Let's go to the Club."

Ariel stiffened in her seat. She immediately thought of the last time she and Jessica had encountered each other at the club. Jessica had practically accused her of murdering Gretchen's mother, just hours before Ariel posted the video

so many times in her head, it was seared into her memory, word for word.

I know you were involved in Gretchen's mom's murder. So if you know what's good for you, you'll keep your mouth shut.

I liked it better when you ignored me, Ariel had responded.

And it was then, at that very moment, that she'd made up her mind to post the video.

Despite the oppressive heat and the warm towel wrapped around her body, Ariel shuddered. "Are you okay?" Nick asked her. "You're shivering."

Ariel swallowed, tried to steady her shaking body. "I'm not feeling that well. I think I need to go home."

"What?" Jessica frowned. "You can't go home! We just got here!"

"I really think I should go. I'll call you later." Ariel could feel the dizziness setting in, her heartbeat quickening. She'd had panic attacks before, but not in a while. Mrs. Lackman had warned her, though, that they could be triggered by stress. Or by a particularly intense, bad memory. She bolted for the door.

Inhale through your nose. Exhale through your mouth. As she walked the familiar route home, Ariel felt herself slowly calm down. The dizziness subsided, her heartbeat slowed, the shaking stopped. But she knew she had to deal with what she'd done. She couldn't pretend any longer.

CHAPTER FOURTEEN

It was Rob who answered the door a few hours later. Tan from lying out at the pool all summer—his dark hair slicked back and two days' worth of grey-tinged scruff on his face—he was still strikingly good looking for a guy in his late-thirties. Ariel, of course, knew who he was from the Club. In fact, Rob was legendary there. The women her mom's age all gossiped about him, how he'd lucked into a marriage with a woman who didn't mind being the breadwinner, how they all felt sorry for him because his music career hadn't panned out. And the high school kids all talked about him, too: how he bought beer for parties, how he'd helped some seniors get a fake ID, how he'd scored backstage passes to some concert down in LA. Even Nick thought he was cool. Ariel had no doubt that at least part of Jessica's easy transition back to popularity had had something to do with the fact that Rob was her uncle.

"Hi, I'm Ariel. I'm a friend of Jessica's. Is she around?" Ariel doubted he would recognize her from the Club, or have any idea who she was.

"Ariel," Rob mused, taking her in in one long, sweeping glance. "You're dating Nick, right?" He studied her for a moment longer. "Didn't you used to work at the Club a few summers ago?"

She blinked. "Um, yeah, Nick and I are going out," she answered, dodging the second part of his question. "Is Jessica here?" she asked again.

He laughed. "Yeah, she's here. Her room's down the hall to the left. Just knock." He stood aside to let her dash past.

She knocked on Jessica's door, and it swung open.

"Oh, hey," Jessica said, puzzled. She was lying on the bed, reading a magazine, headphones stuck in her ears. She pulled them out and sat up, cross-legged. "Are you okay? What happened to you today?"

Ariel felt herself turning red. She took a deep breath. *You have to go through with this,* she reminded herself. *It's the only way.* "I need to tell you something," she admitted. "It's about me. Well, about us."

Jessica nodded. She didn't even blink. "Okay. Tell me."

"Okay." She swallowed and clenched her fists at her side. "When we were in middle school, all I ever wanted was to be popular, and for you and your friends to like me. And I guess, you know, I had a lot of anger about the way you all treated me. So when I caught you and Gretchen on that video, I posted it without really thinking about the consequences, you know? I just wanted to get back at you."

"I know that," Jessica said. Her voice hardened. "I thought we discussed this. You don't need to keep apologizing."

"I know, and I appreciate that, but the thing is, I haven't really forgiven myself." Ariel had never said this before—not to herself, not to Mrs. Lackman, not to anyone—and something about saying the words out loud, about releasing them, brought tears to her eyes. "It's not like I just forgot about you and Gretchen after you left. I mean, I've felt really, really bad for a long time. I'm not the together person that people think I am. Not at all. I've been seeing the school psychologist in secret for two years. I starved myself for most of ninth grade, because apparently, not eating was a way for me to feel in control of myself. And I steal things. I steal food from the 7-Eleven. I steal jewelry and clothes from the mall. I even stole something out of somebody's locker at the Club today. It's, like, I don't know. Mrs. Lackman says that subconsciously I want to get caught, because then I'll be forced to tell the truth."

Jessica opened her mouth to respond, but Ariel cut her off with a sniff. She wiped her moist cheeks with a trembling arm.

"No, wait. Just let me finish before you say anything. When you came back, I was terrified. I was sure you were going to out me to everyone. But at the same time, seeing you here, back in Delphi, was a huge relief for me, because I saw that your life wasn't ruined, you know? I mean, you're still this really cool, beautiful, popular girl, and it might sound selfish, but I'm really glad about that because it means I didn't take all of that away from you. But then Gretchen came back, and she's nothing like who she used to be. I know what happened between you two is none of my business, but I really can't stand seeing her this way, Jessica. She eats alone in the cafeteria, she doesn't have any friends, nobody wants to talk to her. The girl was institutionalized, for God's sake, and I feel like it's all my fault. I feel like I took away everything she was. And, well, I don't how you'll feel about this, but I want to help her. I want to reach out to her and include her again. We have power. If we start talking to her, then everybody will."

Finally, Ariel stopped talking and took a breath. She looked
at Jessica through blurry, teary eyes and braced herself for her
response. Whatever Jessica might have to say about her and
Gretchen, Ariel had decided that she wasn't going to take no
for an answer. Somehow, some way, she was going to make
things up to Gretchen and make things right for herself.

But Jessica didn't say anything. A tear fell from her eye.

"Are you crying?" Ariel gasped.

Jessica didn't answer. A strange, self-satisfied smile crossed
her face as she got up from the bed and walked across the
room. When she reached Ariel, she opened her arms and
wrapped them around her in a tight hug. Ariel was so confused that she almost didn't hear Jessica whisper in her ear.

"You passed the test."

Ariel pulled back from Jessica's embrace. "What did you
just say?"

Jessica still had that strange smile on her face as she reached
out and took Ariel's hand. "I said you passed the test. I knew
you would. Gretchen wasn't so sure, of course, but I knew you
had it in you."

Ariel almost fell backward. She wiped her moist cheeks
again, no longer crying. "What are you talking about? What
test? And what does Gretchen have to do with it?"

Jessica fell back on her bed and patted the space next
to her.

Ariel sat down on autopilot, as if in a dream. Jessica took
her hand again and held it gently, like how a mother might
comfort an upset child. "I know this is going to come as a
shock to you, and I'm sorry about that, I really am. But it was
the only way. Okay?"

"Jessica, I have no idea what you're talking about."

She smiled again. "Ariel, Gretchen and I are still best friends."

Ariel felt the color drain from her face. "What?"

Jessica nodded. "We're still best friends. The whole 'Gretchen as loser' thing is just an act."

The room began to swirl like a carousel. Up felt like down and down felt like up, and Ariel couldn't even understand the words coming out of Jessica's mouth, much less make sense of them.

"I'm really sorry that we lied to you," Jessica was saying. She took a deep breath. "There's a lot to explain."

Ariel's senses slowly began to come back to her, and with that return to reality came anger. "What the hell is going on, Jessica?"

Jessica nodded, as if she understood completely. "Ariel, Gretchen was never institutionalized. You didn't ruin her life. She went to boarding school, just like I did. In fact, we went to boarding school together in England."

Ariel's mouth hung open. She couldn't believe what she was hearing. All this time she'd spent beating herself up about what she'd done to Gretchen . . . but none of it was even true. She didn't say anything as Jessica continued to talk.

"You have to understand, back then, after everything that had happened with her mom, she was already thinking about leaving Delphi. Her dad was depressed and could barely even take care of her, but she didn't know how to tell him that her going away would be the right thing for both of them. So when the video came out, it was the perfect excuse. The Oculus Society was reeling from the video and wanted to distance themselves from her—from both of us—and some of the members convinced her dad that it was the right thing to do. We found a boarding school that could take us both, and I was the one who started the rumor that she'd been institutionalized."

Ariel was crying again. She hadn't even realized it. But anger, relief and confusion were finding their way out, one salty drop at a time. "Why?" she whispered.

"Gretchen didn't want people looking for her," Jessica replied. "But here's the most important thing—and something that very few people can understand . . . her mother had just died. Unless you've been through it yourself, you have no idea what that's like. She didn't want to have to explain herself to anyone. She asked me to make something up that would end her relationships here forever, and it was the best I could come up with."

"So then, why did she come back?"

"She was ready. And she wants the closure. She can't hide from Delphi forever. She belongs here."

"I still don't understand," Ariel said. "Why is she acting like an outsider? Why are you going along with it?"

Jessica laughed. "Really? Come on, Ariel, think about it. Gretchen and I were caught kissing. If we both came back at the same time and were acting like BFFs, everyone would think that we were involved with each other."

Ariel threw up her hands. "Are you?"

"No," Jessica said, as if the very question amused her.

"Okay. But then, I have to ask, Jessica. Why were the two of you kissing that night?"

Jessica's mouth relaxed into a smile again. "Ah. The million dollar question." She stood up and paced the room for a moment. It seemed to Ariel that she was trying to make a decision about something. Finally, she stopped moving and turned to face her. "Do you trust me?"

The question caught Ariel off guard. She admired Jessica, she respected Jessica, and somewhere deep inside of her—in the box where she'd buried the insecure, unpopular girl she used to be—she wanted to be liked by Jessica. But if she was going to be totally honest, the answer was no. She didn't trust Jessica. And that was true even before everything she'd just found out. But then again, Ariel wasn't in the habit of being totally honest herself.

"Yes. Of course I do."

Jessica nodded. She inhaled and loudly let out her breath. "This is going to sound crazy to you, but what you saw wasn't kissing. What you saw was the two of us exchanging souls."

Ariel laughed. But Jessica's look was so sharp, she stopped herself almost immediately. "Are you serious?"

"I'm dead serious. And I'm trusting you with a huge secret here, Ariel. A secret that cuts to the core of the Oculus Society. There are only a handful of people in the world who know that this is possible . . ."

Ariel struggled to listen as Jessica went on. About an ancient Greek philosopher, Plotinus, and his disciple, Gemina. About how the Oculus Society guarded their secret. About how this secret was passed down from generation to generation, along with a mystical phrase that was known only by the one who had been chosen to receive it. And about how she, Jessica, had been chosen as the secret's keeper two years ago. Ariel's mind whirled. Of all the crazy secrets she'd imagined the Oculus Society hid—mostly white-collar crimes and money-laundering—she'd never imagined it was something so off the grid.

"The night you found us, Gretchen and I were trying it for the first time."

Ariel was at a loss. It crossed her mind that Jessica might just be screwing with her, that this was all some sort of elaborate prank and that Gretchen would come popping out of the closet at any minute, surprise! Ha, ha, ha. But something about the look on Jessica's face made her think that she wasn't joking around.

"Did it work?" She felt stupid just for asking.

But Jessica was solemn in her reply. "It did." Ariel figured that doubt must have been written all over her face, because Jessica sighed and shook her head. "Look, I know that asking you to believe this is asking a lot. But I can prove it. Here." She took out her phone and held it out to Ariel. It was cued up to the YouTube video that Ariel had taken of her and Gretchen. Ariel felt her cheeks turn red. She hadn't watched the video since she'd posted it; just seeing it again made her burn with shame. "Watch it," Jessica instructed. "You can see it happen, if you know what to look for. Look at us after we pull back from each other. We're not the same as we were before."

Reluctantly, Ariel pushed the play button.

Before her eyes, thirteen-year-old Jessica and Gretchen came to life. Ariel watched as they sat in the teepee, cross legged with their eyes closed, as if they were meditating. She watched as Jessica told Gretchen to clear her mind, to think about amber, and then said something that, at the time, Ariel had thought was gibberish, but now realized was actually Greek. And then she watched as Jessica leaned in and put her mouth on Gretchen's. But Jessica was right. They weren't kissing, exactly. It was more like they were exhaling into each other's mouths.

Jessica was leaning over her shoulder. "Now watch closely," she said, as the two girls pulled away from each other on the screen.

Ariel put her face closer to the phone.

"*Holy shit,*" Gretchen said. But it was odd, the way she said it. As if her tongue wasn't working right in her mouth.

She watched as Jessica looked down over her body as if she were seeing it for the first time, and how Gretchen examined Jessica's face as if she'd never seen it before. And then, as they noticed the light from the camera and looked directly into it, she saw something else. In their eyes, she could see that they wore expressions of shock. And something akin to fear. They weren't faking.

Ariel's hand shook as she handed Jessica back her phone.

"You had some sort of run-in with Gretchen the next day when she was in my body," Jessica said softly. "It was at the Club. Do you remember that?"

Ariel felt like she'd just been dropped into a bucket of ice. Her whole body went numb as she recalled the incident for the second time in as many days. The odd one-piece bathing suit Jessica had been wearing. The surprise on her face when she saw Ariel turn around in the cabana. The crazy talk about how she killed Gretchen's mom.

I know you were involved in Gretchen's mom's murder. So if you know what's good for you, you'll keep your mouth shut.

Oh, my God, Ariel thought. Was it really possible? Was it actually Gretchen she'd been talking to that day?

"I remember it," Ariel said softly. Jessica studied Ariel's face for a moment, then smiled. "You know I'm telling you the truth, don't you?"

Reluctantly, Ariel nodded. As insane as it all sounded, she was sure that Jessica wasn't making this up. She'd seen it with her own eyes. That *hadn't* been Jessica that day at the Club. Ariel knew this in the deepest part of her core.

"Good. So then, here's the *two* million dollar question: Do you want in?"

CHAPTER FIFTEEN

Castricius heard the news before anyone. He'd been on his way to a meeting at the Curia when one of his bankers approached him in the road. The banker seemed nervous and shuffled his feet in the dirt as he spoke.

"You should know, Senator. Your wife has been arrested."

Castricius casually brushed off the man and his rudeness. "I think you must have mistaken another woman for my wife."

"No, Senator," the banker responded, shaking his head vigorously. "I am certain that it was your wife. She followed me into the bathhouse demanding that I speak to her about opening a bank account." The banker looked at him knowingly. "For a purpose similar to that of your own account."

The color drained from Castricius's face. His account with this banker was a secret. How could Gemina know of it? *And if she knows about the account*, he thought, *what else might she know about?*

"Did she say anything else?" Castricius asked tersely.

"No, Senator. I'm very sorry. I hope you understand that I had no choice but to call the guards. She broke the law in plain view of a dozen men. If I hadn't had her arrested, I would have been myself."

"I understand," Castricius said. "Is she at the jail now?"

"I believe she is, Senator. Again, I'm very sorry."

The young guard at the door nodded deferentially and ushered him in right away. The jail smelled of urine and unwashed bodies, causing Castricius to place the sleeve of his tunic over his nose and mouth. As he passed through the hallway, he stared straight ahead, trying not to look at the thieves, debtors, and tax evaders, miserable in their windowless cells. He couldn't imagine Gemina in a place like this. The thought of her lying on the floor on a lice-infested mat caused his outrage to grow with each step he took.

"Your wife, Senator, is being held in the jailer's private office," said the guard, as if reading Castricius's mind. Castricius exhaled. At least that was something. They reached a door at the end of the hallway that was bolted shut from the outside. The guard slid the bolt back but hesitated before opening the door, as if he were considering something. He reached into a fold of his tunic and emerged with a piece of parchment paper in his hand. "She was holding this when she was arrested, Senator. I thought, perhaps, you might want to have it . . . lest it get into the hands of the wrong people."

Castricius took the paper and skimmed it quickly.

If the perfect life is within human reach, the man attaining it attains happiness . . .

What is this nonsense? he thought to himself. It came from

Plotinus, of that he was quite sure. But as he read the last few
lines, his breath caught in his chest.

> *Why should a woman not own property, or take part*
> *in politics? If she has the same capabilities as man, why*
> *should a woman not become Emperor, even? Is it fear*
> *that leads men to keep the laws of women unequal?*
> *Fear that women might perhaps be better qualified to*
> *govern this Roman Empire?*

This is grounds for treason, he thought with a prickle of
panic. And treason was the only crime in Rome that was pun-
ishable by death. The guard was right to give this to him. With
evidence this damning, even his powerful influence might not
be enough to save Gemina from a public beheading. Castricius suddenly felt guilty. He wanted out of his marriage, it
was true, but not like this.

"What's your name?" Castricius asked the guard.

"Marcus Caelius, sir."

Castricius nodded appreciatively at him. "Your judgment
does not go unnoticed, Marcus Caelius." Castricius took
the paper and placed it in a fold of his own tunic. He would
rip it up once he was alone. "Now, please, may I see my
wife?"

Marcus leaned into the door with his shoulder and pushed
it open. A breeze was blowing through the open window.
Gemina was standing with her back to the door; the sunlight
ensconced her olive skin and bounced off of her shiny, dark
hair. The guard retreated and closed the door behind him just
as Gemina turned around.

"Gemina!" Castricius was furious with her, but at the
moment his predominant emotion was relief at finding her

safe and in an environment that didn't debase her prominent
status. Or his own, for that matter.

"Castricius," she said calmly. "I didn't expect you to be the
first to arrive." This was not the greeting that Castricius had
been expecting. He'd been prepared for her to be trembling, to
run to him and tearfully apologize, to beg him to remedy the situation for her. That was how she'd behaved when her father had
been accused of forgery and faced a lifetime of exile. It was how
she'd behaved when Plotinus had run out of money and was on
the verge of leaving Rome, or when their daughter, Gaia, had
developed a cough as an infant and the doctor couldn't come
as soon as she'd wanted. It was how she behaved whenever
something went wrong in her life that she didn't know how—or
didn't have the power—to fix.

In their relationship, she was the child, and he was the
adult who always came to her rescue. It was why he'd gone
to Lucretia Iusta's bed to begin with. After two years of tol-
erating marriage to a child, Castricius longed to be with a
woman, and Lucretia was certainly that. Years of being
widowed and having to fend for herself had left her strong,
capable, cunning even. She was everything Gemina wasn't.
But this was a Gemina he'd never seen before. Calm, self-
contained, unafraid. Castricius looked into her eyes, and he
knew right away that something was different about her. It
took him a few moments to realize what it was: she seemed
older. If the circumstances hadn't been so dire, he might have
even found it seductive.

He removed the paper from his tunic. "Gemina," he said,
sternly. "What is the meaning of this? Where did you get this?"

She sneered. "I wrote it!" she declared. "And I meant
every word. Do you know why I'm being held here like a
prisoner, Castricius?" She didn't wait for him to answer. "It's

because I'm a woman. I'm a woman, and I wanted to open a bank account."

Castricius lowered his voice to a growl. "Have you lost your mind? How could you possibly handle a bank account?"

Gemina smirked at him. "I'm quite sure it's not so difficult, Castricius. The fact of the matter is, you're sleeping with that traitor Lucretia Iusta, and you're giving her money from my father that was meant for me and Gaia. I'd like it back, and I'd like to put it somewhere that you can't access."

Castricius went pale, and his heart quickened. *So she knows.* Still, there was some relief. *She knows.*

"And," she continued, "in return for me not disgracing you in public, I'd like you to present to the Senate a law that women and men shall be treated equally."

The panic Castricius had been feeling subsided. She was talking nonsense. *There must be something wrong with her,* he thought. *She's been poisoned, or the stress of being in jail is causing her to hallucinate.* It occurred to him that having his wife in a weakened mental state could work entirely to his advantage.

"Gemina," he said softly. He went to her and placed a hand on her arm. "My dear wife, I think you may not be well. I'll explain it all to the authorities, and we'll have you back at home in a few hours. Perhaps I'll consult a priest or doctor for medicine that will help you to think more clearly."

But Gemina shook his hand off of her arm. "I can think just fine!" she roared. "The laws of this empire are an outrage!"

"Shhh! You're going to get yourself executed if you keep talking like that!"

"I will never stop talking like this! I cannot stand by and participate in a society that lives a lie. Rome is so civilized, so enlightened, and yet is so unjust! Why can't women vote?

Why can't women have money of their own? Why can't women imprison men?"

In spite of himself, Castricius was trembling with anger. He found it difficult to keep his voice steady as he answered her. "Because women do not have the sense for such things. Women are needed at home to manage affairs and to raise their children. You're spewing nonsense, Gemina, and if you continue to do so, I can assure you that you'll find yourself in deeper trouble, trouble from which I cannot save you. Now I'm going to leave and see if I can find out a way to get you out of here. But you must not speak of these things to anyone, do you understand? Not to anyone!"

With that, he walked out of the room and brushed past Marcus Caelius, standing guard outside the door. As he heard the bolt on the door slide back into place, he felt the strange mingled combination of nausea and satisfaction.

Amphiclea was in the garden when Plotinus came to tell her the news—or rather, when Gemina came. It was still difficult for Amphiclea to remember that it was her vibrant young friend in that frail, middle-aged man's body.

Gemina trembled in sagging skin as she relayed the story. Plotinus obviously must have forgotten that he appeared to everyone else as a woman. She herself had almost slipped a thousand times that day; she'd caught herself just before curtsying, she'd almost neglected to kiss the hands of other women, she'd nearly declined to discuss business matters. Neither she nor Plotinus had thought enough about how difficult it would be to change them so quickly. But to follow a banker into the men's bath and to try to discuss business right there in front of influential men who knew her and Castricius . . .

"Oh, Amphiclea, what have we done? How will we ever fix this?"

There were tears in Plotinus's eyes. Amphiclea wanted to shout at Gemina for being so careless with her life, for agreeing to something as dangerous and as outrageous as trading souls—and with a man, no less! But she bit her tongue. A reprimand was not what Gemina needed right now. Instead, she reached over and hugged her, feeling the strange contours of Plotinus's body, the thinness of his bones beneath his clothes.

"You must go talk to Castricius," Gemina whispered. "You must tell him the truth. Bring him Plotinus's journal, show him the anklet. Once he understands what has happened, he'll know how to fix this. He always does."

Amphiclea nodded. She'd known from the moment that Gemina and Plotinus had proposed their scheme that somehow it would come to this.

Amphiclea had never been alone with Castricius before. She'd spent enough time with Gemina to have spoken with him, but always in passing and always about benign subjects—like the weather or the sweetness of a particular crop of figs. He'd been pleasant enough, but Amphiclea knew from Gemina that he wasn't always so, and she was aware of his reputation in the Senate for having a quick temper, particularly when matters were not to his liking. So as she waited for him in the courtyard of his home, Plotinus's journal tucked under her arm, the anklet trembled against her skin.

"Amphiclea," Castricius boomed as he entered the courtyard, his large frame draped in a white tunic with silver edging. He was older, in his early thirties, and not particularly handsome. His black hair had begun to recede away from his forehead, like so many soldiers retreating from a hard-fought battle. "Surely you've heard about Gemina?" he asked. He kept his eyes on the ground, never meeting her own.

"I have, Senator," Amphiclea answered, trying to maintain some strength and resolve in her voice. "It's why I've asked to see you."

"Is it now?" he asked, thoughtfully. Suddenly, he seemed more interested in looking at her. "Let me ask you something, Amphiclea. You are her best friend, are you not? The one she shares everything with, perhaps even more than her own husband."

"I am."

"And did you see her today, before all of this happened?"

"I did."

He hesitated, as if he were searching for a diplomatic way to ask what was coming next. "And did you notice her acting . . . perhaps . . . different than usual?" But before Amphiclea had a chance to respond, he threw his hands up in the air. "Oh, I'll just say it! Did you notice that she was acting strange and talking nonsense?"

Amphiclea squeezed the journal with both hands to try to stop them from shaking so visibly. She cleared her throat. "I did notice, Senator. And I believe I may be able to explain it to you." She motioned toward a small garden table behind him, where she and Gemina had shared so many private whispered conversations. "May we sit, please?"

Castricius held out a chair. He waited for Amphiclea to settle in before he sat across from her. His body barely fit in the opposite seat; his large legs took up almost all of the space beneath the table, requiring Amphiclea to sit sideways so as not to rub her legs up against his. She tried not to cry as she laid the journal out on the table between them.

"Senator, what I'm about to tell you defies logic and

reason. It will be hard for you to believe, as it was for me. I must tell you, if I hadn't seen it happen with my own eyes, I still would doubt that it is even possible." She opened the journal to a page she'd marked beforehand. "Senator, Plotinus believed—"

Castricius slammed his hand down on the table, cutting her off. "Plotinus!" he roared, his face turning red with anger. "I knew this was his influence. Filling her head with treasonous ideas about a woman becoming Emperor of Rome!"

Amphiclea steadied herself. She had planned to explain it to him from the beginning: how Plotinus had projected his soul through the Oculus and how he and Gemina had agreed to trade souls with each other. She had planned to tell him of the preparations leading up to their exchange, of the evening she met them at the Pantheon, of the anklet, of the journal . . . and of course, of the need for a witness in the event that something terrible—something like Gemina landing in jail—were to occur. But she realized that Castricius would not have the patience for such a long explanation. Better for them both if she got right to the point.

"No, Senator. I'm afraid that it wasn't her head you saw today filled with those ideas. It was Plotinus. His theories are valid. By the power of the gods, I swear that he is able to project his soul, and he's taught Gemina to do it as well. Oh, Senator! The truth is that Plotinus inhabits Gemina's body, and she inhabits his!"

Castricius's eyes blazed for another instant. For a moment, she wondered if he would strike her. But then the light went out. He slumped back in his chair, as if her words had physically pushed him down. The anger was gone. In its place was an emotion she couldn't read. "So that was her then, at Lucretia's today," he muttered to himself. "Pretending to be Plotinus." Amphiclea didn't know what he was talking about. Had Gemina gone to Lucretia's house? To do what? And why hadn't she mentioned that to her? But Amphiclea didn't dare ask Castricius to explain. He nodded toward the journal. "You have proof of this?" he asked. His voice was low and steady but with a quiet, seething bass note underneath.

Amphiclea slid the journal around to face him. She tapped her finger on the passage about the wearer of the anklet. "It's me," she whispered. She extended her leg to the side of the table and lifted her tunic, exposing the shimmering amber disk beneath it.

Castricius didn't even give her leg a glance. He sat still, quietly staring out toward the horizon. Amphiclea didn't disturb him. *He needs time to think about this*, she told herself. But after several more minutes of his silence, she couldn't take it anymore.

"They can switch back," she finally said. "All you have to do is arrange for Plotinus—I mean, Gemina—to visit him in jail. They need to be alone, but only for a few moments."

Castricius didn't look at her. "I can't," he said.

"Of course you can!" Amphiclea snapped, her voice rising with desperation. "You're a senator. Surely you have influence over a mere guard at the jail!"

But Castricius shook his head. He finally met her gaze, and the vacant look in his eye chilled her. "What I meant is that I don't want to." He stood. "Let him rot in jail, and let her spend the rest of her days in that old fool's body. It's a worse punishment than I could ever dream up for either of them for betraying me like this."

Amphiclea jumped up, horrified. "But Castricius! What about Gaia?"

He shrugged. "Gemina can have her. Or you can take her. It's not like she's a son."

"But how will she provide for her? Where will they live?"

A wicked smile crossed his face. "My wife is in jail, being provided for by the Roman Empire, and whatever money she had from her father belongs to me now. How Plotinus manages from now on is not my problem." He took Amphiclea's clammy hand and held it to his lips. "Good day, Amphiclea. As always, it's been a pleasure to see you."

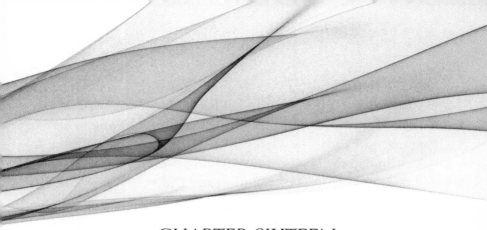

CHAPTER SIXTEEN

The seat belt buckle was directly beneath Ariel's lower back, and the weight of Nick's body kept pushing her down so that it dug uncomfortably into her spine. Normally, Ariel would be clawing at him to get his shirt off, to feel his bare skin next to hers, but today she was hardly responding to his touch. She couldn't concentrate on Nick right now. All she could think about was Jessica's question. *Do you want in?*

Ariel arched her back in an attempt to dislodge the seat belt buckle from her vertebrae.

"I really want to be with you," Nick whispered.

Ariel rolled her eyes. She placed the palm of her hand on the middle of his chest and pushed him off of her.

"No. Nick, I'm sorry." Nick let out a frustrated sigh and collapsed back onto the cushion beside her. "Why? Did I do something wrong?"

She sat up and ran her hand down his arm affectionately. "No. No, it's not you. I'm just distracted."

"By what?"

Ariel didn't know what to tell him. By the idea of switching bodies with another person? By the idea of having to kiss another girl to do it? Or by the idea of doing it with the girl who had the most reason to hate her in the whole entire world? "I don't know," she hedged. "Did you ever . . . did you ever wish you could be someone else?"

Nick looked at her like this was the dumbest question he'd ever heard. "No," he answered blankly. "Why would I want to be someone else?"

Right, she thought. Of course Nick Ford wouldn't want to be someone else. Why would he want to be someone else when he got to be Nick Ford every day? This, Ariel realized, was exactly the problem with their relationship. Nick was perfect. Or at least, he was perfect in his own mind. He was handsome, athletic, wealthy, and well-bred. More to the point he had no idea that he wasn't the brightest white in the laundry. So why, indeed, would he want to be anyone else, especially when he thought that everyone else wanted to be him?

Ariel, on the other hand, had spent most of her life wishing that she could be anyone but Ariel Miller. But mostly, she'd wished that she could be Jessica Shaw. And now—now that she was finally popular, now that she was in a position like Nick, now that other people actually wanted to be *her*—here she was, being given the opportunity to leave herself, to become Jessica. The irony was not lost on her.

"You wouldn't, I guess," Ariel answered him. "But don't you ever wonder what it's like to be Connor?"

Nick laughed. "I already know what it's like to be Connor. It's like walking around in a fog of stupidity all the time."

Ariel laughed, too. She grabbed the back of his neck with

both of her hands and pulled his face down toward hers, kissing him hard.

It was almost eleven o'clock when Ariel climbed back into the front seat of Nick's car. But she couldn't go home. She had to go to Jessica's house.

"I left a book there," she lied. "I need it for a paper I'm writing."

Nick glanced anxiously at his watch. He couldn't be late for his own eleven o'clock curfew or else his dad would make him sit out a practice.

"You don't have to wait for me," Ariel assured him. "Jessica can take me home. I don't want you to be late."

"Are you sure?" he asked.

She leaned over and kissed him on the cheek. "It's fine."

Still, minutes later, as she stood on Jessica's porch, Nick sat in his idling car, waiting until Ariel was let inside. *Does he have to be such a gentleman?* she wondered impatiently. She waved him away, holding up her phone to indicate that she was texting Jessica to come downstairs, rather than ringing the doorbell, and that it might be a few minutes. When he finally left, Ariel waited another minute, then tiptoed away from Jessica's front door and began the three block walk to Gretchen's house. She sent Gretchen a text as she approached her family's long, gated driveway.

Can u come outside? I need 2 talk 2 u. It's imprtnt.

A few moments later, the black, wrought-iron gate swung open. Gretchen appeared barefoot in the driveway, wearing loose white pajama shorts and a white tank top. The path lights lining the driveway lit her from below, casting an eerie glow all around her. Ariel couldn't help thinking that she looked like a ghost.

"I didn't want to wake up your dad by ringing the bell," Ariel explained.

Gretchen didn't say anything. She crossed her arms in front of her stomach.

"Um, I wanted to talk to you about, you know."

Gretchen still said nothing.

Ariel pressed on. "I'm assuming Jessica told you that I know. About everything."

"Jessica told me." She looked Ariel up and down, scrutinizing every inch of her. Ariel sighed.

"Look, if you don't want to talk to me, I understand, okay? I just came here to tell you that I'm sorry about what happened that summer. I'm sorry, and I went to Jessica because I wanted to help you. That's it." Ariel turned around and started walking back down the driveway. Clearly, things with Gretchen were more complicated than they were with Jessica.

"Jessica also told me you steal things."

Ariel stopped walking. Slowly, she turned back around. "Yeah. So what? Are you going to turn me in?"

Gretchen shook her head. "No. I'm not going to turn you in." She walked closer to Ariel until there were only a few feet between them. "I didn't want her to tell you, you know. I thought she was crazy to trust you. But she swore you were different now. That you were dying of guilt." She paused. "If you felt so guilty, then why weren't you nice to me when I showed up at school?"

"I wanted to be!" Ariel pleaded. A dog barked from inside the house next door, and she lowered her voice to a frantic whisper. "Jessica told me not to talk to you. But I couldn't do it anymore. That's why I went to see her today. She must have told you that."

"She told me. She had this idea to test you. If you stuck up for me, then you passed."

"And I did! I did stick up for you! I told her that I couldn't stand seeing you that way anymore. I told her that I wanted to help you."

Gretchen arched an eyebrow. "Took you long enough."

Ariel raised her arms up in defeat. She felt tears spring to her eyes. She was about to turn around and walk away again, but Gretchen reached out and put a hand on her arm.

"It was the stealing that made me believe her about you. People who can afford to buy stuff only steal if they want to get caught."

Ariel looked at the ground. She felt exposed and raw, and she could feel her cheeks turning red. She was glad for the darkness. "That's exactly what my therapist says," she muttered.

For the first time since the eighth grade, Ariel saw Gretchen smile.

Gretchen led Ariel around to the backyard and stretched out on one of the lounge chairs around the pool. Ariel sat beside her.

"What's it like?" Ariel asked, suddenly.

"It's weird," Gretchen answered, knowing exactly what Ariel was referring to. "All of your calibrations are thrown off. You get used to a certain way of walking, of talking, you have an unconscious sense of where your arms and legs end, of how tall you are. And then, suddenly, it's all different, and you're, like, hyperaware of things you never even noticed before. The first time I was Jessica I almost tripped a hundred times because I wasn't used to having legs that long. But mostly, the weirdest thing is that you forget you're the other person. Because your thoughts are still yours, you know? So you'll be talking to someone, and you'll start to refer to yourself, and you really have to force yourself to call yourself by your name instead of saying 'me.' Do you know what I mean?"

Ariel nodded, even though in truth she had no idea what Gretchen *truly* meant. But she had an inkling. "Like that day, at the Club. You were Jessica, but you were still talking like yourself. I always thought that conversation was so strange. Now I know why."

Gretchen didn't reply, and Ariel sensed that maybe she shouldn't have brought that up quite so soon. She quickly steered the conversation in a different direction.

"Are you still in the Oculus Society?" she asked.

"Technically, I'm a member for life." Gretchen snorted. "But no, I don't go to meetings or events anymore, if that's what you're asking. It's too hard to be around all of those happy mothers and daughters. And besides, the whole thing kind of fell apart anyway."

"What do you mean? A lot of the girls at school are still members, and it seems like they have parties every other week."

"They do. I mean, they still exist. It's just . . . it kind of lost its purpose." She gave Ariel a sharp look. "I thought Jessica explained this to you."

Ariel felt like she'd suddenly been put on the defensive. Instinctively, she held her hands out. "She explained to me that the Oculus Society guarded the secret, and that it's been passed down since the early years of the Roman Empire. She explained about that guy, Plotinus, and Jemima—"

"*Gem-ee-na,*" Gretchen corrected.

"Right, Gemina. Anyway, she told me all of that. But

she didn't say anything about what the Oculus Society is doing now."

Gretchen sighed. She seemed annoyed with Jessica for leaving this task to her. "Did she tell you about the anklet?"

Ariel shook her head.

"The night my mother was murdered, she was wearing an anklet. It originally belonged to Gemina. Well, actually, it belonged to Gemina's best friend, Amphiclea. But anyway, when they found her, the anklet was gone. The Oculus Society believes that you can't project without it. They looked for it at first—they called my dad, they sent some people over to look through our yard—but they came up empty. So they stopped the tradition of projecting altogether. As far as the Oculus Society is concerned, their secret agenda died with my mother. Now they just do philanthropy. Now it's just what people always believed it to be: a stupid social club for rich people who want to feel good about themselves, an after school activity that people put on their college applications."

Ariel sucked in her breath. "So they don't know that you and Jessica can project without the anklet?"

"No!" Gretchen glanced up at her house's darkened windows. "And they can't find out, either. That's why it's such a big secret. That's why everyone needs to think that Jessica and I were making out for real on that video, that we were involved and that she dumped me and that I was heartbroken or whatever. It's why I had to go away, and it's why I have to pretend that I'm damaged goods now that I'm back."

When Ariel didn't respond, Gretchen stared hard at her.

"I don't understand," Ariel admitted after a moment. "Why can't you tell them? Why not reinstate the tradition without the anklet?"

Gretchen lowered her voice so that Ariel could barely even hear her. "Because if they find out, they'll take me out of the loop. They all think I was institutionalized. They'll say I'm unstable, and they'll make Jessica project with someone else." She frowned. "Probably her aunt."

Ariel opened her mouth to speak, but then thought better of it.

"What?" Gretchen asked. "What were you going to say?"

Ariel couldn't meet Gretchen's eyes. She looked down at a piece of dirt on the lounge chair. "Were you really not in an institution? I mean, Jessica told me that you guys were at the same school and that you weren't—you know—but I just . . ."

"You just really thought that I was?" Gretchen asked.

Ariel nodded, still looking at the dirt.

"Well, I wasn't. I went to boarding school with Jessica in England."

"But what about summers and Christmas? You must have had breaks. How is it that you never came home?"

"I didn't want to be here, Ariel," Gretchen said with a sigh. "Neither did Jess. And luckily my dad understood. Michelle was just grateful not to have Jess around. In the summers, we both went to sleepaway camps on the East Coast, and during Christmas, my dad came out and visited us." She shrugged. "It really wasn't all that hard to stay away."

Ariel raised her eyebrows. "So did the two of you project a lot while you were away? Did you, like, walk around England in each other's bodies?"

"No. There wasn't any reason to do any of that over there."

Ariel's head was starting to throb. Once, when she was in fifth grade, she'd gone into a corn maze at a pumpkin patch, and she wasn't able to find her way out. She'd turned into every pathway, only to come upon dead end after dead end. This conversation was starting to make her feel exactly the same way.

"Then why do you need to do it here? What am I missing?"

Gretchen threw her hands up. "I need to find out who killed my mother!" The dog barked again, and she lowered her voice. "Nobody's going to talk to me about it. Being Jessica is the best chance I have of finding the murderer." Tears started rolling down her cheeks. "Does *that* make sense to you?"

Ariel swallowed. She'd been so focused on the guilt she was feeling over the video and so worried that Gretchen was going to tell people about what she'd done, she hadn't even stopped to consider that Gretchen might be obsessing over something else entirely. *Way to be self-absorbed, Ariel,* she thought to herself. But then she had another thought, one that horrified her to her core.

"You don't still think that I had something to do with that, do you?" she asked softly. She held her breath as she waited for the answer.

"No," Gretchen said, wiping the tears away. "Of course not."

Ariel exhaled. But her mind drifted to those texts that Gretchen used to send her, texts she still had stored in her phone just in case she ever needed to prove that Gretchen had started the whole thing between them. *It makes sense,* she thought with a shudder. *If she still thinks I killed her mother, that would explain why she wants me involved in this. What's that saying? "Keep your friends close and your enemies closer?" You can't get much closer than taking over another person's body.*

"If you don't think I killed your mom, then why do you and Jessica want to include me in this, Gretchen?" she asked.

Gretchen took in the blank look on Ariel's face and sighed again. "There were three from the very beginning. When Plotinus taught Gemina how to project, he made her include Amphiclea. To be the witness."

"The witness?"

"In case something went wrong, there had to be a third person who knew the truth and who would make sure that no matter what, the two who projected would be able to get back to their rightful bodies."

Slowly the realization dawned on Ariel. "So you want me to be the witness."

"Well, we want you to be *a* witness. The Oculus Society didn't do it this way, but there's no reason why Jessica can't project with you, too. As long as one of us acts as the witness each time, it doesn't matter whether it's you or me."

"But who was your witness before? Why can't that person do it again?"

"We didn't have one before. We were just messing around then, to see if it even worked. But now . . ." Ariel finished her thought. "Now that you're investigating a murder."

Gretchen's lips closed into a thin line. "It seems like the smart thing to do."

"But why me?" Ariel still didn't understand why, of all people, they would choose to trust *her* with a secret this big.

"Well, to be honest, Ariel, we didn't think that Jessica would actually become friends with you."

"What do you mean?"

"I mean, the idea was to blackmail you. You know, you keep our secret, we'll keep yours? I'm pretty sure you wouldn't want anyone to know that you were the one who made that video of us, right?"

The blood rushed out of Ariel's head, making her feel momentarily dizzy. *They've been planning this all along,* she realized. *They've been counting on me to be their third since the day that video went viral.* "So, let me see if I have this straight. The two of you coincidentally show up back in Delphi at the same time. You pretend to be a psycho, and Jessica uses me in order to become popular again. She pretends to be my friend, and then when I least expect it, she springs this . . . this blackmail, on me? Was that the plan?"

Gretchen nodded coldly. "Yeah. Pretty much."

"But you're saying that somewhere along the line, things changed. You're saying that Jessica really does like me, and that now the two of you want me in this for real."

"That's what I'm saying, yes."

Ariel chewed on this for a moment or two. Her mind was going a million miles a minute as she calculated the many different ways they could be manipulating her.

"So how do I know you're not lying to me right now? How do I know that this isn't all part of your plan to blackmail me?" She almost asked how she could know that this wasn't some elaborate scheme to get revenge on her, but she didn't want to give away too much. If this really was an attempt to punish her somehow, she didn't want them to know that she suspected it.

Ariel looked at Gretchen head on, her challenge suspended in the space between them. If Gretchen were to hover above the ground and fly up toward the moon, Ariel wouldn't have been surprised at all. Not even a little.

"You don't," Gretchen responded matter-of-factly.

"And if I say no?"

Gretchen shrugged. "Then we'll have to find someone else." She sat back down on the lounge chair, tucking her thin legs underneath her. "But it would be too bad if you didn't join us, Ariel. It's fun to get to be someone else. You'd be surprised at how much you learn about yourself."

Ariel sat down again, too. She didn't say anything as she mulled it over. If Gretchen was telling her the truth and they really were her friends, then she'd do it for sure. And if they weren't telling her the truth, and this was all about getting revenge on her somehow—which, she suspected, was the more likely scenario—well, then she still should probably do it. After all, if she joined them, she'd have a better chance of figuring out what they were up to, and she might even be able to beat them at their own game.

"All right," Ariel said, definitively. "I'll do it. I'll be your third."

Gretchen smiled. There was relief in her smile, but Ariel thought she saw something else in there, too. Something she couldn't quite put her finger on. "You've made the right choice, Ariel. I promise you, you're not going to regret it."

I wish I could believe you, Ariel thought.

CHAPTER SEVENTEEN

There were only five rules:

1. *You have to be yourself during school hours.*
2. *Texts only; no talking on your own phone.*
3. *No fooling around with another person's boyfriend.*
4. *Don't let anyone know that you're not who they think you are.*
5. *Spill every single thing that happened when you're back in your own body.*

Ariel was sitting next to Connor on the couch in Jessica's den, fuming as Nick and Jessica snuggled on the loveseat across from them. *Rule Number Three: No fooling around with another person's boyfriend!* she wanted to yell out, as she watched her own head rest on Nick's shoulder. That rule had been added as a joke, or so she thought. She still couldn't believe this was really happening. Couldn't believe that this power was actually real and not some sick joke they were trying to play on her.

The sensation she'd felt when she and Jessica had first projected—the overwhelming warmth that seeped into her, like tropical ocean water filling every crevice of the sea floor—it was very much like a dream. So intense during the actual experience and so slippery when it was over. Except for the cold reality: *I am someone else.* Every time she ran her hand through her hair, she was surprised to find a long and wavy tangle with a texture like boar bristles. Every time she looked down at her hands, she was startled to see the ragged fingernails bitten to the quick, instead of her own slender fingers, neatly manicured in pale pink.

They were supposed to be watching a movie—a stupid action blockbuster Connor had brought over and popped into the DVD player—but Ariel hadn't looked at the TV once. Aside from thinking about how weird it was to be Jessica, all she could focus on was Nick cuddled up with a girl he thought was her.

Connor moved closer and placed his arm around Ariel's shoulders. "What's wrong?" he whispered.

Ariel glanced over at Nick again. He was whispering something into Jessica's—no, into *her*—ear. She felt nauseated as she watched herself giggle flirtatiously. It was hard for her to fathom that her body was right there, doing things independent of her. She remembered what Gretchen had said, about how she sometimes forgot that she wasn't herself. But Ariel wasn't having that problem at all. If anything, she was acutely aware of that fact. Then again, Gretchen probably never had to watch while Jessica broke Rule Number Three right in front of her nose.

"Nothing's wrong," Ariel told Connor. She gave him a

weak smile. "I'm just not feeling great. I think I may have eaten something bad."

Connor blew angrily out of his nose. "Last weekend it was cramps, and now it's food poisoning?"

Ariel crossed her arms in front of herself and moved away from him. "You don't have to be such a jerk," she said.

"Guys," Nick said. "Take it easy, okay? We're supposed to be having fun here."

Jessica smiled. "Save my seat," she joked, as she pushed herself off of the couch. "Can I talk to you?" she asked Ariel, grabbing her hand and pulling her up. Ariel misjudged where Jessica's feet would hit the floor and almost tripped as she stood up. That was one thing Gretchen was right about. Jessica *did* have long legs.

"What do you think you're doing?" Jessica asked, once they were locked inside the powder room.

"Me? What are *you* doing?" Ariel studied her own face: nostrils flaring, cheeks flushed, lips pursed. *Is that really what I look like when I'm angry?*

"I'm trying to maintain your relationship with Nick for you. I'm trying to act like you, so that he doesn't think anything's up."

"Really? Because it looks like you're *trying* to steal him from me."

Jessica laughed. "That's the stupidest thing I've ever heard. He thinks I'm *you*. If anything, I'm making him like you more." Ariel watched as her own eyes rolled at her. "Believe me, if I wanted to steal Nick from you, I'd have done it already."

Ariel took a step back. She didn't know what that was supposed to mean exactly, but any remnant of trust vanished completely. You couldn't put your enemies closer than inside your own body. She felt a prickle of fear. "Now why are you fighting with Connor?" Jessica asked calmly in her voice, the voice she'd heard of herself on a hundred vidoes. "What happened?"

"Nothing. He's putting his hands all over me—all over you, I mean. So I told him that I wasn't feeling well because I don't want to fool around with him. Because I'm actually following Rule Number Three." *And because I'd rather have my eyes poked out with sticks than fool around with Connor Matthews.*

"Look, you just need to pretend a little, okay? I know he doesn't act like it, but he's sensitive, and he's insecure. Just pay some attention to him. Tell him—" She stopped talking at the sound of the front door slamming shut. "Shit," she whispered, fumbling with the lock. "They're home." She glanced at Ariel, assessed her anxiously with her eyes. "Try to say as little as possible, okay? But still act like me. Remember, Michelle knows about projection. We don't want her to be suspicious."

Ariel's heart pounded in her ears. She stood back, waiting for Jessica to take the lead and walk out first. But Jessica pushed her out the door. "This is *your* house, remember?"

Right. Ariel took a deep breath and walked out of the bathroom.

She reached Rob and Michelle just as they were about to walk into the den. "Hi," Ariel said, hoping she sounded casual. "You're home early."

Michelle gave Rob a sour look. "Mr. Personality got into an argument with David Carson, so we left before dessert."

"Whatever. The guy's a total prick," Rob sulked. He glanced over at Jessica, standing slightly behind her. "It's Ariel, right?" he asked.

"Yeah," Jessica answered quickly. "Nice to see you again." But Rob was already ignoring her as he noticed Nick and Connor sitting across from each other in the den. His face lit up.

"Hey, dudes," he said. He went over to Nick and engaged him in a complicated looking fist bump/high five combination. His eyes flashed to the TV screen. "I love this movie," he announced, as he plopped down in the spot where Jessica had been sitting. He put his feet up on the coffee table. Ariel smiled to herself, pleased that Rob had hijacked any further cuddling.

"Hi, I'm Michelle," Michelle said, sticking her hand out for Jessica to shake and giving Ariel a look for not introducing her friend.

"I know," Jessica answered, sweetly. "I've seen you on the news. It's so nice to meet you in person."

Michelle beamed. "Oh, really? Most kids your age don't ever watch the news." She shot Ariel another disapproving look. "Jessica certainly doesn't."

Ariel tried to think like Jessica: snarky, borderline disrespectful. "That's because the news is boring," she snapped.

Jessica flashed a surreptitious grin while Michelle's eyes were still shooting daggers at Ariel. When Michelle turned, Ariel grinned back "Oh, well, I've always wanted to be a journalist, so I watch a lot," Jessica said. "I'd love to talk to you about it sometime."

Now Ariel was trying hard not to laugh. She had absolutely no interest in journalism whatsoever, but she admired the way Jessica so skillfully kissed Michelle's ass. She knew exactly what Jessica was doing: if Ariel was going to be hanging around their house from now on, it couldn't hurt to have Michelle like her. "Of course, any time." She turned back to

Ariel. "You know, Jess, I didn't even tell you this yet, but the station is putting me on a new segment. It's called *Behind the Bust*. They're embedding me with a police unit. I'll interview the officers ahead of time, then take a hidden camera crew when they make arrests. The first one is next month. We're going after a ring of car thieves."

"Sounds like *Cops*," Ariel said, flatly, trying to sound like an unimpressed Jessica. "Didn't that show get canceled?"

Jessica took the cue and jumped right in. "That's so cool," she gushed, looking at Michelle with wide, admiring eyes. "That's, like, real reporting."

"I know, right?" Then Michelle lowered her voice, as if what she was about to say was confidential. "I think I could get some national attention from this. I think it could really launch my career and get me into a bigger market."

Her phone vibrated, and she glanced at it. "Whoa," she said, reading from her screen. "There's a fire up in the mountains. Three hundred acres." She put the phone back in her pocket. "I've got to go to the station, they want me to do a breaking news report." She smiled at Jessica. "It was so nice to meet you, Ariel. You know, I was worried about Jessica coming back to Delphi, but it's nice to know that she's making smart new friends."

Michelle turned her attention to the den. Her face darkened. "I'm leaving, Rob," she snapped.

"Bye," he said, matching her flat tone almost exactly. He didn't turn from the TV.

The second the front door slammed, Ariel stifled a laugh. Jessica did, too. It was like looking in a mirror . . . but it wasn't. For the first time since she switched, she felt comfortable—even empowered. *I could be wrong.* Maybe she could trust Jessica. If this was all about finding the person who

killed Gretchen's mom, she couldn't think of anyone besides
Gretchen who wanted that more than she did. And Jessica was
helping to make that happen. Wasn't she? Did Jessica really
think her own aunt was involved?

Rob pointed the remote at the television and stopped the
movie. "I think you're going to have to watch the rest of this
at your house, ladies," he said to Nick and Connor.

"What?" Connor whined. "But there's only, like, half an
hour left. And the ending's the best part."

Rob glanced at Ariel. "Sorry," he said, not sounding sorry
at all. "But I turn into a pumpkin at . . ."—he looked at his
watch—"exactly ten twenty-three. And look at that, it's ten
twenty-three."

Connor opened his mouth in protest, but Nick shot him a
look and stood up to go.

"Come on, Ariel, I'll drive you home," Nick told her. Ariel
started to walk toward him, but Jessica's glaring look stopped
her in her tracks.

"Coming, Nick," Jessica answered.

So that's what Gretchen meant, Ariel realized with a sudden chill. *You just forget that you're not in your own skin.*
This was bad. The deal was that they would switch back by
the end of the night. Now Jessica was leaving her—leaving
with Nick—and she couldn't think of a reason to ask her to
stay without sounding like a freak.

"I have to go the bathroom," Jessica said.

"Me, too," Ariel replied, taking the cue. "There's one upstairs."

Jessica bounded up the stairs of her own home as Ariel ran
to the front hall bathroom. Once alone, behind the locked
door, Ariel took out her phone and sent Jessica a text with
trembling fingers. I thought we were switching back 2nite?

Jessica texted her back. Need 2 get Gretchen. We'll b back soon.

Another text came right after: B careful w Rob. He's smarter than he looks.

Ariel splashed cold water on her face after a quick look at Jessica's reflection. She opened the door to find Connor waiting for her. He put his arms around her neck apologetically. "Sorry about before. Are you mad?"

"Just a little tired," she lied. "I'll call you tomorrow."

Ten minutes later, Ariel found herself pacing Jessica's messy bedroom. She was alone with Rob now. Jessica had told her all sorts of things about him earlier, and she'd taken notes. For reassurance, she took out her phone and reread them.

Rob plays bass guitar and he thinks every pop song is crap. If you say that you like a song on the radio, he'll know something is up. Don't mention his band or he'll rail about it for hours. He hates chocolate. Call him Rob, not Uncle Rob. He doesn't read. His favorite TV show is Sons of Anarchy. *The lead character is called Jax. His birthday is March ninth. He went to college at UC Santa Barbara. We never discuss my parents. He drinks Red Bull and vodka. His favorite beer is Stella Artois. Don't ask him if he wears bronzer. He does, but he thinks nobody notices. We play Halo together.*

Ariel read through the rest of the list, which was, she realized, mostly useless information that would never come up. *But he's smarter than he looks,* Ariel reminded herself. That was probably the most useful piece of information Jessica could have given her. Because honestly, with his slicked back hair and his super-tanned skin (she *knew* it was bronzer), Rob didn't look all that smart.

"Hey," he called upstairs from the den. "Wanna play some Halo?"

"I thought you turned into a pumpkin," Ariel called back.

"Ha ha," Rob said. "Come on, let's play."

Ariel shrugged and headed down stairs. She was actually pretty good at Halo. She used to play it a lot with some gamer guys she hung out with in middle school before she was popular. But she'd always thought of it as kind of a geeky thing to do. She was actually pretty psyched when she'd learned that Jessica played, too. "All right," she said. She picked up one of the Xbox controllers, and she and Rob chose their weapons.

"So, Ariel's the new Gretchen, huh?" Rob asked. "Ironic, isn't it?"

Ariel shot at an alien on the screen. "What's so ironic about it?"

"Oh, I don't know," Rob said sarcastically. "Maybe that you've replaced her with the girl she thinks killed her mom?"

Ariel's heart almost stopped beating. *So Gretchen does still suspect me.* But she wondered how much Rob really knew. After all, if he thought that she'd replaced Gretchen, then he obviously didn't know that Gretchen and Jessica were still best friends. Or maybe he was just baiting her. "I haven't replaced Gretchen with anyone," Ariel said evenly. She shot at another alien and missed. "Ariel is a friend, the way she always should have been. And Gretchen is still a friend, too."

"Really? That's not what I hear. I hear nobody even talks to Gretchen at school. I hear she's a loser with a capital L."

"And you're hearing all of this from who, exactly?" Ariel was trying to sound playful, like they were just joking around. But she was starting to feel uncomfortable. Why would Rob talk to anyone at their school about Gretchen?

"I have my sources," Rob answered. He paused for a moment to throw a grenade. "I also hear the police might reopen the case. Did you know that?"

"No," Ariel admitted. She hadn't heard that. "Why? Do they have a new lead?"

Rob shrugged. "No idea. But I'm wondering if your new BFF has anything to do with it."

"I don't think so," Ariel answered, maybe a little too forcefully. She tempered her tone. "I think you're just hearing rumors."

"Maybe. But rumors or not, Nick deserves to know that he's dating a potential murder suspect."

Ariel tried not to let her annoyance show.

He glanced at her out of the corner of his eye. "You know, most guys would kill to be like Nick." Rob paused, and his voice became serious. "I used to be like Nick. But I got tied down when I was too young. And I can guarantee you that Nick doesn't want to end up like me."

"Why? What's so bad about you?" Ariel asked. Aliens were coming at them now in droves, and Ariel's thumbs were moving like hummingbirds, wildly shooting at everything in her path.

Rob sighed. "Come on, Jess. Don't be a faker with me. I'm thirty-six years old, and I have nothing to show for it. My life sucks."

Ariel looked at him out of the corner of her eye. *Tread carefully,* she reminded herself. "Well, have you ever considered leaving Michelle if you're that unhappy?"

Rob turned his head away from the screen to look at her. "I'm sorry, were you not actually on the phone all of those times that I called you at boarding school to tell you that I wanted to leave her? Was I talking to someone else all those times when I told you that I was trying to save up enough money to live on my own?"

Ariel's pulse quickened. She was quickly losing her hold on Rule Number Four. Better just to stay quiet.

On the screen, their characters got caught in an explosion and died simultaneously.

"Shit!" Rob shouted. He tossed the remote angrily onto the couch next to him. He turned to look at her. "Look, I'm not leaving her. I'll never have enough money to live on my own, and I'm not willing to get a lawyer and call her bluff. She's crazy, and she's got me trapped. End of story."

Call her bluff? Crazy? Trapped? Ariel found herself enraged at Jessica. *She tells me that he hates chocolate and that he wears bronzer, but she couldn't have mentioned this?* But she knew she couldn't risk asking what he meant by these things; if he and Jessica had already had this discussion, then he'd become suspicious. Besides, she knew above all that she had to trust Jessica and Gretchen above anyone. Even if they were still manipulating her, they shared this secret, this *power*. And it was real. It was more real than anything Rob could offer in the way of excuses for getting out of his relationship with Michelle. An awkward silence fell over the room.

Rob chuckled. "Hey, don't get all depressed, kiddo. I've still got a plan."

Ariel raised her eyebrows. "Oh, yeah? What's that?"

"Let's just say that I'm taking steps to improve the quality of my life from within."

"What are you, like, reading self-help books now?" she asked, hoping that it sounded like something Jessica would say.

"Something like that." He wriggled his eyebrows. "I've just realized that I can physically be with Michelle, but still have a life away from her."

"I guess that's a positive way of looking at it," Ariel

offered. She wondered if this was his way of saying that he was having an affair.

Rob nodded. "Hey, if you see Nick tomorrow, tell him I'll hook him up for Saturday."

"Hook him up with what?" Ariel asked, surprised by how quickly he'd changed the subject.

"Whatever he needs. Some dude on the lacrosse team's having a party."

"So why can't you just give it to him? What do you need Nick for?"

"You were gone a long time, Jess. Maybe if you had come home sometimes you would get how things work around here now."

He sighed, and Ariel detected just the slightest bit of hurt in his voice. *He missed her*, Ariel thought. It was kind of sweet, even if he was a weirdo.

"Let's just say that Nick and I have a mutually beneficial arrangement," Rob continued cryptically. "I scratch his back, he scratches mine."

"What do you mean?" Ariel asked.

But Rob just laughed and shook his head. "It's just an expression." He stood up, ending the conversation, and gave her a light peck on the top of her head. "I'm going to bed, Jess. I'll see you in the morning."

The text from Jessica came almost an hour later.

There in 5. Let us in thru the back door.

Finally, Ariel thought. She'd spent the last hour snooping around in Jessica's room, but she hadn't found anything having to do with projection or with Gretchen's mom's murder, or with what their intentions toward her really were. She wasn't sure what she expected to find, though. Jessica knew she'd be in here. It wasn't like she was going to leave her diary open on the desk for Ariel to read at her leisure. She realized that whatever information she was going to get would have to come from other people. People who didn't know they were really talking to her. Like Rob, for example.

Exhaustion swept over her. It was as if she were in some sick and twisted horror movie: trapped inside another girl's body, accused of committing murder, with her accuser walking around as herself, doing and saying God knows what. She sat down on the bed and put her head between her legs, taking deep breaths in through her nose and exhaling through her mouth. She just wanted to get back to herself. If Gretchen and Jessica really were trying to pin a murder on her, they'd come up with a flawless plan. How better to get revenge than to *be* her—rifling through her things, getting to know everyone who mattered to her. If she hadn't been their target, she would admire the fact that they'd spent two whole years plotting and planning this.

Then again, she'd agreed. She'd gone along with them. What did she have to hide? If they suspected her, they would find out she was innocent. The truth mattered more than anything else. She knew that now.

CHAPTER EIGHTEEN

Sunday morning breakfast had only recently become something of a new ritual for Ariel and her mom. It was practically the only time they were able to spend together anymore. Her mom made a big deal of making her favorite things from when she was little: scrambled eggs, bacon, banana pancakes, chocolate chip waffles drowning in syrup. Ariel knew how much her mom loved cooking for her, so she didn't have the heart to tell her that all she really wanted for breakfast anymore was black coffee and dry wheat toast.

"So," her mom began, facing her across the table. "Tell me what happened in your life this week."

That was always what her mom said on Sunday mornings. Usually Ariel would tell her about tests she'd taken at school; she'd give her the dirt on teachers she liked or couldn't stand; she'd tell her a few, well-edited stories about parties she'd been to or guys she'd been hanging out with. But today, Ariel was finding it hard to talk to her mom at all. After all, what was she going to say? *I learned how to trade souls*

*with a girl who I think really hates me and is trying to frame
me for murder? Or, I watched a movie last night with Nick
and Jessica and Connor at Jessica's house, only I was Jessica and
Jessica was me, and I had to pretend that I like Connor?*

"Nothing much," Ariel answered as she pushed some eggs
around on her plate.

Her mom frowned. "Seven whole days and nothing happened to you? Is something going on with Nick? Are you two
having problems?"

"No, it's nothing like that. Nick's great. I'm just tired,
that's all."

"They say junior year is the hardest," her mom offered
sympathetically. "All that homework while you're also trying
to manage your social life and worry about college." She put
her hand on top of Ariel's. "Have you thought about college
at all?"

Ariel shrugged. "Not really. I mean, I have to take the SATs
this year, but I don't know where I want to go or anything
yet. It's only October, mom."

"I know." She smiled and removed her hand. "I loved college," she said, getting a faraway look in her eyes. "All of
that newness and possibility in front of you. You can totally
reinvent yourself. You can become whoever you want to be."

Ariel looked up at her. Interesting that her mom would
pick now to make a comment like that. "I think I just want to
be myself," she replied.

"Of course you do! I wasn't suggesting that you pretend to
be someone you're not. I just meant that in college, you can
put your past behind you, and nobody has to know anything
about what you were like before. It's not coming out right,
but you'll see what I mean." She paused. "I hear you've been
spending a lot of time with Jessica Shaw lately."

"What is it with adults hearing things about people at my school?" Ariel mumbled, suddenly annoyed.

Her mother smirked. "I used to work at Delphi, honey, and I have friends who still do. I can't help it if they tell me things. Anyway, that girl's had a lot of trouble in her life, hasn't she? Her parents died, and she was part of that video scandal a few years ago, right?"

Ariel didn't even know that her mother knew about the video scandal, let alone who was involved in it. It bothered her that her mom had spies at Delphi who kept her apprised of the gossip there. Ariel had always thought that she alone controlled the flow of information. "Yeah, so what?"

"So, nothing. I just hope she's a nice girl, that's all. I wouldn't want to see you getting in any trouble because of her."

"I'm not going to get in trouble, Mom," Ariel groaned.

"It's just interesting to me that you two connected so fast, that's all. You know, you actually have a lot in common, when you think about it. She's an orphan, and you don't have a father." Her mom's tone soured as it always did. "Well, of course, you have one, we just haven't heard from him in almost seventeen years."

Ariel didn't respond. Her dad had taken off before she was born; she didn't know him, didn't know what life was like any other way. The fact that he never contacted them bothered her mom way more than it ever bothered Ariel.

"Anyway," her mom continued, "it's just interesting. And wasn't she friends with that poor Gretchen Harris? She's another one who lost a parent. The three of you could start your own support group."

As much as she wanted to strangle her mother right now, Ariel had to admit that she'd never thought about this before. They did all have that in common. Plenty of kids at school had parents who were divorced, but she couldn't think of anyone else who had lost a parent—literally, like Gretchen and Jessica, or figuratively, like herself. She didn't know why this suddenly mattered so much to her, but it did.

Ariel was in her bedroom studying for a chemistry test when her phone buzzed. It was Nick. Can I come by?

She texted him back right away. Yeah. Meet u out front?

She was waiting outside for him when he pulled up in his black Ford truck.

"Hi," she said. She jumped over to him and gave him a happy hug, but he pulled away uncomfortably. "What's wrong?" she asked.

"I thought we were in a fight," he answered, sullenly. "I didn't sleep last night at all. It obviously didn't mean that much to you, though."

A fight? Jessica didn't mention anything about a fight when they projected back last night. Ariel's insides began to boil over as she realized what had happened. Jessica picked a fight with Nick and didn't tell her on purpose—deliberately breaking Rule Number Five. Jessica was either trying to break them up or trying to test her. Well, two could play that game. Ariel reached out and pulled him to her. "I'm so sorry, babe. I don't . . . I wasn't myself last night. Jessica gave me something when we went into the bathroom together. She said it would make me feel sexy, but I think it had the opposite effect on me. It made me hostile. I swear I don't even remember fighting with you."

Ariel was pleased with how quickly she'd been able to think on her feet—and implicate Jessica, to boot. But Nick gave her a disapproving look and pulled away again. "You're taking drugs now? Ariel, I'm all for partying, but it's not cool for you to take something and not tell me."

Ariel scoffed. "Oh, so you don't think that's cool, but it's okay for you not to tell me that you and Rob are dealing? Don't you think that's a little hypocritical?"

"Is that what Jessica told you? That I'm dealing?" He shook his head angrily. "I'm not a drug dealer, Ariel. Look, people know I'm friends with Rob, so they ask me to ask him to hook them up. That's it. Neither one of us makes money from it."

So then what's the mutually beneficial relationship you have with him? She was dying to ask him, but she could never explain how, when, or where she and Rob might have come to have that conversation.

"Then why does he do it?" she asked instead.

Nick shrugged. "I don't know. I think the dude just likes for high school kids to think he's cool. I don't get the sense that a lot of adults feel that way about him."

"No, I think you're right about that."

Nick moved close to her again, put his arms around her waist. "You really don't remember fighting with me last night?" he asked.

"I swear I don't. But if I said anything mean, I'm really sorry."

Nick sighed. "Okay. But listen, the next time you take something, just tell me, and we can do it together." He shook his head. "Jessica's cool and all, but that girl is trouble. She's perfect for Connor."

Ariel smiled to herself. If Jessica and Gretchen wanted to keep things from her, then they were going to have to re-strategize. The three of them were a team now, for better or worse. But the smile quickly faded. She couldn't ignore the gnawing realization: the only reason they'd break a rule and

still keep something from her or trick her after they'd projected was because they still must have believed, deep down,
that she'd murdered Gretchen's mother.

In English class on Monday, Ariel stared out the window, trying to block out Mrs. Porter's screechy, high pitched voice.
She'd known that Mrs. Porter was originally from Chicago,
but she'd never noticed before how annoying her accent was,
particularly the way she said her Os. *It's Ah-thello!* Ariel
wanted to scream at her. Not *Aw-thello!*

The knot that had formed in Ariel's stomach since Nick's
visit yesterday was still there. And it was showing no signs of
subsiding. She'd barely slept.

"What do we think about Desdemawna?" Mrs. Porter
asked the class. "Is she just a passive victim of Aw-thello?"

Ariel closed her eyes and rested her forehead on her palm.
She'd read the play just last week, but last week felt like so
long ago.

"He murdered her," someone answered. "I'd say that
makes her a victim."

Ariel flinched at the word *murder*. She just couldn't understand why Gretchen still thought she had anything to do with
her mother's murder. Sure, they didn't get along in the eighth
grade, but murder? It occurred to her that maybe Gretchen
really was crazy. Maybe she and Jessica were lying to her
about boarding school. Maybe Gretchen was in an institution, after all. *And if that's the case, what is she planning on
doing to me?*

"Yes," Mrs. Porter answered. "There's no question that
she's a victim. But is she a *passive* victim? When Awthello
verbally abuses her, does she keep her head down and take
it, or does she stand up to him and assert her own beliefs?"

That's it, Ariel thought. She bolted upright, causing her chair to loudly scratch against the linoleum floor. Everyone turned to stare at her.

"Sorry," she said to no one in particular and slumped back down. The class lost interest and went back to discussing Desdemona, but Ariel was energized. *I can't just sit by and let them frame me for this. I've got to* do *something.* In a moment of terrified clarity, she suddenly saw what she had to do: the only way she could prove to Gretchen that she didn't kill her mother was to prove that someone else did. And once she did that, Gretchen would have no choice but to drop this crazy plot of hers to take Ariel down.

But who, she wondered. *Who would have wanted Mrs. Harris dead?*

When class was over, Mrs. Porter tapped Ariel on the shoulder as she was packing up her things.

"Is everything okay, Miss Miller? I've noticed there's been a lot of staring out the window lately."

Mrs. Porter was the second teacher today to ask her if everything was all right. If she didn't watch it, someone was going to call her mom. "Everything's fine."

Mrs. Porter looked at her skeptically. "Nothing's going on at home? No problems with the boyfriend?"

"No, no. Nothing's going on. I'm just . . . feeling a little overwhelmed. Junior year is really hard. You know, college pressure and all."

"We do have a school psychologist, you know." Mrs. Porter's tone had changed from unconvinced to wearily sympathetic, as if she'd heard this story a thousand times before. "You could go talk to Mrs. Lackman. It's all cawnfidential."

Ariel nodded earnestly, trying not to cringe at the

accent. She hadn't gone to see Mrs. Lackman once this year. But she'd learned that with adults, it was easier to say yes and then ignore them than it was to argue.

"That's not a bad idea," she lied. "Maybe I will."

The days were getting shorter now that it was fall, so they were able to meet at the teepee in the park earlier than they had even just a week ago. Dead leaves loudly crunched beneath Ariel's feet as she approached, and when she ducked her head into the teepee, she found Gretchen and Jessica sitting on the ground, their backs leaning against the curved, molded plastic.

"Hey," Ariel said, pretending not to notice the way the air hung with the uneasy silence of people who'd quickly stopped talking.

"Hey," Jessica said hastily. "Listen, I'm sorry about Nick, okay?"

Ariel cocked her head. She didn't believe a word that came out of Jessica's mouth. "Why didn't you tell me you got in a fight with him?"

Jessica sighed. "I don't know. I mean, I knew you already thought I was trying to break the two of you up, so I didn't want to tell you that I'd started some big fight. I figured it would just blow over. It wasn't important. I broke the rule for your sake."

"What did you fight about?" Ariel demanded.

"He wanted to have sex with you! Starting a fight was the only thing I could think of to get out of it. So I said that I thought he had a thing for me and that I didn't like watching my boyfriend flirt with another girl."

Ariel shook her head. *Unbelievable.* "Really. And what did he say to that?"

Jessica frowned. "He said that I'm not his type. And that

the reason he loves you is because you're so sweet and easy-going, while I'm a pain in the ass, and he doesn't know how Connor deals with me."

Ariel tried not to laugh.

"He's not wrong," Gretchen said. "You are a pain in the ass."

Jessica smacked her playfully on the arm. "Whatever. You're just jealous because you never got past holding hands with him."

The two of them laughed.

Ariel glanced from Jessica to Gretchen and back again. "Wait, Gretchen, you and Nick were together? When?"

"We weren't together," Gretchen corrected. "We held hands for five minutes at the end of eighth grade. It was nothing."

Ariel hesitated. *Great. Add one more reason for her to hate me to the list.* "So, are you mad that he's my boyfriend now or something?"

Gretchen rolled her eyes. "No, Ariel. I was gone for two years. I didn't expect him to wait for me, like some girl whose boyfriend has gone off to war. And anyway, I don't care about Nick Ford anymore. Honestly. I mean, yeah, he's hot shit in Delphi, but spend five minutes in the real world, and you might see him a little differently. But whatever. I'm not even interested in guys right now. I'm not interested in anything except finding out the truth."

Ariel recoiled the slightest bit. Gretchen could be so blunt sometimes. But was she was right? Was Nick just some dumb, provincial lacrosse player from Delphi? And was she too dumb and provincial to even see it? Ariel had never been out of California, let alone out of the country.

"Okay. I'm sorry I asked. It's just still hard for me to

believe that we're really friends. You know, after everything that happened."

Jessica reached out and grabbed Ariel's hand. "Look, Ariel, we were really mean to you in middle school. It was stupid. I don't blame you for putting out that video. I probably would have done the same thing if I were you."

Ariel glanced at Gretchen. Sometimes she felt like they were both just being themselves. Sometimes she felt like they were playing good cop, bad cop with her. It was impossible to know what was really going on. She almost said something—almost just blurted out how she was feeling—but she bit her tongue. It was better just to plow ahead and go along with them. Their power was greater than hers.

"Soooo," Ariel said. "It's you and Gretchen tonight, right? I'm going to be the witness?"

Gretchen looked up. "Actually, I was hoping that you and I could project tonight."

Ariel felt a shiver run down her spine. "I don't understand," she said, keeping her voice even. "I thought that Jessica always had to do it. I thought she was, you know, 'the leader.'" Ariel said this last part in air quotes.

"Whatever. I've been Jessica a dozen times!" Gretchen shouted. "I don't need to be Jessica anymore!"

Ariel put her hands up defensively. "You don't have to get upset. I'm just trying to understand how this works."

"Gretchen and I were talking about it, and we both think that there's no reason why it has to be me every time," Jessica explained, her wary eyes on Gretchen, who was staring at the ground. "Gretchen knows the words. She knows how to do it." She shrugged. "She should have been the one who was chosen anyway."

Ariel tapped her fingers up and down on her jeans. Being

Gretchen could be a huge opportunity for her. She could do some snooping, maybe find out what Gretchen was up to. Maybe even get a better handle on who might have wanted her mother dead. But she didn't trust Gretchen, and she worried about what might happen if Gretchen went around pretending to be her. After all, she could do something that might implicate Ariel in the murder. She could confess to the police, even. It was a gamble any way you looked at it.

Ariel's fingers stopped tapping. Her mom had told her very few details about her father, but she knew one thing about him: on more than a few occasions, he'd almost lost everything he had at a blackjack table in Las Vegas. Gambling was in Ariel's blood. It was part of the reason she liked to shoplift. Or so said Mrs. Lackman . . .

She smiled at the two girls sitting across from her. "Okay then. Let's do it."

Jessica grinned and elbowed Gretchen in the ribs. "Just remember Rule Number Three, Gretch. No fooling around with Nick Ford."

CHAPTER NINETEEN

retchen's house was big. Not mansion big—but big
in a high ceilings, spacious rooms, generous backyard kind of way. She walked through the empty
first floor, recalling how she'd stared at the rooms through a
side window three years ago on the night of their graduation
from eighth grade. Of course, Ariel hadn't been invited to
that party. No, Gretchen had made a point of inviting every
single member of their class *but* her (or so it seemed), so she'd
crashed the party in retaliation. Well, if "crashing" could be
defined as sneaking in through the side gate, looking through
the window, and then chickening out and running away.

The only person who knew she'd gone there was her mom.
At dinner that night they'd argued about it. Ariel had wanted
to show them all that they couldn't just keep pretending that
she didn't exist. Ignoring her wasn't going to make her go
away. But her mom disagreed. She thought crashing the party
would just be giving them exactly what they wanted. *Better
to ignore them back*, her mom had said. *Let them think you*

have better things to do than go to their stupid party. It wasn't until Ariel actually got there and saw them all having fun without her, watched them not even giving her a moment's thought, that she realized her mom was right.

She was still standing outside the window when she heard the screams, and she ran away before she even knew what had happened. The next day, when the murder was all over the local news, her mom had burst into her room with a serious look on her face.

Did anyone see you? she'd asked. She'd been hidden in a shadow, and all she'd done was peer through the window. She hadn't seen anyone, and nobody had seen her. She was sure of it.

You were never there, her mother said sternly. *Whatever happens, you were never there.*

And when the police had knocked on their door that night, asking "routine questions" about whether they were at the party and where they'd been that night, Ariel and her mom were as calm as the ocean on a windless day. They'd gone out to a celebratory dinner, just the two of them, then went home and watched a movie. End of story. It wasn't until a few weeks later that Gretchen had started sending her those texts.

At first, Ariel had been freaked out. *She knows that I was there,* she kept thinking. *Somehow, she knows that I was there.*

Every time the doorbell rang, every time she heard a car pull up in her driveway, she expected it to be the police, coming to take her away. But as time went on and the police never came, and as the texts from Gretchen got stranger and stranger— accusing her of murder and of wanting to bring down the Oculus Society—Ariel started to think that maybe Gretchen didn't know anything after all. That maybe Gretchen was just a sad, grief-stricken girl looking for someone to blame. And then Gretchen went away, and the texts stopped coming, and Ariel had nearly forgotten all about crashing the party that night . . . and had almost convinced herself that it had never even happened. Until now.

Now she climbed the sweeping, curved staircase to the second floor, peering into each of the bedrooms. The first one had no furniture, and the brown Berber carpet was barely visible beneath dozens of boxes. Ariel noticed that the boxes bore labels. *Clothes. Shoes. Paperwork.* It took her a second to understand that these were things that had belonged to Gretchen's mother. These boxes held the remains of someone's life. Ariel shuddered and shut the door behind her.

The next room appeared to be a guest room, but it was lived in. A pair of men's pants were on the floor, a razor perched on the edge of the sink. The bed linens were crumpled. A book was on the nightstand. *Living with Grief.*

Her dad sleeps here, Ariel realized. *He probably can't bear to go in the master bedroom, let alone sleep there.* She couldn't blame him, but Ariel felt compelled to see the scene of the crime for herself. She walked down the hall and found a pair of tall white double doors tightly shut. A beige tassel hung from one of the brass doorknobs. Ariel pulled it . . .

Inside was a king-sized bed that had been stripped of its sheets. On one side was a dark wood nightstand with a mirrored top. On the other side was an identical nightstand covered with fashion magazines, a few pieces of mail, an almost empty glass of water, and a crystal bowl cradling a pair of large diamond studs. Off to the side off the room there was a marble-topped vanity strewn with makeup, a hair dryer, and perfumes. On the mantel over the fireplace was a framed picture of Gretchen and her parents on a beach somewhere.

Ariel quickly shut the door behind her. No wonder Gretchen had gone to boarding school. Ariel couldn't imagine having to live in a place like this; part shrine, part storage space. A halfway house caught between life and death.

Finally, Ariel opened the door to the last bedroom. As she peered inside at the walls painted a pale blue, at the full-sized bed draped in a blue-and-white flowered quilt, she felt like Goldilocks. *This room*, she thought, *is just right.*

She stepped inside and took a slow walk around, examining the pictures taped up on the wall next to Gretchen's bed. Most of them were of Gretchen's mom, a few of Gretchen and Jessica from back in middle school. Ariel recognized one from eighth-grade graduation, right after Gretchen had won the Oculus Society award. She felt a pang of regret; Ariel had been on a vengeful binge that day, fueled by envy and jealousy. She remembered how beautiful Mrs. Harris had looked up on the stage in her white dress and beige heels, her shiny dark hair skimming the olive skin around her tiny collarbone. After everything that happened, she'd felt terrible for the things she'd said. But how could she have known that the woman would be killed later that same night?

She searched through Gretchen's desk drawers where she uncovered a few newspaper clippings and Internet printouts. WOMAN FOUND DEAD IN DELPHI; STRANGLED DELPHI WOMAN WAS PILLAR OF COMMUNITY; NO LEADS IN CASE OF MURDERED MOM FROM DELPHI.

Ariel skimmed the articles, but there wasn't any information in them that she didn't already know. She kept digging. She was just about to move on when she came across a manila envelope at the very bottom of the last drawer, buried under a stack of old report cards and AYSO certificates. Ariel opened the envelope and took out seven or eight file folders, carefully making note of the order in which they were arranged.

Her eyes widened as she flipped through the first few folders. Gretchen had compiled files on half a dozen women, all of whom were in the Oculus Society. There was Tina Holt, the current President. There were two other women Ariel didn't recognize . . . Joan Hedley and Kristen Renwick. And to her surprise, there was Jessica's aunt, Michelle. Ariel's heart began to pound as she opened the last folder. Somehow, she knew what she was going to find, and she was right: it was a file on her.

So these are her suspects.

According to Gretchen's notes, all of these women— except for Ariel, obviously—were part of the innermost sanctum of the Oculus Society, the secret group that guarded the Plotinus Ability. And one of them, Gretchen seemed to think, wanted her mother dead. Ariel flipped through her own file first. There were pictures of her from eighth grade, printouts of the texts she and Gretchen had sent each other, the web address of the video that Ariel had released. The last few pages contained police documents. There was a copy of the police report from the night Ariel and her mom had been questioned. And on the final page, there was a statement Gretchen had given to the police on the night of the murder:

Victim's daughter observed a female, approximately 5'5", dark blonde hair (shoulder length), slim build, entering northwest gate of property at approximately 9:00 P.M. Witness believes this person may have been one Ariel Miller, age 13.

Ariel's hands began to shake. Gretchen had seen her. Of course she had.

Her eyes skimmed down to the follow-up section at the bottom of the page, in which the detective had handwritten a note. It was dated July seventh, nearly three weeks after the murder.

No person interviewed could recall seeing Ms. Miller or anyone who fit her description. Further, we could find no reason to doubt the validity of Ms. Miller's alibi. According to interviews with Ms. Miller and her mother, the two were home watching a movie at the time of the murder. Therefore we have no to cause to believe that Ms. Miller is a suspect in this investigation. Recommendation: no further action required.

Ariel took a few deep breaths and tried to compose herself. The detective who interviewed her had never mentioned that anyone thought they'd seen her at the party. But that was probably the point. He wouldn't want to tip her off.

So that's why she thinks I killed her mom. She actually saw me at the party just moments before the murder.

Ariel closed her eyes and forced herself to breathe evenly. She turned to the file on Michelle. Inside was a slick black-and-white headshot that Ariel assumed Michelle used for auditions, and a photograph of Michelle and Rob at an Oculus Society event. The photo was a few years old; Rob was in a suit, but he'd taken off his tie and loosened his collar. His hair was a little bit longer than it was now, but still slicked back in his signature look.

Michelle's hair was shorter, and she looked stunning in a red dress and simple gold hoops. There was another photograph, too, of Gretchen's dad with four other men. All were wearing golf shirts and standing in front of the snack bar on the ninth hole at the Club. Gretchen had circled one of the men's faces with a red pen. Ariel recognized him from when she'd worked at the Club. His name was Mr. Renwick. Mike Renwick. She didn't understand the significance of his presence, though, or why he'd be circled in a picture in Michelle's file. Frankly, she didn't understand why Gretchen would suspect Michelle at all.

Ariel was arranging the folders back in order when a chime rang on an alarm pad in the hallway, causing her to startle.

Garage door open, said a robotic voice. She quickly placed them back inside the envelope and put it back under the report cards and certificates where she'd found it.

"Gretch?" came a voice from downstairs.

Mr. Harris: home from work. Ariel closed the drawer to the desk and took a quick glance in the mirror. There was Gretchen's face, staring calmly back at her. She ran a hand over her hair to smooth it out and walked toward the bedroom door.

"Hi, dad!" she called.

Gretchen's dad had brought home take-out; Caesar salad and *"your favorite, Gretch,"* pizza with olives and green peppers. Ariel tried not to frown as she sat down at the kitchen table. She hated Caesar salad, and olives made her gag.

"So how was your day?" Mr. Harris asked as they settled in.

Ariel wasn't sure how to answer. She didn't know if Gretchen's dad was aware of his daughter's faux-loser status or if Gretchen just lied and told him everything was great. She decided to go with that old, teenaged standby that seemed to work in every awkward parental situation.

"Fine."

Mr. Harris frowned. "More of the same?"

"What do you mean?"

"I mean, the kids still aren't talking to you?"

Ariel shrugged. "Whatever, Dad. I really don't care." She took a bite of the pizza, resisting the urge to pick off the olives first. *Mmm*, she thought, surprised. *This is actually kind of good.*

"I just don't understand why you insisted on coming back, Gretchen. There's nothing here for you. And you and Jessica were doing so great at Chadwell." He smiled ruefully. "To tell you the truth, I was really starting to like England. I'm going to miss having Christmas there this year."

Ariel was glad to know that at least that part of their story hadn't been a lie. She met Mr. Harris's eyes. "You're here," she said.

He sighed. Ariel got the feeling that they'd had this conversation many times before. "I've told you, sweetie, you don't have to worry about me. I'm fine."

"Great," Ariel said, smiling. "And I'm fine, too. So we can be fine together."

Mr. Harris laughed, but his eyes still looked sad. "Touché."

There was a long silence as they both ate their pizza. Gretchen had warned her before they'd projected that she and her father weren't the greatest of communicators, but she hadn't realized it was this strained between the two of them. Ariel thought of her own mother and how she could talk about anything with her. She couldn't imagine things being this tense between them. Gingerly, Ariel broached the subject she was really interested in.

"So, um, have you heard anything about the police re-opening the case?"

Mr. Harris gave her a sharp look. "Gretchen," he said, in a practiced tone, "the police are not reopening the case. They have no leads. They have no suspects. You need to stop obsessing over it. Your mother wouldn't want this. She would want you to go on with your life."

Every muscle in Ariel's body relaxed upon hearing these words. She hadn't even realized she'd been so tense. She wanted to reach across the table and hug Mr. Harris. But he'd become suspicious if Ariel didn't act like his daughter. So she clenched her fists, like she'd seen Gretchen do that night in her backyard.

"Really?" she asked, raising her voice. "You think she'd want her murderer running loose around town? You think she wouldn't want someone to pay for what they did to her?"

Mr. Harris had tears in his eyes. "Honey, we all want justice," he said, his voice hoarse. "But the police can't just go around arresting people without any evidence."

"Yeah? Well, what about Mike Renwick?" Ariel's heart was pounding. She was fishing for information, but it was like fishing blindfolded and with both hands tied behind her back.

"What about him?" Mr. Harris asked. He sounded dumbfounded.

"Where was he the night of the party?"

"He was here. Why? What do you know about Mike Renwick?"

Ariel set her jaw. "I know he has something to do with Jessica Shaw's aunt."

Gretchen's father blushed the color of a Christmas card. *Oh, my God,* Ariel thought, suddenly understanding.

"I don't know what you heard, but Mike had nothing to do with mom. He's a good man, Gretchen. Yes, he made a mistake, but whatever happened between them is over." He lowered his voice. "He's got a wife and kids, honey. There's no need to ruin any more lives, okay?"

Ariel looked down at the floor, chastened. "Sorry," she mumbled. But inside she wondered if Rob knew about the affair. Was that part of the reason why he wanted to leave Michelle? And what *about* Michelle? Had Mike Renwick been her only indiscretion, or were there others?

Mr. Harris suddenly pushed away from the table and stood. For a second, she thought he might leave. Instead, he walked to her and wrapped his arms around her. His hug felt comforting and unconditional, still sturdy beneath his grief. Not like Nick's hugs, with their undercurrent of neediness and sex. It occurred to Ariel that she'd never been hugged by a father before. She swallowed back a hard lump in her throat.

"It's okay," he whispered. "I know you're hurting, sweetie. I am, too. But you have to stop trying to figure this out on your own. The police will find out who did this. I'm sure of it. We just have to be patient."

Even a full twenty-four hours after they'd switched back, Ariel couldn't shake the sadness she'd felt as Gretchen. Everything she'd ever thought about the girl had been turned on its head. Sitting here with Nick in the backseat of his car—as she had so many times before in the past few weeks—she only felt half-present, even as his arm crept lazily over her shoulder. She knew she had to snap out of it.

"Earth to Ariel," he teased.

"I'm sorry," she whispered.

"Are you sure you're okay?"

She nodded. At least Gretchen had made up an excuse

while in Ariel's body that she didn't feel well and couldn't see him. According to her mom, she'd spent the night alone in Ariel's room, feigning illness. Which was fine by her . . .

"What are you thinking?" Nick prodded.

"Is it true that you used to like Gretchen?"

Nick rolled his eyes. "What, so now you think I have a crush on her, too? Really?"

"No. I just heard that you two had a thing a few years ago. Did you like her?"

"Yeah, I guess. She was cool back then." He shrugged. "I feel bad for her. I don't get why Jessica won't talk to her anymore. They used to be inseparable."

Ariel's heart sped up. "I know. I don't really understand it, either," she lied.

Nick gave her a knowing look. "I told you: Jessica's a pain in the ass."

Ariel managed a laugh. "No, she's not."

"Yeah, she is. She's bossy, and she's manipulative, and she doesn't give up until she gets what she wants. But I guess it's understandable, given her situation."

"What do you mean? What situation?"

Nick looked at her sideways. "The girl lost both of her parents, Ariel. And the people taking care of her are certifiable."

"Michelle and Rob? I thought you loved Rob."

"That dude's weird, man. I used to think he was cool, but lately . . . I don't know."

Ariel sat straight and twisted in the seat. "How is he weird? Did something happen?"

He turned his head away so that she couldn't look him in the eye. "He's just . . . I don't know. He's been acting really strange. He keeps talking about this secret he wants to share with me. It's creeping me out."

Now her heart was racing. "Did he say anything else?"

Nick shook his head. "Not really."

"What do you think it is?"

"I don't know. All I know is that he's gotta figure out a way to leave Michelle. He's always talking about how trapped he is, how she makes him feel like a caged animal. Dude's gonna completely lose his shit if he doesn't find a way to get out of there soon."

"Why doesn't he just leave her?" she asked, narrowing her eyes. It hadn't occurred to her that Nick might have the answers she was looking for.

Nick smirked. "Money, for one thing. He hasn't had a real job, in like, ever."

"For one thing," Ariel repeated. "Is there another thing?"

Nick looked uncomfortable, as if he'd been caught telling a lie. "He made me swear not to say anything."

Ariel held her breath. She was on to something here, she could feel it. There was a reason why Gretchen had a file on Michelle, and she was about to find out what it was.

"Come on, Nick," she urged. "I'm not going to say anything."

"Do you promise? Because if Jessica finds out about this, Rob will be pissed *off*."

"I get it. I swear I will not say anything to Jessica or to anyone else."

Nick let out a resigned sigh, as if he knew that he was about to make a huge mistake. "Okay. So, we were hanging out at the Club over the summer one day, and it was happy hour and he starts drinking, and he gets, like, totally shitfaced. And all of a sudden he starts to cry. And I'm, like, 'Dude, what's up with you?' And he tells me that he wants to leave Michelle but he's too afraid, because she's so unpredictable, and he doesn't ever know what she might do. He made it sound like she's unstable, you know? And I'm like, 'Dude, it can't be that bad. If you want to leave her, you just have to do it, and whatever she does won't be your problem anymore.'"

Ariel nodded. "Makes sense."

Nick shook his head. "But he's all, no, you don't understand, it's not that simple. And then he tells me how they got in this fight once, a few years ago, I think. He told her that he wanted to leave her, and she was all, yeah, with what money? And he was, like, with your money. 'Cause California's a community property state or whatever, so she would have to pay him alimony for, like, ten years, I think. And she got all calm and quiet, and she told him that if he ever even thought about trying to leave her, she would kill him. And he said that she wasn't just saying it as an expression. She meant it." He finally turned to look her in the eye. "For real."

CHAPTER TWENTY

G emina was already sitting in the garden, staring down the hillside at the glittering marble of Rome by the time Amphiclea arrived for breakfast. It had been three days since Plotinus had gotten himself imprisoned, and Castricius had shown no sign of changing his mind to help them.

Amphiclea felt sick to her stomach as she took in Plotinus's hunched figure. *Oh, my poor Gemina,* she thought. *Trapped in that old man's body.*

"Good morning," Amphiclea said, hoping that her voice sounded more cheerful than she felt. Her husband Kleitos had agreed right away to allow little Gaia to stay with them while her mother was in jail, but it had taken some convincing before he had agreed to allow Plotinus to stay as well. Amphiclea didn't dare tell him the truth for fear that he might react the way Castricius did, but ultimately, she'd been persuasive.

He's dedicated his life to philosophy, she'd argued. *He has no way to live without patrons.* And when that didn't work, she'd appealed to his insecurities. *He's a great philosopher, known*

throughout all of Rome and Greece. It can only help your repu-
tation to be associated with him. People will think so highly of
us—of you! Do you remember how all the senators and scholars
clamored to be invited to Castricius's dinner table, all so they
could engage with Plotinus? That could be us! Think of it: the
Aristons, exclusive patrons of the brilliant Plotinus.

Kleitos had sent for Plotinus to be moved in the very next
afternoon.

"Good morning," Gemina answered, allowing a weak
smile to cross Plotinus's pale lips. She turned back to where
she'd been staring, and Amphiclea soon saw that she hadn't
been looking out at all of Rome. Rather, she was watching
Gaia toddling through the grass beyond them with one of
Amphiclea's young servants.

"She doesn't want to play with me," Gemina said flatly
without turning to look at Amphiclea. "She doesn't know
that I'm her mother."

Amphiclea's eyes welled up with tears. Though she didn't
yet have a child, this, she knew, was a fate worse than death.
She put her hand on Plotinus's thin shoulder. "We'll get it
straightened out, Gemina. We'll get you back to yourself, and
she'll know you once again. I promise."

Gemina turned to look at her, and Amphiclea was taken
aback by the familiar blaze of her best friend's eyes, staring
out through Plotinus's face. "And then what?" she asked.
"I spend the rest of my life in jail, and she'll know me only
through metal bars?"

Amphiclea swallowed. She'd considered this herself, of
course, but wouldn't allow the thought to take residence.
"Let's get you back to yourself," Amphiclea said, trying to
sound reassuring, "and then we can worry about gaining
your freedom."

"How, Amphiclea? Castricius won't help me. He won't even speak to me. What do you propose we do?"

Amphiclea took a deep breath, then spoke the words she'd spent the whole night before convincing herself of. "Plotinus got you both into this mess for believing that women are just as strong as men. It might not be legal for him to have written what he did, but he's not wrong, Gemina. We don't need Castricius. We can do this ourselves." She reached across the table and placed her hand over Gemina's. "I have a plan."

Amphiclea walked hurriedly to the jail, holding a small lantern in front of her to light the way. In the dark, every noise seemed amplified and threatening, every lamp in every window seemed pointed at her. She put her hand inside the bag she carried—something she'd been doing every few moments since she left her house—and fingered the coins inside. She'd told Kleitos yesterday that she needed some extra money for the market, and he'd given it to her without question, just as she knew he would. He may not be a handsome man, she thought, but he was generous, and he treated her well.

Amphiclea turned the corner, feeling her whole body stiffen and heat up as the dark, looming jail building came into view. She held the lantern she was carrying up high, lowered it for a count of ten, then held it up high again. She did this two more times. A moment later, a hooded, male figure stepped out of the shadows.

Gemina.

Amphiclea resisted the urge to run to her for an embrace.

"You know what to do?" Amphiclea asked. Gemina nodded, and Amphiclea handed her the bag with the coins in it. "Then let's go."

Gemina led the way up the steps to the jail. She walked, as Amphiclea had instructed, confidently and heavily. As a man would. Amphiclea followed, staying a few subservient feet behind. She remained at the top of the steps as Gemina opened the door and disappeared inside.

The jail was damp and foul-smelling, and Gemina's stomach dropped as she imagined Plotinus in such a place, then dropped further again as she imagined herself there. The impossibility of her situation had caused a hard, solid lump to form in her throat, but she pushed it down and composed herself just as the sleepy, rumpled-looking guard noticed her.

"Can I help you?" He was young, about her age. He was handsome, too, with green, almond-shaped eyes that stood out against his dark skin. Gemina reminded herself that to him, she was just an old man. Her feminine charms would be of no help to her in this situation. She pulled the hood off of her head, revealing Plotinus's whole face.

"I am the philosopher Plotinus. Your prisoner, Gemina, is my patron and friend. It's urgent that I speak to her."

The guard shook his head. "I'm sorry, sir, but I can't let you see her."

Gemina had been expecting this. She knew that female prisoners were not allowed to have male visitors other than their husbands. That's why Amphiclea had come. And once Amphiclea had gone in, she would bribe the guard to allow her to accompany her friend.

"No, you don't understand. The woman caring for her child is here, outside. She needs to speak to her. It's imperative."

The guard frowned and shook his head again. "I'm sorry, sir, but I can't allow her any visitors."

Gemina clasped her hands behind her back to keep them from shaking. This was not going as planned. She hadn't counted on the guard being difficult. "What is your name?" she asked, angrily.

"Marcus, sir." He met her eyes, and in them she recognized a quiet outrage. *Something is happening here that I don't understand,* she thought.

Gemina lowered her voice. "I can pay you," she whispered, holding out the pouch with the coins inside.

But Marcus shook his head. He looked at her apprehensively. "Are you really her friend?" The note of tender concern in his voice was unmistakable. A deep blush spread from Gemina's cheeks to the tips of her fingers as she suddenly understood what was going on.

"Yes. I know her better than anyone. Better than she even knows herself. And Amphiclea, the woman outside—they are practically sisters."

Marcus's eyes were moist and had a look of torture in them. "It's all my fault," he moaned. His buried his face in his hands.

"What is your fault?" Gemina asked.

"I thought I was helping her!" he exclaimed, removing his hands. "It was I who gave her husband the paper she wrote. But only because I didn't want it to be used against her! I thought he would tear it up. How could I have known that he would instead turn it over to the magistrate?" He shook his head, agonized. "She'll be tried for treason now, and there's no doubt that she'll be executed."

A rage boiled at the base of Gemina's spine, radiating hot waves of anger through her entire body. She knew that Castricius was a vindictive man, but this was unthinkable. He would have her executed for treason? Did he care nothing for her at all? For their daughter?

"We must see her," she implored.

Marcus nodded. "I only said you couldn't because I was trying to protect her. After Castricius . . . I have no way of knowing who can be trusted."

Gemina pressed the pouch of coins into his hand. "You can trust us."

It was a relief to find the living conditions inside the warden's office to be satisfactory, though as Marcus shut the door behind her and Amphiclea, Gemina felt a wave of panicked nausea wash through her.

I'm going to die, she thought. *I'm going to die, and my own husband is the executioner.*

"It's wonderful to see you both," Plotinus said. His voice was lighthearted, and it struck Gemina as inappropriate under the circumstances. But then it occurred to her that perhaps he wasn't fully aware of the circumstances. Would Marcus have told him about Castricius, or did he think he was he protecting her from the truth as well as from traitors? Gemina was afraid to ask.

"Our guard Marcus is quite taken with you," Plotinus laughed. "He was blinded by your beauty from the moment I arrived. And thank goodness, because he's given me special treatment. I don't imagine the other prisoners receive sprigs of lavender and fresh figs each morning!"

Despite the dire situation, Gemina was flattered; she studied her own face smiling back at her, trying to see what Marcus saw. It was filthy and gaunt. But her cheeks were still pink, and her dark hair still appeared luminous. Of course, that could have been the candlelight . . .

"Well," Amphiclea replied, "that's one kind of power women have that men don't."

At this, Plotinus's expression sobered. "Yes, that's quite true. But it's no replacement for the real thing. I understand you told Castricius about our experiment. I assume you showed him the journal and the anklet?"

Amphiclea nodded. "He was less than sympathetic."

"Yes, his actions with the magistrate led me to believe as much."

So he did know. Gemina was using all her strength to hold back her tears as the reality of her situation took hold. She was going to live the rest of her short life in this tiny room without Amphiclea, without Gaia, without her family. And then she would be dead; hung, or thrown to the bottom of the sea, or worse. It was the cruelest fate she could imagine.

"Let's just do this, Plotinus," she managed to say. She knew that if she uttered another word, the floodgates would open and might never close.

"Do what?"

"Project!" she shouted at him as a tear escaped from her eye and dripped down her cheek. "Amphiclea has done her duty as our witness. She's arranged for us to meet so that we may return to our rightful bodies." She watched as a look of shock crossed her own face.

"And have you face execution?" Plotinus asked. He sounded bewildered. "Is that why you came here? To project?" He crossed the tiny room and put his arm around her shoulder. "My dear Gemina, you brave, brave girl. I would never allow you to take my place here."

"Then what do we do, Plotinus?"

"We stay as we are," he answered, as if the matter were just that simple.

"But I'm you!" she cried.

"And I'm you. And I shall die as you. But I'm not afraid of death, Gemina. Remember what I taught you? Our bodies are merely vessels for our souls. When the body is gone, the soul returns to The One."

Gemina began to shake. She could almost feel the old man's bones rattle around in the saggy bag of flesh that she was forced to negotiate. But the terror began to subside, replaced by black hopelessness. No matter what he said about The One, she would live out the rest of her life as Plotinus, as a philosopher with no philosophical thoughts, as a childless, unmarried man filled with the instincts and love of a mother.

Amphiclea hugged her as if she could read her mind.

"You'll live with me," she said. "You and Gaia. We'll tell her you're her uncle. She'll come to love you."

"No," Plotinus said, interrupting. "No. I will die as you, Gemina, but there is only one thing I ask in return."

"What, Plotinus? Anything."

"We can't allow this to happen in vain. This ability to project . . . I see it now for what it is. It's power. I'm not talking about the magic. In the right hands, it can tip the scales of human justice. Gemina, promise me that you will never tell any man of this power. We men will take it for granted, like everything else."

He took Gemina firmly by the shoulders and looked her in the eye.

"When Gaia is old enough, you must tell her the truth. Tell her who you really are and about what happened to us. And then you must teach her this power, Gemina, and she must teach her daughter in turn. Don't allow it to die with me and you. Let it live for the ages. Let it become a power for the powerless."

Gemina felt a surge of electricity course through her veins. It had never occurred to her to tell the truth, but now the thought of being able to tell Gaia one day—to let the little girl know that her mother is with her—it gave her a glimmer of hope.

"You have my word, Plotinus," she whispered. "This ability—the Plotinus Ability—it will live on. I promise." Before she could dissolve in tears, she turned from her own smile for the very last time.

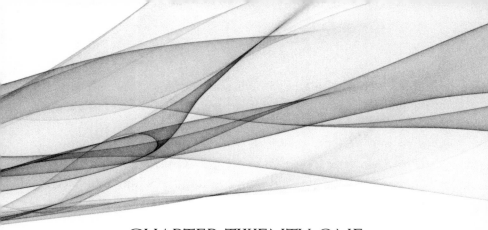

CHAPTER TWENTY ONE

Jessica watched as Tina Holt lifted her crystal gavel into the air above the wooden podium at the front of the room. She found it hard it to take Tina seriously as President. Jessica had seen her dance on the tables one too many times at the annual Oculus Society Christmas party.

"I'd like to call for a vote on the theme of this year's holiday gala. All those in favor of a masquerade ball say 'aye.'"

A chorus of 'ayes' broke out among the members of the Oculus Society, all of whom were sitting on plastic folding chairs that had been set up in the small room where the monthly, Thursday afternoon meetings were always held.

Jessica had a vague, hazy memory of an Oculus Society meeting taking place at her old house, where she lived with her parents before they died. She must have been four or five at the time. Still, she remembered the smell of fresh flowers and the hurried sense of importance that her mother carried as she readied the house. The images were fragmented: silver, metal folding chairs; the parquet wood of the dining room table laid out with fancy bowls and platters; coats piled up in the guest bedroom. It must have been one of the last meetings they ever held at a member's home, because a few months after her parents' accident, the Oculus Society bought a former Masonic lodge. Once suitably renovated with cream-colored walls, dark wood floors, and tufted white upholstery, the building became the new headquarters for all Oculus operations.

"All those opposed?" Tina glanced around the room, the look on her face daring anyone to utter a 'nay.' Once the requisite period of silence had passed, Tina lowered the gavel with a soft *thud*. "Masquerade ball it is, then."

The official Oculus Society bylaws stated that members were expected to refrain from using cell phones during meetings. Jessica disregarded this rule, as she felt that the Oculus Society should refrain from making meetings so painfully boring. Still, she didn't want to flaunt her disobedience. As she alternately texted Connor and checked Instagram, she held her phone behind the meeting agenda, which she'd propped up vertically in her lap. A text appeared from Connor:

I want 2 hump u.

Jessica rolled her eyes. Connor did have a sweet, endearing side to him, but then he'd bust out with something like this that just made her want to smack him. The guys in Delphi were so lame. Even Nick had turned out to be a huge disappointment. To think she'd been so jealous the night of Gretchen's graduation party, when Nick had held Gretchen's hand. And they had flirted with each other that summer at the Club, and Gretchen was furious, even though she'd never said so. Jessica would be a liar if she didn't admit she hadn't thought about him while she was in England. She'd built him up to be some kind of god: hot, athletic, popular.

So of course, Ariel had fallen for him. She'd never left Delphi, so she still believed in the myth of Nick Ford. Jessica knew that Ariel would start to see the cracks in Nick sooner or later—she wasn't stupid. And in the meantime, if Jessica wanted to keep hanging out with Ariel and Nick, she would have to suck it up and pretend that she was into Connor Matthews. It was the only way the plan would work.

There was a tap on her shoulder, and Jessica quickly shoved the phone underneath the paper she was holding. *Michelle.* Jessica looked up guiltily, expecting to be reprimanded—her aunt took the Oculus Society *so* seriously—but Michelle didn't comment on the infraction. She didn't say anything at all, just tilted her head, signaling that Jessica was wanted in the back room.

Jessica raised her eyebrows.

There hadn't been a backroom meeting since the video of Jessica and Gretchen kissing had gotten out two years ago, and it had been suggested that Jessica "distance" herself from the Oculus Society for a while. Michelle shrugged, as if to say that she had no idea what was going on, either.

Jessica held her breath as she followed Michelle down a narrow passage behind the main stage. Joan Hedley handed them white robes as soon as they stepped inside, and Jessica immediately slipped hers over her jeans and T-shirt. She was nervous, though she couldn't put her finger on exactly why. Joan and Kristen Renwick were already robed, and they took their places at the table. A few moments later Tina Holt joined them and took her spot in the middle of the group. Jessica could hear the muffled sounds of women talking in the other room now that the meeting had been adjourned.

Tina cleared her throat and took a sip of water from a

glass she'd carried in from the general meeting. She held a piece of folded-up paper in her other hand.

"Ladies, welcome back. I've called this meeting to let you know that we're officially dissolving the board, as its purpose of protecting the Plotinus Ability is no longer required."

Michelle interrupted with a question. "Sorry, but didn't that purpose end two years ago when we lost the anklet? Why are you doing this now?"

Tina nodded. "As you know, we've been actively searching for the anklet since it was lost."

Jessica raised her hand. Her heart was wildly beating, and she desperately hoped no one else could hear it. Tina nodded at her to speak. "What does that mean, exactly, that you've been 'actively searching' for the anklet?"

"While you were away, Jessica, we were in contact with the police regarding the anklet, and we also hired a private investigator on behalf of the Oculus Society to try to find it."

Jessica blanched. The police? A private investigator? She was horrified. *Gretchen must not know about any of this.* Of course not. She tried to stay calm and to appear only mildly interested. "And did they find anything?"

Tina shook her head. "Nothing. I've been arguing with the police to try to get them to reopen the case, but until someone produces a real lead, they're not willing to—and I quote—'invest the resources.'" Tina sighed. She looked sad and tired. Jessica realized that it must be killing her that this happened on her watch as President. After thousands of years of protecting the Plotinus Ability, Tina Holt was the woman responsible for its demise.

"Anyway, I think it's time for us to move on. The anklet has vanished, and as such, so has the Plotinus Ability. However, I'd like to propose that we create a document compiling all of the known information about Plotinus, the anklet and the role the Oculus Society has played in protecting it. There's nothing written down in the archives about how all of this works. One day the anklet might find its way back to us again, and it will be important that whoever is in charge then knows what to do with it."

Jessica felt sick to her stomach. She wanted to shout out to them that the Plotinus Ability was alive and well, and that the anklet had nothing whatsoever to do with projecting. *It's just an anklet,* she wanted to scream. *It doesn't have magical properties!* But of course, she couldn't say anything. Not unless she wanted to admit to everyone that she'd lied two years ago when they'd asked her why she and Gretchen had been kissing late at night in a plastic teepee on the far corner of a playground.

We were just experimenting, she'd been forced to say. *We were curious.*

And never mind how angry they would be if they knew that she'd told Gretchen about the Plotinus Ability in the first place. She couldn't even begin to imagine what would happen if they knew that she and Gretchen had been projecting all this time. Not to mention that they'd recruited a girl *not* in the Oculus Society both to project and to be a witness. The very girl who videotaped them and accused the Oculus Society of terrible hypocrisy in the first place . . .

Jessica sat rigid in her chair and didn't say a word.

"I propose the following division of labor," Tina continued. "Each of us will be responsible for one section of the master document, and each of us will retain a full copy." She slipped on a pair of reading glasses and smoothed out the paper she'd been holding. "I'll deal with the actual process of projecting: how it's physically accomplished, what needs to be said, the anklet, etc. Kristen, you do the history of how the Oculus Society came to be in possession of the anklet. Joan, you report on the OS members who were formerly chosen to project. I think you only need to go back ten years or so, and, um,"—she cleared her throat—"don't include anyone who isn't living. Michelle, since you're a journalist, I think you'd be best to handle the murder and the subsequent investigations. Request copies of the police reports, and I'll get you the file from our private investigator. And Jessica, I'd like you to research Plotinus's life."

Jessica stared at her. "What do you mean?"

"I mean, treat this like the research project that will get you into the college of your choosing," Tina snapped.

Glaring back at Michelle's friends was something Jessica had never had trouble with. But for the first time in her life, she saw Tina's face. The crow's feet. The purple under her eyes. The quivering lips. And still, the authority.

"I'm sorry," Jessica whispered.

"Save it," Tina said. "I want you to access his beliefs, how he came to project, who he projected with, and his death. Our archives will be totally available to you." She gravely looked around at them all. "I can't stress to you all how important this is. We are the keepers of an ancient secret. It's our responsibility to preserve it in whatever way we can."

Tina hit the light switch and gave a curt nod, signaling for them all to clasp hands with each other. She closed her eyes and spoke softly in Greek.

"*Empistosýni mas kai ti n písti mas tha férei ti dikaiosýni. Af tí eínai i ypóschesi pou pani gyriká kratí sei.*"

"Our trust and our faith shall bring justice. This is the promise we solemnly keep," translated the rest of them in unison.

Jessica opened her eyes and took a furtive glance around; they were all beautiful women, made even more so by the flickering candlelight. *Is it really even possible,* she wondered, *that one of them is a murderer?*

Just before lunch the next day, Jessica met Gretchen outside the boiler room of the school on a small patch of grass sandwiched between a brick wall and a tall, leafy hedge. It was one of the few spots at Delphi where they could talk unseen by anyone else.

Jessica had noticed that Gretchen had been even more down than usual lately; she was upset, of course, that they hadn't found her mother's killer yet. But there seemed to be more. Her usual slouch had turned into more of a slump, and her eyes seemed dull and almost always on the verge of filling up with tears. All of the sparkle that Gretchen had once had—even after her mother had died—seemed to have completely deserted her. So Jessica was relieved to see Gretchen's face perk up as she heard the news about the private detective; the color came back to her cheeks, and she lifted her head straight. She began to pace the grass.

"The most important thing," Gretchen said, jabbing her finger into the air, "is that you get a hold of whatever they give Michelle." She clenched her hands into fists. "I can't believe they had a private investigator looking for the anklet! You've got to get those files, Jess. I've got to know what this guy was looking into. *Who* this guy was looking into—"

"But he didn't find anything," Jessica reminded her. She was worried about not being able to manage Gretchen's expectations. She didn't know how well Gretchen could handle being disappointed again. "I'm not sure it's going to be the smoking gun you think it is."

"No shit, Jessica. But there might be something that I missed or something that means something to me that meant nothing to him. I just want to see it." She looked pointedly at Jessica, her face a steely mask of resolve. "And if you can't get it, then we'll project, and I'll do it myself."

Jessica chewed anxiously on her lower lip. She loved Gretchen like a sister, but her obsession had become exhausting. Obviously, she empathized with her. After all, Jessica had lost both of her parents, and if there had been someone to blame—if it hadn't been a simple car accident in the rain—she would have been the first one to try to bring them to justice. So she supported Gretchen in her quest to uncover the truth, she really did. But two years had already come and gone.

Granted, life had been easy and almost surreal while they were at Chadwell. They'd lived and plotted together all that time, day in and day out. Together they'd built Ariel up in their minds into a kind of mythic, menacing evil. And while they were there—thousands of miles away from Delphi and everyone associated with it, deliberately off of Facebook, off of Twitter, off of Instagram, so that nobody from Delphi could contact them or find out where they were—Jessica had been able to buy into the idea that Ariel might have been . . . well, if not responsible for the murder, then at least involved, somehow. And so she went along with Gretchen's plan. Go back to Delphi pretending to hate each other. Lure Ariel in with the prospect of popularity. Make her feel like they're really friends, then blackmail her into projecting with them. Use her to get information, and when the time was right, exact revenge for what she did to them. And if they were able to prove—as Gretchen suspected—that Ariel had something to do with the murder, then they'd turn her in to the police.

But the plan had gone awry from day one. For one thing, Ariel wasn't the monster that they'd imagined her to be. It was obvious that she regretted what she'd done to them—had been suffering for what she'd done to them. And worse, at least from a certain point of view and to her own great surprise, Jessica actually *liked* her. Ariel was funny and cool and fearless, and she'd been honest with Jessica about her problems: her shoplifting, her absentee father, her feelings about Nick. Jessica had wanted, a few times, to tell Ariel what she really thought—that Nick was kind of a meathead and that she was, frankly, too good for him—but she'd restrained herself. Rather than being angry about what Ariel had done to them, Jessica had ended up feeling badly about how she had treated Ariel in middle school. They hadn't counted on her already being popular, either, although ultimately, that had worked to their advantage. As an outsider, Ariel had nothing to lose if she said no to their offer. But as the most popular girl in eleventh grade . . . well, she couldn't afford to say no to them and risk losing her social status if they told everyone what she'd done. And it was obvious to both of them that, until now, Ariel cared more about her social status than just about anything else. Although, who could blame her, really, after all those years spent as a social outcast?

And they still had no proof whatsoever that Ariel had anything to do with the murder. Nor had she provided them with any leads on who did.

"I'll bet you anything he's got something on Ariel in that file of his. I can feel it," Gretchen said. Her eyes were gleaming and she rubbed her hands together like she was kindling wood.

"I have to go," Jessica muttered. "Lunch started five minutes ago, and they'll be wondering where I am." She couldn't bring herself to say what she really wanted to say: *Let it go, sweetie. Ariel isn't the murderer. And we may never find out who is.*

Gretchen waved her away with an exaggerated flick of her wrist. "Go, then. Go have fun, and be popular."

Jessica gave her a weary look. "This was your idea, Gretchen. You were the one who thought it made sense to pretend that we hate each other. You were the one who thought it would be better if only one of us was popular."

"But you never argued that it should be you, did you? Admit it Jessica, weren't you just a little bit worried that I might be more popular than you if we came back? Weren't you just a little bit concerned that Nick Ford might pick me over you again?"

"I was, until I spent five minutes with him," she said with a laugh.

But Gretchen wasn't smiling.

Jessica's cheeks flushed. "No, Gretchen. The only thing I was concerned about was finding your mother's killer. About being your friend."

Now Gretchen turned red, but not with anger. Something in her face told Jessica that she was embarrassed. Embarrassed and exposed. Jessica shook her head and let out a loud sigh before walking away, leaving Gretchen alone again as she retreated to the ruling table in the olive grove.

Ariel was already seated at their table along with Molly Carson and a couple of other girls from the Oculus Society. Nick and Connor and some of their lacrosse team buddies were there as well.

"Where were you?" Ariel asked her. Jessica thought she sounded suspicious, prompting her to consider, as she often did, how much Ariel really knew. Did she know that Gretchen still suspected her? Did she realize that this whole thing was one big set-up? Or that it was trying to be, at least?

"Nowhere," Jessica said with a casual shrug. "I had to stay after class for a few minutes." Jessica saw Ariel's attention shift to something behind her, and she turned. Gretchen was crossing the olive grove; she took a seat at an empty table in the sun. Her face was red and blotchy; it was obvious that she'd been crying. *Great,* Jessica thought. *Now I've gone and upset her.*

Ariel shook her head and fixed her eyes back on Jessica. "It's enough," she said quietly but firmly. "This is ridiculous." She stood up purposefully, but Jessica grabbed her arm.

"Don't," she hissed. "You don't know what you're doing." Ariel hesitated, and Jessica knew she had her. "Just sit down, Ariel. This is what she wants."

But Ariel shook free of Jessica's grip. "Maybe it's what she thought she wanted, but I don't think it's working out quite like she planned." Jessica watched helplessly as Ariel strode over to Gretchen's table and sat down next to her. People instantly began elbowing each other—*look at this*—and within seconds, the grove had become silent.

Molly Carson leaned across the table. "What is she doing?" she whispered to Jessica.

But Nick responded before Jessica had a chance to answer. "She's being nice," he said. He shot Jessica a dirty look. "She's doing what we all should have done when she first came back here. The girl's mother was murdered, for God's sake." Then he picked up his lunch and went over to join them. A few seconds later, everyone else followed him. Only Connor and Jessica were left at the table.

"Shit," Connor said. He glanced anxiously at the other table, then at Jessica. "Why do you hate her so much?"

Jessica flushed. She wasn't prepared to answer this right

now. She and Gretchen had managed to create enough spec-
ulation over their supposed former romance, they'd never
needed to explain themselves. Whenever people had asked
about it, she just said that she didn't want to talk about it;
that alone had always been enough to make people think
they'd had some sort of lover's quarrel. Leave it to Connor
not to pick up on the signals.

"I don't hate her," she admitted. "It's complicated."

"Well, you look like a huge bitch right now." He picked
up his lunch and stood up, but he didn't go over to the other
table right away. He just stood there, glancing back and forth
between Nick and Jessica.

Jessica sat for a second or two, trying to decide what to do.
It doesn't matter anymore, she finally realized. *Ariel's right.*
She got up and joined Connor at the other table. Soon after,
the noise in the olive grove returned to normal.

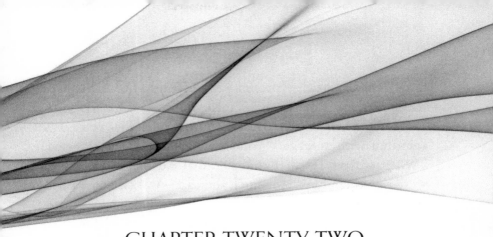

CHAPTER TWENTY TWO

It was only later, after school—when the three of them were alone at the teepee in the park—that Jessica realized how much rage Gretchen still had bottled inside her. Her face was nearly purple, and her hands were balled up so tightly that her knuckles were white. "What were you thinking?" she shouted at Ariel. "Why did you bring all those people over to my table at lunch today?"

Jessica sighed. She'd been listening to Gretchen rant and rave all afternoon. "Look, Gretchen, for the last time, Ariel wasn't trying to mess things up on purpose. She cares about you. For real."

But Gretchen could not be assuaged. "She was there," she said, lowering her voice, looking only at Jessica.

"Where?" Jessica asked.

"The graduation party. She was there."

Jessica pursed her lips. They'd been through this so many times. "You don't have any proof of that," she reminded her.

She glanced at Ariel, expecting her to protest. But Ariel's face had turned the color of an eggshell.

"Yes, I do." Gretchen turned to Ariel now. Her voice was calm but with an edge. "Your mom told me," she revealed. "When we projected. I told her that I'd heard the police were thinking about reopening the case. And she said that I shouldn't worry about it. She said that the police had already questioned her twice and that there was no reason for them not to believe her about where you were that night. She said it was a good thing that nobody saw you at the party. But I did see you."

Jessica's hands suddenly felt clammy. She could hear the blood pounding in her ears. She turned to Ariel. "Is that true?" she breathed. "Were you really there?"

Ariel looked down at the ground. "Yes, but it's not what you think—"

"Enough!" Gretchen cut her off. She was hysterical again. "You killed my mother!" she screamed. "I knew it was you!" Without warning, she lunged forward and grabbed Ariel by the throat. Ariel lost her balance and tipped backward, catching herself with her palms. Unable to use her hands to fight back, she drew her knees up to her chest and kicked Gretchen in the stomach with the soles of both feet.

"Stop it!" Jessica shouted, planting herself between them. "Both of you, stop it!"

Gretchen let go of Ariel, clutching her stomach as she returned to her spot on the ground. Ariel rubbed the red, irritated skin around her throat. They both glared at each other. Jessica crossed her arms in front of her chest.

"Ariel, you'd better have a good explanation."

Ariel swallowed a few times and cleared her throat. In a hurried and embarrassed jumble, the story came out: how she'd come to Gretchen's house that night to crash the party, how she'd peered through the window, how she'd changed her mind and left . . . how she was already running away when she'd heard the screams.

"That's bullshit," Gretchen spat.

But Jessica held her hand up. It wasn't bullshit. She could tell from the terrified look on Ariel's face. "Think about it, Gretchen. Yes, you saw her. Your suspicions are confirmed. But still, you only saw her outside, and only for a minute. Nobody saw her inside the house. Nobody. Her story makes sense."

Ariel took a deep, shaky breath. "I just don't understand why you think I would have wanted to kill your mother."

Jessica kept quiet. This one was for Gretchen to answer. After a long silence, she finally spoke.

"Because you hated me. And because you hated the Oculus Society."

"But there are other people you suspected," Ariel pointed out. "I saw the files in your desk."

"Their alibis all checked out," Gretchen answered. "Yours was the only one that didn't. I knew I had seen you that night. I was positive. So I never believed that you were home with your mother." She paused. Her eyes had become watery. "But if you didn't do it . . . then there's nobody left to suspect."

"I don't understand," Ariel murmured. "Why are you so sure that it only could have been me or those other women in your files?"

Gretchen shrugged. "Because you were the only one who hated me, and they were the only ones who knew about the anklet. And hating me or getting the anklet are the only motives I can think of for killing her. The police have questioned practically everyone else in town, and there's nobody who would have wanted her dead for any other reason."

Ariel looked confused. "But how do you know that nobody else knew about the anklet? Couldn't someone in the Oculus Society have told someone else?"

"Only five other people in the Oculus Society knew about it," Jessica said, "and they're all sworn to secrecy. You don't understand how seriously they take this. Nobody would tell. They just wouldn't."

"You did," Ariel pointed out.

Jessica shook her head. "It's different."

"Not really. Doesn't everyone rationalize why it's okay to do something they're not supposed to do? Couldn't someone else think that their situation is different, too?"

"I guess," Jessica said, but she didn't really mean it. She simply couldn't imagine any one of the other board members telling someone else about the Plotinus Ability.

"What about Michelle?" Ariel asked.

"She didn't do it," Gretchen said resignedly. "She was fooling around with some other guy."

"Mike Renwick," Ariel said, nodding. "I saw the picture of him in your files. Is that where she was at the time of the murder? With him?"

Gretchen nodded.

"That's where she *said* she was," Jessica corrected. "But we don't know that for a fact."

Gretchen rolled her eyes. "I caught her with him at the Club, remember? It makes sense."

"Of course it makes sense. She's smart. She wouldn't tell a lie that doesn't make sense." Jessica exhaled loudly. Nobody understood just how cunning Michelle could be.

Ariel met Jessica's eyes with a solemn, questioning stare. "I know you think she's awful, but do you really think she's capable of killing someone? I mean, she is your family."

Jessica's emotions rose up in her without warning. Her voice broke as she answered. "She's *not* my family. My parents were my family. Michelle's just a relative who's raising me out of a sense of obligation." Jessica wiped the tears from her eyes roughly, furious with them for being there. "The only family I have now is Rob." She let out a harsh laugh. "And that's pretty pathetic."

Ariel opened her mouth, then closed it. She looked frightened about what she was about to say. "Let's say Michelle didn't do it. Could she have told someone else about the anklet?"

Jessica shook her head. Michelle was certainly capable of murder, but she was loyal to a fault—she would never betray a secret like this. Never. "No. She couldn't have." Jessica said it forcefully, as if it were the end of the discussion.

But Gretchen cocked her head to the side, as if she'd heard something in Ariel's question that interested her. "Why?" she asked. "Is there someone you think she told?"

Ariel's face turned grave. "Yes. I do." She looked Jessica dead in the eye. "I'm sorry, Jess. But I think she told Rob."

Shortly after the philosopher's last diary entry, there is evidence that his patron Gemina was imprisoned for treason, though there are no existing accounts of what led to her arrest . . .

Jessica had read this sentence three times already, and yet the words couldn't register. She was still fuming from the accusation that Ariel had made against Rob yesterday. She'd barely slept the night before, replaying it over and over again in her mind, and now, no matter how hard she tried, she still couldn't concentrate on anything else. Yes, Rob was a lost soul. But he was harmless. He was *her* lost soul. She knew what people thought: that he was a fool who'd wasted his adult life. But he was smarter than anyone gave him credit for. More sensitive, too. Accusing him was, in Jessica's mind, almost the same thing as accusing Jessica herself. He was, after all, the closest thing she had to a parent. Michelle had never bonded with her the way that Rob had.

Besides, Ariel didn't even have any evidence. Absolutely nothing to go on. Just *a feeling,* she'd said, based on nothing but the fact that Rob buys alcohol for high school guys, and a secondhand conversation with Nick Ford when Rob had let his guard down and admitted that he wasn't happy with his life. And really, how many adults *were* happy with the way their lives turned out? There'd be a lot of murderers running around if that were the only criteria. At least when they'd accused Ariel of the murder, they'd had a reason for doing so. Gretchen had seen her at the party that night, and Ariel had lied about being there. *That* was evidence. A feeling was just bullshit.

Jessica sighed. She knew that this was just Ariel's way of getting back at them for suspecting her. She was hurt, and she wanted to hurt Jessica right back. Well, it wasn't going to work. Ariel was *not* going to make her doubt Rob of all people. The only thing was, now that Gretchen had it in her head that Rob was a potential suspect, Jessica knew she'd never hear the end of it. This, she thought, is how celebrities must feel when the tabloids just make up a story about them, and everyone in the world believes it.

There was a quick knock at her bedroom door, and then Michelle's face was peering in at her.

"Can't you at least wait for me to say *come in?*" Jessica asked.

The left side of Michelle's upper lip rose as if it were attached to a string held by an invisible puppeteer. "This is my house that I pay for, and I'm entitled to go into any room that I want, whenever I want. You're lucky I even knock at all."

Jessica sighed. "What do you want?"

"You have to drive me to the office. The bust I'm reporting on is on Monday, and I've got a meeting in twenty minutes that I'm not prepared for. I need to read some things on the way over."

"I'm busy," Jessica protested. "I'm working on the thing that Tina asked for."

Michelle frowned. "God. I haven't even looked at that yet, and Tina gave me the file three days ago. It's still sitting in my office." Her anxious expression suddenly gave way to a self-satisfied smile. "Hey, I know. Take me to the office and just work on it there. You can use my computer. I'll only be an hour." She preemptively wagged an index finger at Jessica. "And before you try to come up with a lame excuse for why you can't do it, just know that there's only one ending to this conversation, and it's you asking me where the car keys are. So let's go."

The **NBC affiliate station** in Delphi occupied three stories of a squat, nondescript building in the center of town. What made it stand apart from the rest of the squat, nondescript buildings on the block was the oversized peacock logo affixed to the stucco, along with a massive billboard that seemed to rise out of the roof, emblazoned with a horribly airbrushed picture of Michelle and the rest of the News-on-Nine Team. This heightened version of Michelle—with the overly white teeth, the impossibly unblemished skin and the helmet of too-perfect hair—still made Jessica cringe.

Inside, the office was frantic. Interns rushed with stacks of paper; people in cubicles urgently shouted across the room. *The husband in the domestic dispute was thirty-four, not thirty-seven! The teacher charged with molestation had a prior arrest for engaging in lewd acts! The mother of the little boy rescued from the fire spent time in rehab last year!* Nobody said hello as Michelle and Jessica walked down a carpeted hallway toward the row of offices that lined the back wall.

"They're not very friendly," Jessica observed.

"They're news people," Michelle quipped, as she opened the door to her office. "Lacking social skills is a job requirement. Haven't you lived with me long enough to have learned that by now?"

Jessica almost smiled. *At least she's self-aware.*

The office was cramped and cluttered with DVDs and stacks of accordion folders everywhere. There was a television atop a black metal stand in the corner and a rectangular, curtainless window along the back wall. The front wall was dominated by a large window overlooking the rest of the office—shielded by blinds that had been lowered to half-mast, so that Jessica could only see the legs of the people scurrying past. On the desk were several pictures in silver frames: one of Michelle and Rob on their wedding day, one of Michelle with some of her friends at an Oculus Society event, one of Michelle and Jessica's mother from when they were children. And there was a candid one of Jessica at her eighth grade graduation. She was wearing her cap and gown, laughing at something off camera.

Jessica had never seen the photo before. She hadn't even known that it existed. She'd never been in this office for longer than fifteen seconds at a time, and usually those brief periods where spent buried angrily in her phone—anything to escape. But inside of her, in the icy place where she stored her feelings about her parents—about Michelle, about how sad it was that there was nobody who really, truly cared about her—a tiny little piece chipped off and melted.

Michelle eyed Jessica as she took in the photo, but didn't comment on it. "Just stay in here," Michelle instructed. "You can use the computer, but Do. Not. Touch. Anything else. I'll be back in an hour." She smoothed her hair and smiled into the full-length mirror hanging on the back of the door. "Thanks for telling me that I had lipstick all over my teeth."

"Well, I'm thinking about becoming a news person myself," Jessica answered dryly.

Michelle smirked and pulled the door shut behind her.

Jessica sat at Michelle's desk, waiting. As she studied the photo of herself, doubt began to pry its way under her convictions, lifting them up and unsettling them, like tree roots beneath concrete. *Is Michelle capable of killing someone? Could she really have murdered Gretchen's mom?*

Finally, the coast was clear. She pulled open the top desk drawer: mints; a light blue, suede makeup case; a travel-sized toothbrush. In the drawer beneath that were a company handbook, a folder of HR materials, and a black address book filled with the names and numbers of various public officials, police officers, newspaper reporters, union leaders and CEOs of local companies. Jessica picked through some of the accordion folders lying on the floor, keeping one eye on the legs moving around outside the window.

She was just about to give up when she found a single manila file folder leaning against the side of the desk. The words *Oculus Society* had been typed onto a thin label that ran across the tab of the folder. She picked it up and sat back down at the desk.

Inside was a memo written to Tina Holt from a Ralph
Sheasby, Licensed Private Investigator.

I regret to inform you that after a lengthy and compre-
hensive investigation, I have found no further relevant
information regarding this case. Although I know how
much you and your family may want closure, it is my
professional opinion that continuing this investigation
will be a costly and, ultimately, futile exercise.

Jessica's heart sank a little. She had heard Tina say that the
private investigator had found nothing, but seeing it in writing—so stark and bleak—drove it home. She flipped through
the rest of the file. Tina Holt had supplied Mr. Sheasby with
a list of people who were aware that the anklet was a "rare
and ancient artifact," and he had compiled a dossier on each
of them. Tina's list matched hers and Gretchen's exactly,
with the exception of Ariel, of course. But she frowned when
she saw that Ralph Sheasby had extended this initial list to
include the husbands, families, and close friends of each of
them, as well. Jessica turned straight to the page on Rob.

There was a photograph of him outside of the Club—taken,
it appeared, at long range and without his knowledge. And
Mr. Sheasby had also delved into his finances, as evidenced
by a spreadsheet detailing his assets, liabilities, and bank
accounts. As expected, he had next to nothing in the asset col-
umn and just a few credit cards with small balances. He had
two bank accounts: a joint account he shared with Michelle
and another account in his name only. There was also a
safe deposit box at the Delphi Bank and Trust. *He probably*
keeps his pot there, Jessica thought. *Or maybe he's finally*
started squirreling away some cash so that he can leave her.

Jessica glanced at her watch. It had been almost ten minutes since Michelle had left, and she hadn't done any research
on Plotinus yet. She knew that Michelle would be suspicious
if she hadn't produced something, so Jessica carefully put
the file back and logged onto the computer as a guest. She
returned to the Wikipedia page she'd found at home.

*Shortly after the philosopher's last diary entry, there is
evidence that his patron Gemina, wife of the wealthy
Senator Castricius, was imprisoned for treason, though
there are no existing accounts of what led to her arrest.*

This time, the words sank in.
Treason? Jessica opened a new window and typed a search:
treason in ancient Rome.

*During imperial Rome, charges of treason were rare
but could be imposed for the following offenses: the
questioning of the emperor's governance or choice of
a successor, the murder of high-ranking magistrates,
incitement to sedition, and falsification of public documents. The punishment was death, usually by hanging
or beheading, and confiscation of property.*

She wondered if Gemina might have been involved in a
murder somehow. How fitting, she thought, given the circumstances under which her anklet disappeared almost two
thousand years later. Jessica clicked back to the original passage she'd been reading.

*Gemina was found guilty of treason and was sen-
tenced to death by hanging. There are reports that,*

subsequently, Plotinus became depressed and slowly went mad.

In an account by the Roman philosopher Porphyry, who is known to have studied under Plotinus in the early years of his career, there were claims that Plotinus was "often confused" and that at times he "behaved as if he believed himself to be someone else." Based on these and other descriptions, many scholars believe that Plotinus may have been exhibiting signs of schizophrenia.

Plotinus spent the remainder of his life at the estate of Amphiclea Aristos and her aristocrat husband, Kleitos. Amphiclea Aristos had been a close childhood friend of Gemina's, and after her death, she raised Gemina's daughter, Gaia, alongside her own daughter, Alexia.

Jessica's brain hurt from trying to read between the lines in front of her. The facts, she knew, were the facts, but the real story lied in the details, details she could only guess at. Over and over she kept returning to the quote from Porphyry about how Plotinus believed himself to be someone else. She tapped her pen against the side of Michelle's desk. *He believed himself to be someone else. He believed himself to be someone else.*

Jessica dropped the pen. A sickening idea had begun to form in her mind. Was it possible that Gemina and Plotinus had somehow gotten stuck in each other's bodies? Could Gemina have been executed before they'd had a chance to project back to themselves? It would certainly explain why Plotinus believed himself to be someone else. It was because he *was* someone else. He was Gemina.

Jessica felt like she was going to throw up. She remembered back to the first time she and Gretchen had projected, how panicked she'd been when she'd realized that there was no guarantee that it would work a second time. How terrified she'd been that she might be stuck in Gretchen's body forever. But then it had worked, and they'd never really given it a second thought. All of those times with Gretchen, with Ariel . . . if she'd have known that it could really happen—that you could get stuck like Plotinus and Gemina—she'd never have taken the risk.

I'll never do it again, Jessica swore to herself. *Never.*

CHAPTER TWENTY THREE

Rob was in the den playing Guitar Hero when Jessica returned home that afternoon. Michelle had dropped her off at the house and had gone straight out again. The police were making her wear a bulletproof vest for the bust, and she needed to go get fitted for it ASAP. The brand was called Dragon Skin, Michelle had told her. Jessica had had to bite her tongue to keep herself from saying that it was aptly named: Dragon Skin for a Dragon Lady.

Funny: Jessica couldn't remember the last time Rob had played Guitar Hero. He usually said it made him too depressed to pretend to be a rock star on the way up after his real band had come so close and failed. It had hardly been close, though. It made her a little sad to think about how much Rob had hung his hopes on that one A&R guy—some jerk had come out to hear the band as a favor to the drummer's college roommate.

He'd given Rob his card after the show, told him they had a great sound, said he should give him a call. Rob had been out of his mind with excitement. He went out and bought an expensive leather jacket and a new guitar he'd had his eye on for years; he told everyone that he was getting signed to a record label, that he'd be moving to LA. But the guy never called back. Ten, twelve, twenty phone calls . . . and he never returned any of them. Rob had been devastated. The feeling of sadness around the house was almost as bad as when her parents had died.

"Hey," she said. Rob looked away from the screen and grinned at her without missing a note. His grin reminded her of the old days when the two of them had been inseparable. He used to take her out for ice cream after school, and he'd work with her on her bike riding or teach her how to throw a football like a guy. He was the only one in those first few months after the accident who could make her laugh. She realized that she hadn't seen his grin in a long time. She missed it.

Jessica watched as Rob played out the last few notes of the song, holding the final one for a good ten seconds as he raised the neck of the guitar above his shoulder. The audience in the video game roared their approval.

YOU ROCK! appeared on the screen.

"Damn right I do!" he shouted back at the TV.

"You're in a good mood," she observed. "What's the occasion?"

There was the grin again. "Things are looking up for me, Jess."

She raised her eyebrows. "Oh, yeah? Why's that? Did something happen?"

Rob shrugged. "No, nothing happened. It's just a feeling."

Just a feeling, she repeated to herself. She hated those words. "Okay, well, it's nice to see you happy again. It's been a while."

"Yeah, it has. Listen, Jess, I know I've been kind of a bear since you came back, and I'm sorry about that. I just . . . I've been really unhappy, and I didn't . . . I didn't mean to, you know, to take it out on you." He looked down at the floor, as if there he might find the words he was fumbling for. "I just . . . I want you know that you mean a lot to me. More than a lot. I mean . . ." He looked back up at her now. "I'm just really glad you came into my life, and I want you to know that."

Jessica furrowed her forehead. "Are you leaving or something?"

"What? No. I told you, I'm not leaving her."

"You did?" This was news to her. Rob's plan had always been to save up enough money of his own to leave Michelle. He'd called Jessica at boarding school at least a dozen times to lament the fact that it was taking him so long. "When did you say that?" she asked.

He gave her an exasperated look. "That night we played Halo, remember? After Nick and Connor and Ariel left. We had a whole discussion about it. I swear, sometimes you act like you have amnesia or something."

Ah. That was why she didn't remember. He'd said it to Ariel the night they projected. But Ariel never mentioned that she'd had a heart to heart with Rob. Jessica wondered what else they'd talked about. Here was one more reason never, ever to project again: too many secrets.

"No, sorry. I just . . . So you're really not leaving?"

"I'm really not leaving, Jess. What made you say that, anyway?"

"I don't know. What you said to me sounded a lot like a goodbye speech. Like, either you're leaving or you're dying."

Rob laughed. "I'm not leaving or dying. Like I told you

before, I've just decided that it's time for me to move on from all of this unhappiness. I'm making changes from within."

"So you're only leaving metaphorically, then," Jessica clarified.

"How come you're so smart?" he asked, smiling.

"Probably because I'm not related to you," she dead-panned. At that, Rob grabbed a couch pillow from behind him and threw it at her. Jessica ducked, but it still grazed the top of her head. She reached down to grab it and throw it back at him, but Rob was already in front of her. He snatched it before she had a grasp on it and smacked her in the head with it, laughing. Jessica put one hand up to defend herself and lunged toward the couch, seizing hold of a throw pillow. She fought back, landing a few good whacks to his arm, but mostly she just hit the pillow he was holding. "I have to go," Jessica finally said, once she stopped laughing and was able to breathe again. "I don't have time for these childish activities of yours, Rob."

"Why?" he asked, still panting. "What do you have to do that's more important than pillow fighting with me?"

Jessica stuck out her tongue at him. "I have to do this stupid research project for the Oculus Society." The words were out of her mouth before she had a chance to weigh them, and she wondered if maybe she shouldn't have mentioned the project. "It's just for the archives," she added, quickly.

Rob raised his eyebrows. "I didn't know that social clubs gave out homework. What's it on?"

"Oh, you know, the history of the Oculus Society, blah, blah, blah. Ancient Greek guys and stuff."

He nodded. "Plotinus, eh?"

Jessica cocked her head. "How do you know about Plotinus?"

Rob's face flushed, and he coughed loudly into his hand twice, and then a third time. "Sorry. My throat's so dry."

"How do you know about Plotinus, Rob?" Jessica asked again.

He shrugged. "They gave out that award at your eighth grade graduation, remember? The Plotinus Award. Gretchen won it, and her mom presented it to her." He shook his head, sadly. "It's so weird, I can't remember what I ate for breakfast this morning, but I remember every detail of that day. I think it's, like, post-traumatic stress disorder or something. Like, because I was there when she was killed, I can remember everything that happened. Is it like that for you?"

"No," Jessica answered. She tried to adjust the levels of suspicion and mere curiosity in her tone of voice, just like how she adjusted the treble and bass on the car stereo. "But how did you know that Plotinus was an ancient Greek guy? I mean, how did you know that Plotinus wasn't a city or something?"

Rob gave her a look like she was being weird. "I don't know." He seemed to be thinking for a moment. "Oh, wait, I think it said it in the graduation program. It kind of, like, explained who Plotinus was in the description of the award."

Of course it did.

Jessica exhaled, rebuking herself for letting Ariel get to her. Her eyes wandered to his hands. They were small and delicate, with long, thin fingers: artist's hands. How many hours, she reminded herself, had those hands spent coloring with her, or making Play-Doh animals with her, or playing video games with her? It simply wasn't possible that those same hands could have strangled another human being—let alone her best friend's mother. Jessica realized now that she'd misjudged Ariel completely. She'd just been lonely, and she'd let her loneliness get in the way of common sense. The two of them were never meant to be friends. As far as Jessica was concerned, Ariel could go to hell.

Jasper Carey was having a party that night; his parents were out of town, and he'd been talking a big game about how it was going to be a rager that would make Nick's Labor Day party seem like something for little kids. Jessica was looking forward to it. There hadn't been a big party to go to in a while, and frankly, she was looking forward to getting drunk. Whatever Ariel might think about Rob supplying alcohol to their guy friends, Jessica was grateful for it. After all, without Rob, parties like this would be nearly impossible to pull off.

Jessica checked her watch.

Rob had left over an hour ago—to go run an errand, he'd said, with a wink—and she was all alone in the house. It had been nearly four hours since Michelle had gone to get fitted for her bulletproof vest, and Jessica was beginning to get anxious. Michelle had promised that she could use the car tonight in exchange for having driven her to work earlier in the day, and she was supposed to pick up Connor in less than an hour. She wondered if they were skinning actual dragons while Michelle waited.

Jessica had just finished blow drying her hair when she heard Michelle come in through the garage door. *Finally.*

She listened to Michelle's footsteps as she walked into the kitchen to put down her stuff, and waited for the sound of the refrigerator door opening. Michelle never ate during the day—too busy, she claimed—so she was always famished at night. During the week, when she came home after doing the eleven o'clock news, the first thing she always did was open the refrigerator and inhale whatever leftovers she could find.

She didn't even heat them up or anything. Just stood in front of the open fridge and ate the food cold with her fingers. It was gross, really.

But tonight the refrigerator door didn't open. Instead, Jessica heard the sound of Michelle's footsteps stomping toward her bedroom door.

The contents of Jessica's stomach began to swirl, like leaves blown about by a strong gust of wind. She could sense the anger in those footsteps, and she knew, instinctively, that it was directed toward her. *She must know that I was snooping in her office,* Jessica thought. *She must know that I read through that file.*

Jessica braced herself as her door opened without even the customary warning knock. *Uh-oh.* But Michelle didn't yell or scream or anything. She just walked in and sat down on the edge of the bed. Her face was red.

"The bastard's leaving me," she announced.

Jessica drew in a sharp breath of air. The room felt as if had been turned upside down. "What? He's not leaving you. He just told me tonight that he's happier than he's ever been." But Michelle shook her head.

"He's lying." She unzipped the black, patent leather briefcase she'd been holding and removed a plain manila folder. Jessica recognized it immediately. She couldn't image what in that file suggested that Rob might be leaving her. As she well knew, there was hardly anything on Rob at all. But Michelle turned to the page listing Rob's assets and held it out for Jessica to see.

She peered at the spreadsheet as if she'd never laid eyes on it before. "I don't understand," she finally admitted. "How do bank accounts and some credit cards prove that he's leaving you?"

Michelle's finger shook as she pointed to the line that listed their joint account. "I never added him to this account," she said. Her voice sounded careful, measured, as if she was taking pains to stay in control of it. "Joint bank accounts need to have signatures from both parties, but I never signed anything." She removed another paper from her briefcase, a fax from the Delphi Bank and Trust.

Jessica's eyes flashed over the paper: an agreement authorizing Rob as a signatory to the account, signed by Michelle. She started to feel sick. "I called the bank right away, and they sent this over to me," Michelle went on. She looked Jessica in the eye. "He forged my name, Jess. On my own bank account. The account into which all of my paychecks are deposited." Now her voice began to tremble. "And the worst part is, he's been stealing money from me. He's been making withdrawals for two years and transferring them into his own account. He knows that I always forget to balance my checkbook, so he's been withdrawing money every day in small increments, knowing full well that I'd never notice."

Jessica lifted her hand to her mouth. "Are you absolutely sure?"

Michelle nodded. "Positive."

"How much did he take?"

Michelle pushed her lips together so that they disappeared completely. "Almost twenty thousand dollars."

Jessica didn't know what to say. Her first instinct was to defend Rob, but she couldn't think of any actual defense. "Could there be another explanation?"

Michelle rolled her eyes. "I know he walks on water as far as you're concerned, but you need to wake up, Jessica. There's no other explanation. It's no secret that he's not happy with our relationship. I just . . ." Michelle's eyes were tearing up, and she took a moment to compose herself. "I just never thought he'd *steal* from me, you know? I thought he respected me more than that."

"You cheated on him," Jessica blurted out, angrily. "Maybe he thought the same thing about you."

Without warning, Michelle began to sob. She buried her face in her hands. After a moment, she stood up and yanked the briefcase off the bed. "I don't know why I thought that you might have some sympathy for me," she choked out. "You always take his side over mine. You and your amazing Uncle Rob. Let's see if you ever hear from him again, once he's gone." She slammed the door shut behind her.

In the darkest corner of her heart, Jessica knew that she was right.

Rob was going to leave, and he wasn't taking Jessica with him or even telling her where he was going. That speech tonight *had* been a goodbye.

Jessica jumped up from her bed and ran out into the hall-way. Michelle was standing against the wall, sobbing, her shoulders heaving. She'd never seen Michelle so vulnerable before. Suddenly, her perspective seemed to shift, as if she were looking at an optical illusion. Only, instead of seeing a vase where a woman's profile had been, she could see life from Michelle's point of view instead of her own. Married to a guy who wouldn't grow up, burdened with the child of her dead sister. Supporting them both all by herself. It was a lot to deal with. Jessica didn't know if she would have handled it all any better.

"I'm sorry," Jessica said softly. "I'm so sorry." She reached out to pat Michelle consolingly on the arm, but before she could, Michelle stepped into the open space and collapsed against Jessica, burying her face in her niece's shoulder. It was such a strange feeling that it took Jessica a moment to respond. Finally, she patted Michelle on the back. "Come on," she said, leading her back toward her room. "Let's go talk."

After a half hour of calling Rob every name under the sun—threatening to kill him, or at the very least to cut off various parts of his anatomy, raging about what a mistake it had been to marry him in the first place—Michelle finally seemed spent.

"So what are you going to do?" Jessica asked from the edge of her bed, once she felt it was safe enough to speak again. Michelle fell into Jessica's desk chair.

"I don't know." Her voice was hoarse. Her mascara had run. "I want to throw him out of the house, but I also want my money back, and I need to file a formal complaint with the bank before they'll begin an inquiry."

"Then you shouldn't say anything," Jessica recommended. "Not yet. If he thinks you're on to him he'll take off and you'll never see your money again. You have to just act normal for a few days."

Michelle nodded. "I know." Her face began to turn red again. "I pulled up his credit card information online . . . He's so stupid, he uses the same login and password for everything. Do you know what he's been buying?"

Jessica shook her head. She couldn't begin to imagine.

"He's been buying clothes from Abercrombie. At first I thought, you know, he's always hanging around with those high school kids. Maybe he's dating one of those little idiots and buying her stuff. In which case I'd have him arrested for statutory rape. So I called the store, and I had them pull up the receipts and read to me what he'd bought."

Jessica tried not to balk at this suggestion. She couldn't think of anyone at her school who would possibly want to

have an affair with Rob. For one thing, they'd all be too terrified of getting caught by Michelle. She bit her lip to suppress
the smile tugging at the corners of her mouth. "And? Was it
girl's clothes?"

"No. It was all guys' stuff. Jeans, T-shirts, hoodies, cargo
shorts." Michelle let out a bitter laugh. "Like he's preparing
to be Mr. Single Guy, and he thinks he's still a seventeen-year-
old. Does he really think women won't realize he's almost
forty if he dresses like he's in high school?"

The *click* in Jessica's head was almost audible. She stared
at Michelle. "What did you just say?"

"I asked you if he thought women won't realize he's almost
forty if—"

"No," Jessica interrupted, waving her hand impatiently.
"Before that."

"That he thinks he's still a seventeen-year-old?"

Jessica nodded. "Yeah," she said, so faintly she almost
didn't hear herself. She sprang up from the bed. "Get up,"
she commanded to Michelle. "I need the chair."

Jessica snatched the chair from under her as she stood,
almost knocking Michelle off-balance. She placed it in front
of her closet and climbed up onto it.

"What are you doing?" Michelle wanted to know.

But Jessica just held up an index finger as she pulled a
shoebox down from the top shelf of her closet. "Come on,
come on, be in here," she said to herself as she rifled through
the contents of the box. Pictures of her parents, certificates
from when she used to take gymnastics, a ticket stub from a
Black Keys concert she'd gone to with some girls at boarding
school. "There you are," she breathed.

She lifted up a booklet of cream-colored paper that had
been stapled down the middle.

Michelle peered over her shoulder. "Why are you looking at your middle school graduation program?"

Jessica held up her finger again as she scanned the pages, looking for the list of awards.

Outstanding Eighth Grade Boy . . . . given by the faculty to the boy with the most all-around achievements in the eighth grade class.

Outstanding Eighth Grade Girl . . . . given by the faculty to the girl with the most all-around achievements in the eighth grade class.

Plotinus Award . . . . given by the Oculus Society to the eighth grade girl who best demonstrates the values and community-mindedness espoused by that organization.

The color drained from Jessica's face as she looked up at Michelle.

"Jessica, what is going on?"

She could barely even manage a whisper. "Michelle, did you ever tell Rob about the Plotinus Ability, or anything about Plotinus at all?"

Michelle looked at her with disdain. "What? No, of course not. What does that have to do with anything anyway?"

Jessica ignored her question and asked again. "Do you swear? Do you swear on your career that you never told him?"

"Yes, I swear *on my career*," Michelle answered with an eye roll. "What's going on?"

But Jessica shook her head. "I have to go out."

Michelle's mouth opened. She looked Jessica up and down, taking in her tight black jeans and low-cut tank top, as if just realizing that she was dressed for a party.

"What do you mean, you have to go out? Cancel! What I'm going through right now is more important than some date with Connor Matthews!"

"I'm not going on a date with Connor. I mean, I was, but not anymore. Look, there's something I have to do, but I can't tell you what it is right now. Not until I'm sure. But it has to do with Rob leaving you."

Michelle's eyes flashed. "Jessica, tell me right now!" she commanded. "Right now or so help me God, you will not leave this room until you go to college!"

"I'm sorry, but I can't." She reached out for Michelle's hands and held them. "Look, I know that we haven't always seen eye to eye, but I'm on your side with this. I swear I am. I just need for you to trust me right now, and I'll explain everything to you as soon as I get back. Please, Michelle. I need you to let me go out right now."

Michelle's narrowed eyes searched Jessica's, then softened. She dropped Jessica's hands. "Be home by midnight. And you tell me everything the minute you walk in that door."

"Fine. Deal." She smiled at Michelle and put her hands together under her chin, bowing slightly at her. "Thank you. Thank you so much."

CHAPTER TWENTY FOUR

Dozens of cars lined the street outside Jasper's house; Jessica had to park almost two blocks away to find a spot. She texted Connor as she walked on the sidewalk toward the sound of a thumping bass.

Can't pick u up. So sorry. Will explain l8r. Meet me @ Jasper's. xo

Inside, the house was packed with people from school; mostly juniors and seniors, but a few bold sophomore girls had shown up as well, overdressed in short skirts and their mom's high heels. Jessica pushed through the crowds in the hallway, turning her head in every direction as she looked for Ariel. She spotted Molly Carson in the living room and made her way toward her.

"Molly!" she shouted. "Molly!" The music was so loud Molly couldn't hear her, so Jessica grabbed her arm.

"Oh, hi, Jessica!" she yelled. Her eyes were glassy and Jessica could tell she was already drunk. "Where's Connor? You two are so cuuuute together!"

"Have you seen Ariel?" she asked, ignoring the Connor remark.

Molly snorted. "Uh, *ye-ah*. She came with *Gretchen*. Can you believe that? I mean, talking to her at lunch was one thing, but bringing her to a party? Seriously?"

Jessica took a step back, trying to hide the surprise she was feeling. She hadn't known that Gretchen was coming tonight, but she didn't want Molly to know that they'd left her out of the loop. Or that she was suddenly feeling insecure about having been left out. But she didn't need to worry; Molly wasn't paying attention to her at all. She'd closed her eyes and was swaying drunkenly to the music.

"So have you seen them?" she asked.

Molly moved her head up and down in an exaggerated motion, as if her neck muscles had turned to jelly. "They were in the kitchen before."

And they were still, Jessica discovered, as she made her way past the double islands and found Ariel and Gretchen standing near the stainless steel, sub-zero refrigerator. They both gave her the same wary look as she approached them.

"Hi," she said, taking an accusatory tone.

"Hey," Ariel answered coolly.

"I need to talk to you both. In private." She looked around for somewhere quiet where they could talk, but every square inch of the house seemed to be filled with people. "Can we go outside?"

They found a secluded spot on the side yard under a small, covered area where Jasper's parents kept the trash bins. It smelled of wet paper and rotting vegetables. Jessica crossed her arms and eyed them both suspiciously.

"So, what, you throttle her, she kicks you in the stomach, and now the two of you are going to parties together?"

"I called Gretchen to apologize to her," Ariel explained. "And I invited her to come with me. I thought it would help her to take her mind off things, even if just for tonight." She looked down at the floor. "I wanted to apologize to you, too, but I didn't think you'd want to talk to me."

"No," Jessica said with a sigh. She slumped her shoulders and dropped her arms to her sides. "You don't need to apologize. I think you might actually be onto something."

Gretchen's eyebrows shot up. "What do you mean?"

"I'm not sure exactly. Look, Ariel, I need to talk to Nick, but he doesn't trust me. The only way he'll tell me anything is if he thinks I'm you." Jessica shook her head ruefully. "I promised myself I would never do this again, but I need to project with you. Tonight. Now."

Ariel made a *yeah, right* face and took a step away from Gretchen. "Did you know about this?" she asked. Gretchen shook her head no, but Ariel made a face like she didn't believe her.

"Ariel, it's over," Gretchen said gently. "You didn't kill my mom. I know that now. And we don't want to get revenge on you anymore. We're your friends. For real. What you did at school the other day . . . it was really nice of you. I didn't think you'd changed, but I see now that you have. You can trust us." She lowered her voice to a whisper. "For real," she added.

Jessica nodded in agreement. "No more secrets between us, okay? No more secret plans, no more hiding things from each other. From now on, we tell each other everything." She exhaled slowly. "I'll start. When Gemina and Plotinus projected, they got stuck in each other's bodies. Forever."

Gretchen's face went white. "Oh, my God," she whispered.

"That can happen?" Ariel asked. Her eyes had nearly

doubled in size. "How come you never warned me that that could happen?"

"I didn't know that it could happen until today. It's not like I want to get stuck."

"We shouldn't do it, then," Ariel insisted. "I'll talk to Nick. What do you need to know about that's so important?"

"I need to know what Rob's been talking to him about. Look, I think Rob's planning to leave Michelle, and I think he's planning to use Nick to help him. But you can't do it. There's no way that I can explain to you what the right questions are to ask about Rob. It has to be me." She looked at them both with a serious stare. "But this has to be the last time, and we have to do it completely by the book, with Gretchen as the witness."

"I don't know," Ariel hedged.

"Look, I don't want to get stuck, either. But it's always worked for us before." She glanced at Gretchen. "And if I'm right . . . well, then we'll finally know the truth."

Gretchen gasped, then quickly put her hand over her mouth. "You don't have to, Ariel," she said. "I'll understand if you don't want to do it."

But Ariel was silent. They both watched her as she took a few moments to think it over. Finally, she nodded. "I'll do it."

Gretchen began to softly cry. Jessica grimaced. "Okay. We change back the second I get what I need from him. Deal?"

"Deal."

Jessica's heart pounded in her ears. "All right. Close your eyes, and try to clear your mind."

Ariel did as she was told, and Jessica whispered the words in Greek. "*Écho exorísei aíma egó dió xei ostó n, prollálloun ti n psychí mou se állo spíti.*" Then she leaned in and put her mouth on Ariel's soft, gloss-sticky lips.

• • •

"There you are," Nick said, grinning as she walked over to him. "I've been looking for you all night."

Jessica put Ariel's arms around his neck and pecked him on the cheek. "Sorry. Girl issues." She rolled her eyes.

"Yeah, I heard you came with Gretchen. How's Jessica taking that?"

She tried not to flinch at the knowing look he gave her. The look that said: *Jessica is such a nightmare. I'm sure she's being her usual nightmare self.*

"Oh, you know, she's Jessica, but she's handling it okay."

"Did you ever find out why she hated Gretchen so much?" He raised his eyebrows and lowered his voice to sound mock-seductive. "Were they together?"

He's such a dolt, Jessica thought. She chose her words carefully. "No. And I don't think she actually hated Gretchen, either. I think she was just embarrassed about that old video, and she was worried that if people saw them hanging out together, they'd think . . . well, they'd think what you're thinking. But she couldn't win, because people just thought that anyway."

Nick shrugged. "I guess." He pulled her closer to him. Jessica could sense that he was losing interest in talking.

"Oh, hey, speaking of Jessica, is Rob at this party? Apparently he went out hours ago, and nobody's been able to get a hold of him. Jessica thought that maybe he was here. Have you seen him?"

Nick frowned but didn't answer her.

"What's wrong?" she asked. He pursed his lips and looked down at the ebony-stained, hardwood floor. "Nick, what's going on? Did something happen with Rob?"

"That guy's an asshole," he finally said.

"Why?" Jessica asked. The word came out of her mouth slowly, as if it had been marinating there in molasses.

Nick glanced at the people standing around them in the hallway. "You can't tell anyone about this," he urged. "Do you understand?" Jessica nodded. He bent his neck forward so that the top of his head was touching the top of hers.

"He's blackmailing me," he whispered. Jessica could smell the beer on his breath. She looked at him with wide eyes. "He's going to walk out on Michelle. Just disappear. He has some money—I don't know how he got it—but he said she'll freeze his bank account as soon as she realizes he's gone. 'Cause, you know, technically it's half hers, so legally she can do that. But he wants to hide the money in my savings account, just for a little while, until he gets situated in a new city. I'm supposed to wire it back to him when he contacts me."

Jessica could feel her blood running hot and fast in her veins. "And what if you say no?"

"Then he'll tell coach about how he gets us alcohol for parties. He has pictures of almost every guy on the team drinking, sometimes on the night before a game."

Jessica shook her head. She didn't understand. "So what?" she asked.

Nick glared at her. Their faces were so close, she could almost feel the annoyance emanating from his eyes. "So what? Ariel, we'd all get suspended from the team, and the season would be over. No chance of state. No chance of divisions, even. And forget about getting recruited for college."

She closed her eyes. So *that* was why Rob was always so eager to supply liquor to her friends. She'd always thought he just wanted them to think he was cool. She would never have guessed that he was really trying to collect damning evidence against them. *Well played*, she thought.

"When is he doing this?" Jessica asked. "When is he leaving her?"

"Monday. I'm supposed to meet him at the bank right after school to transfer the money, and then he's taking off."

"Are you going to?" Jessica held her breath as she waited for him to answer.

"What choice do I have? I either help him to commit a fraud that nobody will probably ever find out about. Or I don't, and he ruins my lacrosse career and my chances at getting into a decent college. What would you do?"

Jessica lifted her head up and pressed her body against his. "I'd go to the bank," she whispered in his ear.

Gretchen and Ariel were waiting for her in the backyard. Ariel nearly pounced on her as she approached. "Well? Did you get what you needed?"

Jessica felt a little unsteady on her feet—Ariel's feet—as she grappled with the emotions that were just now starting to hit her. She hadn't known Rob at all. Everything she'd built him up to be was a lie. He was a fake, a fraud, and worst of all, she was pretty sure that he was a murderer. But she'd been right about one thing: he was smarter than he looked. A hell of a lot cleverer than she'd ever given him credit for, in fact.

"Jess," Gretchen said, looking carefully at her. "Are you okay?"

She sat down on the stacked bluestone that ran along the edge of the patio and leaned forward so that her head was parallel to the ground. Ariel's thick blonde hair fell like a curtain around her face. "Yeah. I'm okay." She glanced around at the yard, making sure no one else was in earshot of them. "Come on," she said, standing up and walking back toward the garbage area, motioning for them to follow her. "We need to switch back. Now."

Jessica couldn't kiss Ariel fast enough; her heart was pounding and she was starting to sweat as she thought about Plotinus and Gemina. *What must that have been like for her?* she wondered. *How did she survive it?* But Jessica knew that she'd never be able to clear her mind enough to project if she kept dwelling on it; she shook her head to try to make the thought go away.

"*Écho exorísei aíma egó dió xei ostó n, prouálloun ti n psychí mou se állo spíti.*"

Jessica felt the strange, overwhelming warmth rush into her throat and spread out through the rest of her body. She exhaled. *Thank God.*

When she opened her eyes, Ariel was staring back at her with a relieved expression on her face. "Never again," she affirmed.

"Agreed," Jessica responded.

"So, did Nick tell you what you wanted to know?" she asked.

Jessica bit the skin around her thumbnail. *Her* thumbnail. "Yes," she said.

"And what do you think?" Gretchen asked.

She met Gretchen's eye and held her gaze, but she couldn't bring herself to say the words out loud. Gretchen's face seemed to crumple before her eyes.

"You really think he did it?" she asked. The words came out sounding choked. Ariel put her arm around Gretchen's shoulder as Jessica nodded.

"And I think I know how we can catch him," she said quietly. "But we're going to have to tell Michelle about everything. We can't do this without her."

Ariel took a small step forward. "Well, let's go get her, then."

The teepee was not designed for four. If it hadn't been for the circle of night sky that appeared through the top of the curved roof, Jessica would have been too claustrophobic to stay inside. As it was, her left knee was practically on top of Michelle's right one, and her right one was smushed under Gretchen's left, as if they were lasagna noodles layered in a casserole dish.

Of course, they'd prepped Michelle in the car.

We're going to tell you some things, Jessica had explained, *and you're going to be mad. But just try to remember that we were only trying to do what was right.*

And Michelle had agreed to be open-minded. She'd promised to listen to the whole story before she said anything or made any judgments. But now that they were actually explaining it to her in this tiny space—where the kissing crime had occurred, no less—Jessica realized that Michelle was going to be furious on many, many levels. No matter what. She was starting to wish that she *had* gotten stuck in Ariel's body after all.

"It all started with the meeting where they told me about the Plotinus Ability," Jessica explained, keeping her eyes on her flats, crossed in front of her in the darkness. "I did some research afterwards, and I read something about how the anklet might not have any power, it might just be part of the ritual. So I wanted to see if it was true. Plus, Gretchen and I thought that if we could just be each other for a little bit, we might be able to snoop around and figure out who might have killed her mom."

Michelle blanched. "And who were you planning on snooping on?"

Jessica gnawed on the skin around her nails.

"Ariel," Gretchen said, stepping in. "I saw her at my party that night, and I was convinced that she had something to do with killing my mom."

"I never went in the house, though," Ariel said, quickly. "I just looked through the window, and then I ran away. But Gretchen didn't know that."

Michelle narrowed her eyes. "*That* was your suspect? A thirteen-year-old girl who crashed a graduation party?"

All three of the girls looked down at the floor.

"Well," Jessica said, in a meek, apologetic voice. "We might have also suspected you."

Michelle recoiled, as if an invisible force had pushed her shoulders back. "Me! You thought *I* killed Gretchen's mom? Why? Why would you think that?"

"I don't know!" Jessica shouted. "You were so insistent about Gretchen not being the leader, and then you volunteered to take her place . . . I'm sorry, okay? It just seemed suspicious at the time."

"But I told you where I was when she was killed!" Michelle yelled back. She caught herself and glanced at the other girls. Jessica knew that she was wondering whether or not they knew about her affair with Mike.

"Actually," Gretchen said calmly, "you told me."

Michelle's mouth fell open. Her eyes got huge, and her cheeks turned bright red. She blinked three or four times in a row. "It worked? It actually worked?"

Jessica and Gretchen nodded.

Michelle slumped against the back of the teepee, shaking her head as she spoke her thoughts out loud. "I always thought it was just a metaphor for the Oculus Society's power. I only wanted to be the leader because I thought it would give me more cache. I never actually thought it was real." She focused on Jessica, her eyes suddenly full with understanding. "Oh, my God. That video. Was that the two of you . . ."

"Yeah," Jessica answered.

Michelle sat up with a jolt, as if she'd just remembered that she was supposed to be angry. "Why didn't you say anything? Why didn't you tell anyone in the Oculus Society?"

"We couldn't," Gretchen pleaded. "They would have made us stop, and I needed to do it. I needed to try to figure out who killed my mom."

"Then what about her?" Michelle asked, pointing at Ariel. "What does she have to do with any of this now?"

"She's been projecting with us," Jessica said, trying not to wince. Best just to plow forward. And so she went on—all the way through the entire two years of scheming, the plan that she and Gretchen had cooked up at boarding school, and how it had all fallen apart since they'd been back.

When she was finished, Michelle squeezed her head with both hands, as if she were trying to steady her brain. "So, let me get this straight: she videotapes you projecting and runs you out of town. You two come back and pretend to hate each other all this time. But really, you're in cahoots with each other to find proof that Ariel committed the murder. And in order to get the proof you need, you bring her in to project with you. But now you don't think she did it anymore. Do I have that right?"

They looked at each other and nodded. Jessica wondered if she looked as sick and embarrassed as her friends. "More or less," Jessica answered.

Michelle flashed a brittle smile. "Great. So, you"—she pointed at Jessica—"are grounded for, like, the rest of your life."

Jessica's stomach dropped. "What? Why?"

"Why? Shit, Jessica! You let me think that she was you, and I don't even know her! Who knows what I might have said if we'd been alone? What if that had been her, tonight, when I came in your room?" She shook her head. "And you're going to get kicked out of the Oculus Society for sure—"

Ariel cleared her throat.

"*What*?" Michelle spat.

"Um, I understand that you're upset, but I think you're kind of missing the point."

Oh, God, Jessica thought. *This should be interesting.*

Michelle smiled in mock amusement. "Really, dear?" she asked. "And what point is that exactly?"

Ariel gave her a skewering look.

You've got to hand it to her, Jessica thought. *This girl cannot be intimidated.*

"The point is not what happened before, but what's happening now," Ariel said. "It's only because they projected—with an *outsider*—that Gretchen and Jessica were able to uncover things that the police couldn't. Things that not even your private investigator could find."

Michelle didn't say anything. Jessica couldn't believe it. She'd never seen anyone render Michelle speechless before.

"What kinds of things?" she finally asked.

Ariel opened her palm in Jessica's direction, ceding the floor back to her. Jessica took a deep breath. "I think there's more to Rob leaving you than you think," Ariel said.

Michelle's eyes widened. "You told them?" she asked angrily. "You told them he's leaving me?"

"Listen, Michelle," Jessica pleaded. "Just listen, okay?"

Michelle crossed her arms in front of her chest. "Okay. But this had better be *really* good, or I will think of punishments for you that you didn't even know existed."

Jessica took a deep breath. "So, I was doing research about Plotinus today for the project that Tina assigned to us. Anyway, he wrote in his diary about how he and Gemina were planning to project, and then right afterwards, Gemina gets thrown in jail for treason—I don't know why—and she gets executed. And after that Plotinus stops writing in his diary, after writing in it every day for years, and suddenly there are accounts of him acting schizophrenic and behaving like he's someone else."

"Wait, what?" Michelle asked. Jessica could practically see the wheels turning in her head as she put the pieces together. "Do you think . . . ?"

Jessica finished her thought. "Yes. I think they got stuck in each other's bodies, either by accident or on purpose, it doesn't matter. But it got me thinking, what if that happened to one of us? What if we projected, and we couldn't switch back? We'd have to live out the rest of our lives as someone else. It would be awful. Unless—"

Ariel's face went pale. "Unless you wanted to escape your life."

Jessica touched her index finger to the end of her nose. "Bingo."

"Oh, my God," Ariel whispered. "But it won't work, right? The anklet isn't enough to make it work. Not by itself."

Michelle's ears perked up at the mention of the anklet. "I'm not really following all of this, but do you know where the anklet is?"

Jessica sighed. She didn't know how to put this delicately, so she wasn't even going to try. "I think Rob has the anklet. I think he killed Gretchen's mom for it."

Michelle scoffed. "You think Rob killed Octavia? Come on, Jessica, that's ridiculous. He might be an asshole, but he wouldn't murder someone any more than I would."

"Actually, I think he would."

Michelle stared at her, disbelief moving across her face like clouds crossing in front of the sun. "Are you serious?"

She nodded. "Listen, he knew who Plotinus was. He mentioned him to me this afternoon when I said I was doing research on the history of the Oculus Society. I was surprised, and I asked him how he knew about that."

"And what did he say?" Michelle asked.

"He said he remembered hearing the name at my eighth grade graduation. And that the graduation program explained who Plotinus was. But I checked the program, remember? I looked at it while you were in my room."

"It didn't explain . . ." Michelle's voice faltered.

"No, it didn't. So he must have looked it up on his own. Look, I think it probably started out innocently. At graduation, he saw Mrs. Harris give Gretchen the Plotinus Award, and it piqued his interest. You know: a secret society that all of the women in his life are members of but that he can't know anything about? It must have driven him crazy. So he hears about this Plotinus Award, and he thinks, what's Plotinus? Maybe it'll give me some clues about what they do over there . . ."

Jessica paused. Together in this tiny plastic teepee, with only the moonlight and the crickets, she was suddenly aware that not a single one of them was breathing. All eyes were on her.

She went on: "So he goes home, and he Googles it. And he reads about projection and the amber anklet. Most people would be like, okay, whatever, this Plotinus guy was crazy. Only he remembers that Mrs. Harris was wearing an amber anklet just like it at graduation that day. I mean, I remember seeing it on her; it was blinding when the sun hit it. And so he puts it all

together, and he thinks, hey, maybe this isn't just some old philosopher who was losing his mind. Maybe this is real, and it's
why the Oculus Society is so secretive. He starts to think about
what he could do if *he* had that anklet. And that night, at the
party, when he sees Mrs. Harris wearing it again . . . well, he
probably figured it was his only opportunity."

Jessica stared at her aunt as she processed the information.
For a second, she looked like she was going to cry. But then
she took a deep breath and pushed her shoulders back.

"So what is it you think he's planning to do?"

Jessica knew that she had to say it now. It was time. "I think
he's planning to project with Nick Ford. And I don't think he
plans to project back."

"The clothes!" Michelle gasped, stricken.

"Exactly. But what he doesn't know is that the anklet isn't
the key to projecting. It's just a symbol. And he can't possibly know about the words. It's not in any of the research I
did. Plotinus must not have written it in his diary because he
was worried that it could fall into the wrong hands. He had
to have taught them to Gemina, and she must have passed
them down to her own daughter, and on and on. But spoken.
Always spoken. It's why Tina couldn't find anything written
about it in the Oculus Society archives."

"But if he thinks that the anklet is the key, then he'll have
to wear it when he tries to project with Nick," Gretchen said.

"So then we'll have to catch him," Ariel added. "We'll
have to catch him while he's got it on."

"He's meeting Nick at the bank on Monday right after
school. Nick thinks Rob wants to transfer some money into
his account for him to hold onto until Rob gets settled in a
new city," Jessica explained. "But I think it's just a ruse to get
Nick alone."

Michelle nodded. "He's got a safe deposit box at the bank," she offered. "It was in the file from the PI. I'll bet you that's where he's keeping the anklet." She tapped on her leg as she tried to think like Rob. "He'll go to the bank early, to get the anklet out of the box, and then he'll go back outside and wait for Nick." She paused. "It would be a genius plan, actually, if the anklet really worked. God, you'd think if he was that smart, he would have been able to find himself a job in the last ten years."

Jessica almost laughed. Ariel cracked a smile. But Gretchen's face darkened, and Jessica swallowed. She reached out and placed a hand on her friend's shoulder.

"So how do we get the police there?" Gretchen asked. "It's not like we can call them up and tell them our theory. They'll think we're insane." She lowered her voice. "And I'm finished with people thinking I'm insane."

Jessica looked at Michelle, waiting to see if she'd come up with the idea on her own. It wasn't even a second before Michelle locked eyes with her. They both smiled.

"I know exactly how," Michelle said.

CHAPTER TWENTY FIVE

At exactly 3:10 P.M. Monday afternoon, Gretchen pulled up across the street from the Delphi Bank and Trust. None of the girls had said a word since bolting from school minutes earlier. Jessica snapped off her seatbelt and glanced at Gretchen, then Ariel. They nodded. The white van that Michelle had described was inconspicuously parked about half a block behind them. As they approached it on foot, the door to the van slid open and Michelle waved them inside, sliding it shut again behind them.

The inside of the van had been reconfigured. The back seats had been ripped out, and a long, wide shelf that functioned as a table had been connected to one wall. On it sat two small video screens and a large computer monitor.

Three men wearing black pants and black jackets, lettered on the back with the word POLICE, huddled around the screens. Michelle was also in black pants, but instead of a police jacket she had on a black windbreaker over a white shirt.

"This is Jack, Mitch, and Finn," Michelle said, pointing at each of the officers. Jessica looked them over. Jack was an older guy with a neat, greying mustache and sharp blue eyes. The self-confident air about him told her instantly that he was the guy in charge. Mitch looked to be about Michelle's age, and he could have been a movie star. He was tall with close-cropped dark hair and a chiseled jaw line covered with a few days' worth of stubble. Finn was clearly the rookie. He didn't look much older than they were, and he had the same goofy, dumb jock expression that she always wanted to wipe off of Nick and Connor's faces. "This is my niece Jessica, and her friends Ariel and Gretchen. They've been briefed on protocol," she assured them. "They won't get in the way."

Yeah, we've been briefed, Jessica thought. Michelle's instructions had been to say nothing and to touch nothing. *These guys are doing me a favor*, she'd told them. *They're squeezing this in before the real bust they have to do on Monday night. So don't screw it up.*

"Is he inside?" Jessica asked in a quiet voice.

"He got there at two forty-five on the dot," Michelle answered. "Went right into the bank and asked to be taken to his safe deposit box."

Gretchen's mouth fell open. "How do you know? Do you have someone on the inside?"

Michelle smiled mischievously. "Mitch gave me a button with a pinhole camera in it. I replaced one of the buttons on Rob's shirt collar with it last night. We can see everything he's seeing."

Jessica leaned in to look at the video monitor. "I don't see anything but static."

Jack leaned back in his chair and stroked his mustache

with two fingers. "Unfortunately, the safe deposit box room is underground, and it's heavily insulated. We can't get a signal from there. But as soon as he comes back to ground level we'll pick him up again."

Ariel sighed. "So we have no idea if he has the anklet."

Mitch whirled around to look at Ariel. "What anklet?" he asked. He turned to Michelle. "I thought we were looking for money," he said to her.

Ariel's eyes got huge as she realized her mistake. Michelle had been very clear with them. *Don't say anything about the murder or the anklet. All they think we're doing is stopping Rob before he transfers his money to Nick.*

"We are," Michelle said, gritting her teeth. But before she could go on, Jack was calling them back to the video screen.

"He's back!" he hissed.

Jessica held her breath. In silence, she and the others watched the backside of a bank officer as he pushed open a metal door and held it open. The camera seemed to pass through the door, then past half a dozen people. It was disconcerting, watching it like this, a disembodied eye floating along. The exterior door to the bank pushed open, and there on the screen was the street, trees, some cars passing by. The camera stopped moving.

"He's waiting," said Mitch.

Finn had gone up to the driver's seat. He peered through a pair of binoculars. "He's still carrying the bag," he informed them. "Whatever he took out of the box is in there. He didn't come out with anything different." Jessica climbed into the passenger seat next to him. She could make out a person standing on the corner, but from that distance she couldn't see his face. Jack handed her the binoculars. "Here, take a look."

She held them up and squinted through the holes. There was Rob, as sharp and crisp as if he were standing two inches in front of her. He was holding a small duffle bag—she'd seen him carry his things in it to the Club before—and he was wearing an open blue button-down with a white T-shirt underneath. Jessica quickly tilted the binoculars so she could see his feet. Grey Jack Purcells stuck out from the hem of his jeans. His ankles were concealed. She handed the binoculars back to Finn.

"Here comes our guy," he announced a few moments later.

Sure enough, Jessica saw Nick rounding the corner, approaching the spot where Rob was standing. She went back to the other end of the van to watch him on the monitor.

Nick was about half a foot taller than Rob; when Rob looked up at him, the bottom half of Nick's face appeared on the screen.

"Hey, man," Nick said.

"Hey. Thanks for coming."

Nick frowned. "Don't pretend that I'm here because I want to be. This isn't a favor."

"Whatever, dude," Rob answered. "I was trying to be friendly, but we can do it this way if that's what you want."

"Can we just get this over with?"

"Yeah, sure. Come on." The camera began to move in the opposite direction from the bank.

"Where are you going?" Nick asked. "The door's over here."

The camera stopped. "We're going in through the back," Rob said. "I don't want the security cameras to get us on video together. You know, just in case."

Nick's chin bobbed up and down. "All right." He paused. "There's a back door to the bank?" he asked, sounding skeptical.

"Yeah, just follow me."

Jack jumped up from his seat at the table. "They're on the move!" he shouted. "The transfer's about to happen!"

Everyone looked at Michelle. "What do you want to do?" Mitch asked her. "We can go in now, but if the money's not in the bag we don't get him. Or we can watch, but then we run the risk of losing him if we move in too late." He lowered his voice and looked intently at Michelle. "We can't engage in a chase, because that would mean calling for backup. This isn't an authorized operation. This is a favor."

Michelle nodded. "I know." She hesitated for a split second. "I'm going in. Myself."

Mitch stepped forward to block her. "I don't advise that."

She sighed and pushed him out of the way. "He's my husband. He's not a gang member. I just want to confront him. If I need backup, I'll signal for you. Okay?"

The three men looked at each other, talking it over silently with their eyes. They all nodded.

"All right," Mitch agreed. He grinned. "But remember, you have to say it casually. Work it into the conversation. If you just shout it out he'll know something's up. Do you remember the signal word?"

Michelle rolled her eyes. "Thumbelina."

The officers all burst out laughing. Jessica snickered as she tried to imagine Michelle casually working that word into a confrontation with Rob. She looked at Mitch again; he was still grinning at Michelle. "Don't get in some big fight, though," Mitch warned. "We don't have time for a lover's quarrel. We need to be in place for tonight in an hour."

"Don't worry," Michelle answered. "You need to have love for there to be a lover's quarrel."

Jessica realized suddenly that Michelle and Mitch were flirting with each other. For a second, she wondered how long that had been going on. But then she reminded herself that Rob was a murderer and that Michelle should be flirting with whomever she wanted. Without any further discussion, Michelle slid open the door to the van and jumped out. Mitch slid it shut again behind her.

"Your aunt's a cool lady," he said to Jessica.

"Yeah," Jessica responded. "I know."

The camera bobbed along the alleyway behind the bank. Neither Nick nor Rob had said a word since they'd started walking, but as they approached the solid, steel door at the bank of the bank, Nick spoke up in a worried voice. "Um, I don't think anyone's getting in that way," he said.

"Is this kid stupid, or what?" Mitch wondered aloud.

"He's not stupid," Ariel replied defensively. "He's confused. Rob told him they were transferring the money inside the bank."

Mitch turned around to look at her. "And you know that how?"

"He's my boyfriend," Ariel admitted. "He told me."

Jessica cleared her throat. "Now is probably not the best time to bring this up, but um . . . Ariel? You can probably do better than Nick for a boyfriend."

"Hey," Jack interrupted. "Look at this. What the hell is he doing?"

Jessica's eyes flashed back to the screen. Nick's back was pushed up against the wall, and Rob had reached out with his right hand and had grabbed the back of Nick's head.

"Dude, what the hell?" Nick asked. He put his palm out and tried to push Rob away from him, but Rob grabbed it with his other hand and held it down by Nick's side.

"This will only take a second," Rob breathed. He pushed Nick's head forward. The underside of Rob's chin appeared on the screen. Nick struggled to get free, turning his face from side to side as Rob moved closer. "Hold still!" Rob commanded.

"Is he trying to kiss him?" Finn asked, incredulous.

"Oh, my God," Gretchen whispered.

"We should go in," Jack said, standing up. "Where the hell is Michelle?"

On the screen, Rob had finally succeeded in getting his mouth on top of Nick's, muffling his screams.

"Wait," Mitch instructed, holding up one finger without taking his eyes off the screen.

"This kid's getting molested," Jack pleaded. "We have to go in."

"Just give her ten more seconds," Mitch insisted firmly. Jack looked at his watch, his eyes fixed on the second hand.

Rob exhaled loudly into Nick's mouth. His fingers dug into the back of Nick's head.

"Five seconds," Jack warned.

Rob exhaled again.

"It's not going to work, Rob," came Michelle's voice off screen.

Rob turned his head toward her voice, giving Nick the opportunity to shove him off of him. The camera jolted as Rob stumbled; he must have fallen to the ground because Michelle suddenly appeared to be hovering above the camera.

"Are you okay?" she asked Nick.

Nick spit three times and wiped his mouth with the back of his hand. "Stay away from me!" he shouted at Rob. "Dude, you tell my coach about the parties, and I'll tell everyone you're a pedophile! How's that for blackmail, asshole?"

Rob sputtered. "I'm not—I was just . . ."

"Nick, you should go," Michelle told him. "I'll deal with him."

Suddenly, Rob's right leg stretched out, filling up the screen. The duffle bag had fallen to the ground a few inches away, and he pointed his foot, looping the front of his sneaker though the handle of the bag and sliding it toward him. The hem of his jean rolled up. There, around his ankle, was a thin gold chain attached to an amber disc.

"There it is!" Jessica cried out, pointing at the anklet on the screen.

Gretchen started to cry quietly in the corner of the van.

Jack looked at the screen, then at Gretchen. "What is that?" he asked her.

She dabbed at her eyes with her index fingers. "It's proof," she answered. "Proof that he murdered my mother."

Jack, Finn, and Mitch exchanged glances. "What's going on here, girls?" Jack demanded.

"I'm getting the distinct feeling that we weren't told the whole story," Mitch said tersely.

But before they had a chance to exchange glances of their own, the camera bobbed again. "No!" Rob shouted to Nick. "Don't you go anywhere!"

On the screen, they had a visual of Michelle's waist and the right half of Nick's torso, slightly behind her.

"Whoa," Nick said, quietly.

"What are you doing, Rob?" Michelle asked. Her voice sounded deliberately calm.

"Tell me how it works!" he shouted at her. "Tell me!"

"It doesn't work," she answered. "It's just a legend."

"No!" he yelled. "It does! I read about it! Plotinus and the anklet! It's why the Oculus Society is so hush-hush about everything!"

"I'm sorry to disappoint you, but it's just a story. Plotinus was crazy. He made it all up."

"I hate you!" he screamed at her. "I never should have married you! You ruined my life!"

"Please, Rob," she said. She had slipped into her TV voice, over-enunciating every syllable. "Please take your little Thumbelina off of that gun."

"He's armed!" Mitch shouted.

"Move, move!" Jack yelled. In one swift motion, the three of them had drawn their weapons, slid open the door, and taken off running down the sidewalk.

"Stay there!" Finn commanded them over his shoulder. It had all happened so fast, Jessica hadn't even realized that she'd started to cry until Ariel quickly slid the door, to the van shut again with a loud *swoosh*.

"She's going to be fine," Ariel assured her.

"I don't have anyone else," Jessica whispered. It was the first time that she understood this to be the absolute truth. Rob was a criminal. Michelle was the only family she had in the whole world.

"I know," Ariel said. "I'm in the same boat. I get it."

"Me, too," Gretchen seconded.

Suddenly, a shot rang out. They heard it in stereo, both from outside and through the audio of the camera. On the screen, they watched as Michelle collapsed.

Jessica's hands flew to her mouth. "No!" she screamed.

"Drop your weapon!" came Jack's voice. They heard the clatter of the gun as it hit the ground; a split second later, Jack and Mitch were in front of the camera. It jostled, then went black.

"I'm going," Jessica heard herself say. She was out of the van before she even realized what she was doing. Gretchen and Ariel leapt after her. Her ankles felt like jelly as she rounded the corner into the alley. Time seemed to freeze. Sirens wailed in the distance.

When they reached the scene, the first person they saw was Rob, lying facedown on the ground, his hands cuffed behind his back. Jack was standing guard by his side. Behind him, Nick was sitting on a concrete step beneath the bank's huge steel door. He looked pale and shaky. Ariel ran to him. And just few feet away, Michelle was stretched out on her back, her head resting in Mitch's lap. Jessica held her breath as she searched for the pool of blood that would indicate where Michelle had been shot. But there was nothing. She kneeled down next to Mitch. Michelle's eyes squeezed tightly shut.

"Is she okay?" Jessica said in a terrible whisper.

Michelle's lids flew open. "I'm fine," she said, coughing as she spoke. "I just got the wind knocked out of me." She made a fist with her right hand and rapped on her chest with it. "Thank God for Dragon Skin," she said.

"Best invention since sliced bread," Mitch agreed.

Jessica's legs finally gave out from under her. She collapsed on her rump at Mitch's feet. Tears fell from her cheeks.

The sirens were almost on top of them now, and within moments two police cars had screeched to a halt in the alley, followed by an ambulance. As the EMTs examined Michelle, one of the policemen questioned Nick, while the other hauled Rob to his feet. He kept his eyes glued to the ground as the officer read him his rights. It was only as he was being led toward the police car that he finally noticed Jessica standing there, watching him. His eyes lit up when he saw her. The policeman opened the door and pushed Rob toward it.

"Jess! You're still on my side, right?" he shouted at her, his voice full of hope.

Jessica turned back around toward Michelle. From behind her, she heard the door to the police car slam shut.

CHAPTER TWENTY SIX

The lights were dimmed in the back room of the Oculus Society building; white candles on silver trays cast a pale yellow glow on the walls. The white, silk curtains were drawn tightly, like lips set in a grim line, refusing to talk. The last two times she'd been back there, Jessica hadn't even noticed that there *were* curtains. She glanced around, taking in the other details that had escaped her before . . . the two matching, narrow bookcases running from the floor to the ceiling. The dusty hardbacks that lined its shelves. The pale blue patterned rug spread over the white washed, hardwood floor. The large, black-and-white photograph of what remains of the Roman Pantheon . . .

At the center of the table that dominated the room sat Tina Holt. Her crystal gavel rested atop the table beside a rectangular, black velvet jewelry case. To her right was Michelle; to her left, Kristen Renwick. Jessica sat at the end, with Joan Hedley at the other end. Before them stood Gretchen, wearing a white robe, just like the rest of them. Her dark hair had been blown out into shiny, long waves, and she stood up straight, her shoulders back, her head raised. She looked, Jessica thought, strikingly like her mother.

Tina banged her gavel against the table once, then twice, bringing the meeting to order.

"As you know, Gretchen, your mother had a long history of service to the Oculus Society. It is with great pleasure that we welcome you to the board, where you may continue in her footsteps." Tina's voice broke just the slightest bit. "It's all she ever wanted for you."

"With a seat on the board comes great responsibility," said Joan. "This group was created specifically to protect the secret of the Plotinus Ability, which has existed under the sole province of women for over two thousand years. Thanks to you and some fellow board members, the secret is safe once again." She nodded to Jessica and Michelle.

Jessica smiled back at her.

Kristen Renwick stood up from the table and stepped forward. "Please raise your right hand," she instructed Gretchen. Gretchen did as she was told, and Kristen began to read from a sheet of paper.

"The board of the Oculus Society operates in total secrecy. Do you solemnly swear not to divulge or admit the existence of the board to any non-member, even if such non-member is a general member of the Oculus Society?"

"I do," Gretchen answered.

"The existence of the Plotinus Ability is known only by members of the board. Do you solemnly swear not to divulge or admit the existence of the Plotinus Ability to any non-member, even if such non-member is a general member of the Oculus Society?"

"I do," Gretchen said again.

"Then by the power vested in me as Vice-President, I hereby declare you a member of the board of the Oculus Society."

Jessica snapped her fingers in congratulations along with the other board members. She could see the tears in Gretchen's eyes as she bowed her head.

Tina lifted her gavel again and banged it lightly on the desk. The snapping subsided.

"Since we've had some, ah, *special circumstances*, I think we can dispense with the formalities from here on out. Gretchen, Jessica has requested that you take her place as the rightful holder of the Plotinus Ability. We obviously don't need to explain to you what that means, or what's involved with projecting. We just need to know that you accept this designation as the Leader."

"I do," Gretchen said.

"Excellent. And I understand you've already decided on a partner."

"I have. I'd like for Jessica to be my partner."

"Agreed and accepted," Tina said. Jessica smiled. It was such a relief to be doing this the way it was supposed to be done, in accordance with the rules, and not in secret, sneaking out to the teepee after dark. She'd been worried that they were all going to get kicked out of the Oculus Society for what they'd done, but Tina was so relieved to have the anklet back in her hands, she was willing to forgive everything.

"So, then. Who will be your witness?"

Gretchen glanced anxiously at Michelle. Michelle smiled and nodded to her encouragingly. "I respectfully request that Ariel Miller be allowed to join the board as my witness," she said.

Tina looked down the table to her right, then down to her

left. "Let's take a vote, please. All those in favor of admitting Ariel Miller to the board, say 'aye.'"

"Aye," they all responded in unison.

"All those against?" Silence.

"Very well, then. Bring her in."

Michelle stood and took off her robe, then left the room. A moment later she came back with Ariel. Jessica looked her over. Her hair, too, had been blown out for the occasion. Straight and thick, curling up just the slightest bit at the ends. But Jessica noticed that her face looked blotchy, and her eyes were red-rimmed. She knew that Ariel had ended things with Nick last night. It must have been hard. He may not have been the god they'd dreamed him to be, but he was a good guy. It wasn't enough, but it was something.

Michelle slipped her robe back on and handed one to Ariel, then led her to the spot in front of the table where Gretchen had stood just moments before.

"Well, Ariel," Tina said. "It's very unusual for someone to be initiated into both the Oculus Society and the board on the same day. But then again, everything's been pretty unusual around here lately, I suppose." She let out a long sigh. "Joan?"

Joan stepped forward and administered the same oath to Ariel that she'd just given to Gretchen.

When it was over, Tina asked Gretchen and Jessica to stand with Ariel in front of the table. Jessica stood to Ariel's right, and Gretchen stood to Jessica's left, so that Jessica ended up sandwiched between them

"Ariel," Tina continued, once they were assembled, "since you're already familiar with the Plotinus Ability, we'll get straight to the point. You've been brought onto the board to serve as the witness for Jessica and Gretchen. Now I know the three of you had your own way of doing things while you were—shall we say a rogue operation—but we have a system in place for everyone's protection. If you're the witness, then you're only the witness. You don't project. Is that understood?"

Ariel nodded. "Yes," she said. "I really have no desire to ever project again," she added.

Tina chuckled. "That's excellent to know." She picked the jewelry box up off the table and opened it, revealing the anklet and its disc of translucent amber.

"Ariel," she said. "As the witness, I present you with this anklet that was handed down with the Plotinus Ability, from Gemina to Amphiclea, to their daughters Gaia and Alexia, and to their daughters, and on through the ages. Though we know now that it holds no power it still serves as a symbol of protection to those who project, so that they will always be able to find their way back to their true selves."

She handed Ariel the box.

"Gretchen and Jessica," she continued. "As the keepers of the Plotinus Ability, you must only project in the presence of your witness. As we know from the unfortunate fates of Plotinus and Gemina, projection is not something to be done at whim. It may only be exercised with the express permission of this board, and only when the circumstances are such that they adhere to the spirit of the ritual. Namely, to right a wrong done to a woman who is unable to help herself. Because of this rule, projection has not been practiced for several generations. You are the first to have achieved it in recent memory. And although you went outside the rules, we believe that it was in this spirit that your projection took place. Therefore, we pronounce you the Leader and the Partner, and we trust that it is only in this spirit that you will project again, if ever."

Jessica closed her eyes and exhaled. Her stomach, which had been swirling with anxiety, suddenly became still. *They have nothing to worry about,* she thought. *My days of rogue projecting are over.*

When she opened her eyes again, Tina was smiling at her, as if she knew exactly what Jessica had been thinking. "Let's say the oath," she directed.

Tina, Michelle, Kristen, and Joan joined the girls in front of the table, and they all joined their hands in a circle.

"Empistosýni mas kai ti n písti mas tha férei ti dikaiosýni. Af tí eínai i ypóschesi pou pani gyriká kratí sei."

"Our trust and our faith shall bring justice," they translated together. "This is the promise we solemnly keep."

Jessica squeezed Gretchen's hand, then Ariel's. She glanced at Michelle, standing across from her, and smiled.

Michelle smiled back. Her mascara was running again.

Jessica held her gaze. There was no doubt that Michelle would always be who she was. Difficult, narcissistic, impatient: a bitch. But not evil. There was a difference. She'd assumed Michelle was what she'd wanted Michelle to be. Wasn't that what projection meant, really? These women and girls around her, they were imperfect, every single one. *We've all lost so much*, Jessica thought. Mothers, fathers, sisters, husbands, boyfriends . . .

Looking into her aunt's eyes, she saw the truth of the Plotinus Ability. She and her friends had traded places to find what had been in front of them all along, all that remained, and in the end, all that mattered.